WE, THE JURY

Also by Robert Rotstein

Corrupt Practices

Reckless Disregard

The Bomb Maker's Son

The Family Lawyer (with James Patterson)

WE, THE JURY

Robert Rotstein

Published in 2018 by Blackstone Publishing
Cover design by Daco Auffenorde and Sean M. Thomas
Book design by Tom L. Williamson

Printed in the United States of America

First edition: 2018
ISBN 978-1-5385-0772-8
Fiction / Thrillers / Psychological

1 3 5 7 9 10 8 6 4 2

CIP data for this book is available
from the Library of Congress

Blackstone Publishing
31 Mistletoe Rd.
Ashland, OR 97520

www.BlackstonePublishing.com

For Daco

How little do they see what really is, who frame their hasty judgment upon that which seems.

—Daniel Webster

THE COURTROOM CLERK

MICK REDMOND

Memorandum

To: The Honorable Natalie Quinn-Gilbert
From: Mick Redmond, Clerk to Hon. Natalie Quinn-Gilbert

Judge,

As you requested, what follows is a summary of the undisputed material facts:

- David Sullinger (hereinafter "David") killed Amanda Sullinger (hereinafter "Amanda") on a Tuesday at 3:40 p.m., the day before their twenty-first wedding anniversary.
- Amanda died of massive brain injury that resulted from a blow to the head from a sharp object.
- The instrument that caused Amanda's death was an ax.
- Amanda had been twenty-eight and David had been nineteen on their wedding day.

- Amanda had previously been David's eleventh-grade history teacher.[1]
- Amanda was the sole source of the Sullingers' income.
- After two years of marriage, Amanda obtained her real estate broker's license and quit her teaching job. Within five years, she was a member of her firm's *Million Dollar Club*, handling only high-end properties for well-heeled clients.
- At the time of Amanda's death, she and David were living in an 11,955-square-foot home on Bedford Road, located in the bluffs overlooking the city.
- After dropping out of the local community college his sophomore year, David had many different occupations, including, but not limited to, bartender, luthier, dog groomer, apprentice real-estate agent, sous chef, Pilates instructor, and graphic artist.
- As of the afternoon of the homicide, David was unemployed.
- The Sullingers' daughter, Lacey, was seventeen at the time of the homicide, and their son, Dillon, was sixteen.
- During testimony, the Sullinger siblings both referred to their family home as "Hell on the Bluffs."
- The Sullinger kids disagree on which parent was Satan.

Apologies for the last bullet point, Judge. My dark sense of humor rears its ugly head. But you know what? That last bullet point *does* belong in there. It's why we're having this trial.

[1] The parties dispute the year in which Amanda and David first had sexual relations.

THE HONORABLE

NATALIE QUINN-GILBERT

When I first took the bench, my husband, Jonathan, a trial lawyer himself, gave me advice that I've invariably followed during my twenty-two years as a judge: when you instruct a jury, don't read to them; speak to them. It's human interaction, not dry, legalistic recitation, that fosters justice.

Now I look up from my three-ring binder and make eye contact with each juror in turn. "To kill with malice aforethought means to kill either deliberately and intentionally, or recklessly with extreme disregard for human life. David Sullinger killed Amanda with malice aforethought."

Jenna Blaylock, the defendant's lawyer, leaps out of her seat as if someone had just told her it was electrified. "Your Honor, may we approach?"

Interrupting a judge's charge to the jury is exceedingly rare, appropriate only when a judge misreads an instruction, which I didn't. I wonder if this is another Blaylock ploy. Over the past four weeks, she's tried to bully the prosecution's witnesses, assistant DA Jack Cranston, and, occasionally, me. (No one gets bullied in my courtroom.) She's made unnecessary objections designed to disrupt Cranston's examination and confuse the jury. She's pranced and preened like a manipulative show horse—all tactics that most judges can't stand, including this judge.

As much as I want to dislike her, I can't. I doubt I'm alone in that reaction. I think the jury loves her. It's a cliché, but she has presence. Maybe because those intelligent, incisive hazel eyes convey a gentleness even when she's in bulldog mode. Or maybe it's her rich contralto voice, a gift from God that, even when she's borderline shouting, reminds you of a melodious woodwind. (No one shouts in my courtroom.) Or maybe it's the perfect posture, which conveys confidence and credibility. Blaylock is one of those rare people who can behave badly and yet charm you, who can use her bad behavior as a *way* to charm you—which makes her an effective trial lawyer and a dangerous person.

My husband, Jonathan, was an effective trial lawyer, as good in his prime as Blaylock, but he never behaved badly.

I beckon the attorneys and the court reporter to the bench. My clerk, Mick Redmond, pushes a button that creates white noise so the jurors can't hear us talking. Mick looks tired, even pained. Understandable. It's been a long, grueling trial. I'm tired. The heater in this ramshackle building is on the fritz, it's February, and I'm cold.

"This had better be good, Ms. Blaylock," I say.

"Apologies, Your Honor," she says. "But you just misstated the malice-aforethought instruction."

"I certainly did not," I say.

Blaylock brushes away a loose strand of blond hair—an anomaly because usually there's not a hair out of place. "With respect, you did, Judge Quinn-Gilbert. You told the jury that

David Sullinger killed Amanda with malice aforethought. You left out the words 'It is for you to decide whether.' You've essentially instructed the jury to find David guilty."

She gazes at me, her eyes wide, the knuckle of her left index finger in her mouth—a childlike pose of anticipation. Blaylock is a young woman, but before now there hasn't been anything child-like about her. Her cheeks are pink. This is the first time since this case started that she looks as if she's not playing a role. In fact, she appears shaken.

I look at Cranston, her adversary, certain that he'll disagree with her.

"Unfortunately, counsel is accurate, Your Honor," he says, shrugging one shoulder. Even when he's not advocating, he has an edge. His droopy eyelids make him look bored; his acne-scarred cheeks give him a thuggish mien; his thinning black hair clashes with his ashen complexion. Jonathan would say Cranston was the only person he knew who could sound snarky and smarmy at the same time. If Jenna Blaylock is someone you want to dislike but can't, Jack Cranston is a man you want to like but can't.

I look at the court reporter. "Christina, did I ...?"

"I'm afraid you did, Judge," she whispers back.

"Oh, my. I didn't realize ... Apologies, counsel." I lean in toward Blaylock. "Are you up here to seek a mistrial?"

"No, Your Honor. I'm up here to ask you to fix the problem."

Blaylock believes she's winning. Otherwise, she would have moved for a mistrial. She's right; she is winning. If Cranston were quicker on the uptake, he'd try for a mistrial even though my error worked in his favor. I wouldn't grant it, but he should have tried.

"I'll fix it," I say. "Please take your seats. I will fix it."

Now I'm the one who's shaken. In my years on the bench, I've stumbled over jury instructions, of course, but I've never made a blunder like this. I pride myself on being a meticulous judge. I have high ratings from posters on the Robing Room and Above the Law—unusual because those sites most often attract harsh critics. I know it's egotistical to care about my website ratings, but I do. How did I botch a jury charge? Few tasks are simpler for a judge. You just have to flip sheets of paper in a three-ring binder and parrot the words that the judicial council has set out in standard-form jury instructions.

My God, I just told the jury that David was guilty!

Yes, I've been forgetting things, and no, it's nothing to worry about. Stress, anxiety, grief—mostly grief. My husband died four months ago. Or has it been five already? I miss him. Yes, he's dead, but no, he's not gone. He's here with me at this very moment. The cliché is that the loss of a loved one leaves a huge void in your life, but that isn't right. After Jonathan died, his presence expanded to inhabit every molecule of my being. Despite his presence, he's a nanometer out of reach. His inaccessibility is like an unscratchable itch in the deepest chamber of my heart.

My OCD kicks in. *One hundred minus seven is ninety-three, minus seven is eighty-six, minus seven is* … The serial sevens. Yes, I've researched dementia online, and if you can subtract from a hundred by sevens accurately, you're good. I'm good.

… minus seven is thirty, minus seven is … Stop being ridiculous, Natalie. Stop distracting yourself with nonsense. Maybe you made the error because you were distracted with just this sort of nonsense.

I shiver slightly. It's not dementia; it's that this courtroom is like an icebox. That's what my parents called a fridge: an icebox. Who cares if I forgot the word *citronella* the other day? I remembered the word ten minutes later without googling "scented candle that repels bugs." I'm sixty-four years old, this trial has been exhausting, and I miss my husband.

When the attorneys are seated at their tables, I say, "Members of the jury, counsel pointed out to me that I misspoke in giving this last instruction. Apologies. You will disregard what I said and draw no inferences from my mistake. Here is the proper instruction. To kill with malice aforethought means to kill either deliberately and intentionally, or recklessly with extreme disregard for human life. It is for you to decide whether David Sullinger acted with malice aforethought. That's the key. That's what I left out—that the issue is for *you* to decide."

The jurors look at me impassively, which is exactly what I want. A good group, this jury. Smart. Attentive. Capable of ignoring my error. I fixed it. Have I? It was just a slip. I hope the jury doesn't think it was a Freudian slip.

In those online brain-function tests, I was also able to draw the hands and numbers on a faceless clock and to identify a volcano.

I tap my pen on the desk three times, a technique Jonathan uses—used—when he was arguing a court case. Calmed his nerves, he said. Got the jurors' attention, he said.

His little self-help trick works, and I'm back on track. "An issue in this case is whether David Sullinger justifiably killed Amanda Sullinger in self-defense. The use of deadly force is justifiable only if David reasonably believed that such force was necessary to prevent imminent death to himself. If David had a lawful right to be in the Sullinger residence, he had no duty to flee an attack. Rather, he would have every right to stand his ground."

I pause, take off my readers, rub my eyes, and take another long breath, then say, "Evidence that David suffers from battered-person syndrome was admitted for your consideration regarding his claim of self-defense. The standard is whether the circumstances were such as would excite the fears of a reasonable person possessing the same or similar psychological and physical characteristics as David and faced with the same circumstances surrounding David at the time he used force."

Circumstances were such? Excite the fears of a reasonable person? Who writes this gibberish? *I* wrote that gibberish yesterday, though I was following the guidelines of the judicial council and the case law. I guess when it comes to instructing a jury, I'm a parrot with some discretion. I'm tempted to add, "Members of the jury, in English, this last instruction means that you have to figure out whether Amanda was so abusive that David killed her because he legitimately thought she was going to kill him first." I can't. The powers that be abhor plain English.

I recite the next instruction by heart. "Ladies and gentlemen, in a moment, the bailiff will take you to the jury room. Your verdict finding the defendant either guilty or not guilty must be unanimous. You must follow the law spelled out in these instructions. Even if you don't like the laws, you must use them. For over two centuries, we Americans have lived by the Constitution and the law. No juror has the right to violate the rules we all share."

THE COURTROOM CLERK

MICK REDMOND

Wonderful uncle that I am, last Christmas I bought my four-year-old nephew a set of colored ink stamps (ideal for three and up). My sister-in-law gave the little pecker some sheets of blank paper and told him to go to town. First thing, he made a colorful zoo. He was calm, a model child. But he'd been eating gingerbread men and candy-cane drops all morning, and when the sugar high came on, he was suddenly on overload. In a frenzy, he stamped not only the paper but the table cloth, the dining-room wall, and his left forearm. All the while, his eyes were filled with that lunatic gleam that little kids get. I had two thoughts: (1) the look in this kid's eyes is demon-seed terrifying; and (2) welcome to my world, adorable little buddy, because I stamp paper all day for a living, except that the asshole attorneys charge eight hundred and fifty dollars an hour to prepare the paper *I* stamp. I have the ultimate power, though. If I decide not to put my official seal on the legal papers, the attorneys' pleadings are worth less than my sugar-crazed, ADHD nephew's ink elephants, monkeys, and giraffes—in short, *nada.*

Processing legal pleadings and scheduling hearings and trials isn't my main job. My main job is protecting Judge Natalie Quinn-Gilbert. I felt this way even before she went out on a limb and officiated at my husband, Eric's, and my wedding, one of the first gay marriages in Sepulveda County. Not a big deal, since we live in a progressive state? Wrong. We have neo-Nazi–alt-right bikers in residence, and our county's voting pattern resembles that of rural Indiana.

Now I'm worried because the judge botched up the jury instruction and didn't catch it. Judge Natalie Quinn-Gilbert doesn't do that. She tried to fix it, but if Sullinger is convicted and Blaylock appeals, who knows what those intellectual snobs on the appellate court will do? Who knows what they *should* do?

Because the trial is over except for the verdict; the attorneys' lackeys gather up the litigation bags, laptops, and demonstrative exhibits, like circus roustabouts packing up to move on to the next town. Blaylock is a bombshell in a St. John's suit, with the face and figure of an actress—which she is, both during a trial and on those cable news appearances. She's resting her hand on her client's shoulder, guiding him toward the corridor, where she'll undoubtedly hold yet another impromptu victory press conference.

Sullinger shuffles up the aisle with head down and eyes focused on his shoes—the beaten-beagle look. Since day one, the man has kept his head and eyes down, even when sitting at counsel table, even on the witness stand, and that's a bad thing to do if you're a defendant trying to win over a jury. Or maybe it's a brilliant thing, because this doleful passivity makes him seem harmless, even gentle. You'd never know that poor, sweet, mild-mannered David buried an ax in his wife's skull. Not that Amanda didn't ask for it.

David's daughter, Lacey, runs up to her father, throws her arms around him, and says, "Oh, Daddy," more like an eight-year-old greeting her favorite parent after a long business trip than a twenty-year-old who has watched her father's trial for killing her mother. The tabloid journalists sure jumped on that one—whether David and Lacey have a sick relationship. Yes, I'm talking incest. Mercifully, that word was never uttered in this room, because when Jack Cranston tried to explore the idea while cross-examining Lacey, Judge Quinn-Gilbert exploded in front of the jury and threatened to sanction him if he said another word. I guess she did the right thing by shutting down the questioning, although I was curious about what Lacey would say. But I also think the judge firmed up the possibility of incest in the jury's mind. Juries remember when judges get mad, and they try to figure out why, and that leads to speculation about what they're not supposed to speculate about. (Don't think about a pink-and-blue-striped elephant.)

The Judge Quinn-Gilbert I know can be stern and tough but is rarely temperamental. I can remember only two other times when she lost her temper. The first time was at a shyster who missed a filing deadline, offered me a bribe to backdate my time stamp and, after I reported him to the judge, claimed I had solicited the bribe. Luckily, the jerk was already under investigation by the state bar and the sheriff's department, so his credibility was nil. The second time, she lost it with a biker on trial for felonious assault, who told her she was biased against him because she was married to a "kike." After calming down, the judge denied a motion to disqualify her, and after the thug was convicted, she had the pleasure of sentencing him. Except that it wasn't a pleasure for her. Sentencing criminals never is. Cranston's infraction in this trial, if it was that, didn't come close to those prior instances. The Judge Quinn-Gilbert I know would have called a recess and used a verbal spindle to ream Cranston a second anus for trying to pursue the perverted stuff, but she would have kept her wrath hidden from the jury. It has to be Jonathan. She's still in mourning. I told her to take time off, and so did some of her fellow judges, but she wouldn't hear of it.

"I'll lose myself in the work I love," she said. I think she's really trying to *find* herself in the work.

Speaking of Cranston, he catches my eye and shakes his head sadly. It's not clear to me whether he's commenting on the judge's error, Jenna Blaylock's sharp tactics, his own sorry courtroom performance, or the demise of his political aspirations because Blaylock kicked his ass in this trial. I respond with the curt nod I learned at bureaucrat school. Cranston thinks I'm his friend because we've had maybe a dozen trials together, and he's not a bad person. Not a good person, either. But he's not my friend—no attorney is. It's a matter of principle.

One of those media jerks, a tabloid blogger named Kelsi Cunningham, lingers after everyone has left the room. The media infested the Sepulveda County Courthouse over this case, and Cunningham is the queen roach. *People v. Sullinger* is the trial of the century in our county, the biggest since 1928, when a silent-movie comedian sued a local newspaper for libel after it accused him of engaging in sodomy with a male gaffer—though I doubt there were any female gaffers back then, so maybe I'm being redundant. In those days, our county was a resort, a place where the elite could come and live out their fantasies by the river. The poor guy, who called himself Porky Potter, ironically, was more Oscar Wilde than Liberace. A jury found the article to be true, and truth is a defense, so there went Potter's career down the American Standard.

The Sullinger case is much bigger, even accounting for inflation in the public's appetite for sleaze. *Sullinger* has sex, gruesome violence, deceit, and family tragedy. But there's something else. This trial involves an important legal issue—namely, whether a man can beat a murder rap by claiming he's a battered husband. Should there be such a defense? Judge Quinn-Gilbert said yes in her jury instructions. That's good enough for me.

As I said, I don't like any of the media, but Cunningham is the worst sort. (Yes, I'm repeating myself, but the judge's husband, Jonathan, once told me, "Why say something once when you can say it twice?") If there's testimony about sex, it'll be the lead headline on her website. If there's testimony about *violent* sex, it'll get forty-point type. She sidles over to my desk and says, "The way your judge instructed the jury—what a clusterfuck." The woman has a potty mouth, piercings in more places than just her earlobes, and a tattoo on her ankle. So much for journalistic dignity.

"I'm locking up," I say as I stamp FILED on an emergency motion for another case, which the defendant's lawyer should have filed downstairs in the main clerk's office, but which I'm accepting in the courtroom out of the goodness of my heart—because the main filing window is closed, and this goof attorney will blow a deadline if I don't.

"Oh, come on. Are there issues with her … mental acuity? Others in the courthouse say so. Talked to me on background. The trial's over, and everybody saw and heard—"

It's bullshit. The judge has been under great stress, and the bailiff, Deputy Kobashigawa, and I have had her back.

Cunningham is on a fishing expedition. Well, this fish isn't going to bite rotten bait. I assault her with my most withering glower. "I'm locking up *now.*" I stand, walk over to the door, and hold it open for her.

As she passes, she says, "My company pays its sources, you know. Nothing illegal about it. A courtroom clerk can't earn much."

Nothing illegal about paying off a county employee? Yeah, right. As soon as she's clear of the door, I shut it and turn the lock hard.

My desk phone buzzes, and as always, I answer before it buzzes a second time. I'm proud of never keeping Her Honor waiting. I've even raced across the room to get the phone on the first buzz.

"Yes, Judge?"

"Is there anything on the calendar this week I need to prepare for?" she asks wearily.

"Zip, Judge. Just waiting for the Sullinger verdict."

"Good. That's good." There's silence, but I never hang up on a call with her until I hear a goodbye or a dial tone. She breathes into the phone. I hear a snuffling, then a long, labored breath. Finally, she says, "Well, that wasn't my finest hour, Mick." The statement isn't an observation but a question, and I answer the only way I can.

"You made it right," I say, though how can you ever know if that's true? "This has been a long, hard trial, a real bear. Not made easier by the broken heating system. I'll get maintenance to fix the thermostat tonight. If they don't show, I'll fix the darn thing myself."

"You're a good man, Mick," she says.

THE HONORABLE

NATALIE QUINN-GILBERT

Traditionally at common law, a jury of twelve veniremen decided a criminal case, and their verdict had to be unanimous. Then, in *Williams v. Florida*, 399 U.S. 78 (1970), the United States Supreme Court concluded that the twelve-person jury was a historical accident born out of superstition and mysticism—twelve apostles, twelve stones, twelve tribes—and that a jury comprising as few as six citizens could insulate jurors from outside intimidation while at the same time allowing for adequate deliberation and providing an adequate cross section of the community. Legal scholars who favor a jury of fewer than twelve people argue that six-person juries promote efficiency. Those who oppose smaller juries fear that the more powerful jurors will prevail over the weak at the expense of justice. Our state's compromise is to require a minimum of eight jurors and a unanimous verdict. If two drop off, however, the remaining six may decide by unanimous vote. I have faith in these jurors. A good group. I wish there were twelve. If the choice is between cumbersome and unjust, I'll take cumbersome. But I'm obviously in the minority.

THE BAILIFF

BRADLEY KOBASHIGAWA

I won't turn in my sheriff's badge. It's shaped like the Star of David and has a blue cross at the top point. The combination means we serve everyone. The division chief wants me out. That's why he assigned me to be a courtroom bailiff. No matter. I won't resign. I'll remain a deputy sheriff no matter how bad the assignment.

Most of the time, I feel like a custodian. I clean up the courtroom. I lock and unlock doors. During trial, it's different. During trial, I'm a police officer again. It's my job to make sure the courtroom is secure. To make sure no one is stalking the judge. There are haters and lunatics out there who would just love to kill a judge or a lawyer or a defendant. This Sullinger case is tough. So much publicity. The crazies came out to root for their favorite side. Like they're watching a football game. No, more like they're watching a video game, where the characters look just like real people but exist only to kill or be killed. The people in a trial are human beings, not pixels.

Once jury deliberations start, I'm a babysitter. Or maybe one of those—what do they call those hotel guys? Concierges? Don't get me wrong, I take this trial and my job serious. It's my job to get the eight jurors through this. Also, I enforce the law by making sure they don't violate the rules. Like Judge Quinn-Gilbert says, I'm their connection to the outside world.

They line up in numerical order. I don't even have to remind them anymore. They wait for me to unlock the door. Juror No. 1 is grinning. She looks like she's first in line for a Disneyland ride. She's about to decide a man's future. There's no reason to grin. She should take this proceeding serious. Since the first day of jury selection, she's acted like she earned the right to be number one. Really, she just got the number assigned from a computer in the clerk's office. She's a records manager at an insurance agency. She's in her midfifties and has never been married. She has a twenty-four-year-old son who works on a golf course in Scottsdale, Arizona. She loves her cats. The second I open the door, she rushes inside and takes the chair at the head of the table.

Juror No. 6, the Architect, and Juror No. 17, the Housewife, go in next. They sit side by side. They always eat lunch and get afternoon coffee together. The Architect looks at me a lot. Checks me out. Once, she said, "I can tell you work out, Deputy Kobashigawa." Hot smile. She's my type. Tall, athletic, not too curvy. A yoga- or Pilates-teacher look. Pretty face that doesn't look as hard when she's flirting. Divorced, which I don't mind, because so am I. In her forties like me, which I don't mind, either. Tempting, but I can't. It's not about the conflict of interest. Trials end fast. It's just that she's way too rich and smart for me. She minimizes rich and smart by saying she designs public toilets for a living. Funny. But really, she designs all kinds of buildings for parks and recreation. Most women I meet don't want to be smarter or more successful than men. It's not because I'm old-fashioned that I believe this. I wish it was different. I think it's in female genes to feel that way—not their fault. Probably all the Architect wants is sex.

The Housewife is a stay-at-home mom. In her midthirties with three children. The oldest is five years old. How does she manage? I have one son, and when he was that age, he put a strain on my marriage. My bad. I was always patrolling the streets at night.

The Housewife doesn't work out at the gym. I'm sure she has no time, but it would be good for her to work out. Chasing kids isn't enough. She's round all over. No more than five-two, with a round face, round eyes, round figure, round arms. Baby weight. Every day, she comes to court dressed in a white blouse and blue jeans. Like a uniform. She's smart like the Architect. She has a master's degree in communications. She made such a big deal about that during voir dire. I felt sorry for her. She's very uptight. Working out would help that. My workouts help me blow off the steam. As soon as the jury is discharged for the day, I'm going to the gym.

I know why the Architect and the Housewife are drawn to each other. Each has what the other wants. Sometimes that results in friendship; sometimes it results in enmity.

I don't work out at the Sepulveda Gym anymore. Too many deputies there. Ever since the incident, they treat me different. They nod, grunt hello, but that's it. No dinner and a beer after, no conversation that lasts longer than a minute. Not even an offer to spot me—not that I would trust them to. So I go to the 24/7 fitness place by my house. It's not ideal. They don't have hundred-pound dumbbells there, but I make do.

Juror No. 11, an anthropology major at the local college, stops at the door. So does Juror No. 29, a jury consultant with a PhD in statistical psychology. Together, they help Juror No. 33, a grandmother, into the room. The Grandmother is a retired high-school teacher and vice principal. She's seventy-eight, wears a hearing aid, and walks with a cane. She's been married fifty-seven years. Her husband has Alzheimer's. My dad's dad had it. Forgot he was in the Manzanar internment camp during World War II. Forgetting has a silver lining.

Judge Quinn-Gilbert offered to excuse the Grandmother for cause on the grounds of family hardship. For most of the jurors, that offer would've been manna from heaven. The Grandmother said no because jury service is her obligation as an American citizen.

Mick, the clerk, thinks different. He thinks the Grandmother doesn't care that much about public service, just needs a break from taking care of her husband. I don't agree. I'm a romantic. Not many people would think a former patrol cop could be a romantic, but I am. Not just a "flower-and-candy husband" romantic, but a romantic toward life. My ex-wife hated that about me.

Mick and I seem like different personalities, but we're friends. We both served our countries—I was a marine, and he was in the army—and now we both serve the same judge. Mick is worried about Judge Quinn-Gilbert. I think it's just the stress. She's been under a lot of it with this trial.

The Student helps the Grandmother into a chair.

"You're a very sweet girl," the Grandmother says.

The Housewife and the Architect look at each other, and the Housewife rolls her eyes, I guess because the Grandmother just referred to a twenty-year-old African American woman as a "girl." The Student smiles a thank-you to the older woman. The Jury Consultant and the Student take seats flanking the Grandmother.

Juror No. 43, the Clergyman, sits at the far end of the table. A big man from Texas or somewhere in the South, if I have his accent right. You'd think a man of the cloth would have people skills. Not this one. I overheard the Architect whisper to the Housewife, "He thinks he's holier than thou." The Housewife laughed. People even talk behind the back of a Methodist minister. People talked behind my back during the internal-affairs investigation. They still do, even in the courthouse. I'd like to say I don't care, but I do. I'd like to think it doesn't matter, but it does. Malicious gossip is sometimes the truest assessment of a person. Raw, unfiltered, harsh, intoxicating, like a rough-fermented brew. Maybe most times. That's why the words hurt so much.

Mick admires the Clergyman, who quit his church and started his own independent congregation because the Methodists keep deferring approval of gay marriage. This fact didn't come out in voir dire, so the other jurors don't know about it. The Clerk knew about it before, independent from this jury. Maybe the others would be kinder to the Clergyman if they knew. Others might dislike him more. I wouldn't say this to Mick or the judge, but I'm not sure about gay marriage. That doesn't mean I don't admire the Clergyman for standing up for what he believes.

Last to come into the room is Juror No. 52, the Express Messenger. He calls himself an actor. He looks around and mouths the words *This sucks.* He's used those two words so often that the Grandmother threatened to report him to the judge. "That would suck," he replied. After that, the Express Messenger whispered the words so the Grandmother couldn't hear. What he didn't know is that the Grandmother reads lips. She didn't report him to the judge. She reported him to me. I had a little talk with him. He doesn't say "this sucks" in the Grandmother's presence anymore. Except now.

The Express Messenger is thirty-one, but he reminds me of my twelve-year-old. Dreaming impossible dreams without understanding that they're impossible. Oh, I know you're supposed to keep dreaming, reach for the stars, grab the brass ring, seize the day, never give up, never give in, and all that. *The biggest risk in life is not risking.* I read that on the cover of a Spanx underwear box. You know who preaches stuff like that to ordinary people like us (underwear companies aside)? Extraordinary people who are already on top, who are living their dreams; lucky, talented, blessed people; pampered pop stars, successful authors, rich actors, superstar athletes, billionaires, politicians. That's who tells us this stuff. Sure, they might've worked hard. But I hate to tell you this: they didn't get where they are only because of hard work. In high school, I worked hard to throw a ninety-mile-an-hour fastball. Couldn't have worked harder. I maxed out at eighty-four and blew out my arm in the process. How cruel of the top dogs to tantalize us when they know quite well that few of us can be them. My twelve-year-old doesn't need to know this yet. The thirty-one-year-old Express Messenger does. It might not be fair, but that's the way it is.

Then there are those of us who don't ask for the stars, who just ask for a tiny piece of our own planet, get it for a while, and have it taken away. After I threw out my arm, all I wanted to do was be a cop, not a courthouse custodian and babysitter. But it's my duty to do those things, and Brad Kobashigawa does his duty.

Maybe I'm not such a romantic about life anymore.

"Okay," I say. "Everybody's seated. Through those doors are the restrooms. One for the men and one for the women. You have pitchers of water and the evidence binders and pencils and pads of lined paper. You know the rules. Please refrain from using your cell phones in here." I walk over and stop at the door to the courtroom. "All right. There are two buttons. One is green. That's to notify the judge that you have a question. The other is red. Press that button only if you've reached a verdict. There's no yellow. It's not like a traffic light. Go, stop, and nothing in between. I'll be outside in the courtroom if you need me. I'll be back at five-fifteen to send you home for the day if you haven't reached a verdict. Any questions?"

The jurors look at each other and shake their heads. The Clergyman doesn't look at anyone. He just keeps his head bowed, as if in prayer.

THE HONORABLE

EDISON HALLECK

As presiding judge of the Sepulveda County Superior Court, I'm responsible for arranging tours of the courthouse for county residents. This tour business is a misguided outreach program that my predecessor conceived as a way to make the court system less byzantine and more accessible to ordinary citizens. As it transpired, ordinary citizens have no desire to spend time touring a building that has only unpleasant connotations. People must come to court because bad things have happened. You'd do better arranging a tour of an endodontist's suite.

Alas, the Norman Patrick Gleason County Courthouse and Hall of Administration has no charm. Constructed in 1959, the building occupies an entire block in the town's center. Because the courthouse was built on a slope, its two main entrances open onto different floors, the third and the fourth, confusing visitors, who often look in vain for a particular courtroom or administrative office, only to discover they're on the wrong floor. The several architects responsible for designing the building proclaimed that it would stand as a marvel, but they couldn't have been more mistaken. Citizens consider the building—a drab, rectangular middle-rise constructed of a glass curtain wall and concrete—to be an eyesore. Those who care about such things look at vintage photographs of the old courthouse, a wonderful art deco building constructed in the 1920s, and curse the city fathers of yore who demolished it on the grounds that it was gauche and outdated. This edificial carnage wasn't an isolated incident. During the 1960s and '70s, big cities as well as small towns in our state thoughtlessly destroyed its best architecture: art deco; programmatic-architectural buildings shaped like hot dogs, Dalmatians, derby hats, and doughnuts; Googie coffee shops, motels, and drive-in theaters.

The courthouse was named for Norman P. Gleason, a famous judge who became a justice of the state supreme court and, later, an unsuccessful gubernatorial candidate. As a judge, in 1928 Gleason ordered integration of a public swimming pool for the first time in the county and took on a corrupt mayor and city council. He survived a car bombing. But in the early 2000s, a graduate student at an upstate university published a master's thesis positing that during the 1920s Gleason had taken bribes from employers trying to suppress union activity in local factories. That was the least of Judge Gleason's crimes, however. It turned out he was the likely perpetrator of a murder that occurred in a riverside bungalow in 1931—the consequence of a quarrel with a man whom Judge Gleason accused of committing sexual indiscretions with the second Mrs. Gleason. The victim was found dead, lying facedown. An unidentified doctor arrived on the scene and declared that the poor fellow had died of a stomach hemorrhage. Only after the "doctor," who was never seen again, left the scene and the coroner arrived was the body turned over to reveal three gunshot wounds to the abdomen. Through correspondence, heretofore undiscovered police records, and newspaper reports, the grad student concluded that Gleason had done the shooting and that the supposed doctor was a confederate. Unsurprisingly, the reputation of the courthouse suffered. Out of either embarrassment or lethargy, the county board of supervisors has yet to schedule a vote to change the building's name.

When you walk through the courthouse, you encounter a fusty smell of mold and disinfectant, dank corridors leading nowhere, and gloomy faces of attorneys and litigants. By the time of the Sullinger trial, a study by the court's general administrative offices concluded that most jurors find the courthouse difficult to access, the jury deliberation rooms too small, the restrooms rundown and unsanitary, and the parking garage dirty, dark, and potentially dangerous. Some of the more superstitious and cynical court watchers posit that justice can't be done while the tainted ghost of Judge Norman Patrick Gleason inhabits the building.

I don't believe in such hogwash. Still, lately I've found myself wondering whether Natalie Quinn-Gilbert's courtroom is haunted by the ghost of her late husband. What else explains the goings-on in there?

THE PROSECUTOR

JACK CRANSTON

The fucking jury is deliberating, that asshole Jenna Blaylock is somewhere preening and making money, the judge is probably on her way home, and I—who'd like nothing better than to go home, pour myself a Scotch, and crawl into bed—am back in my shit hole of an office on the eighth floor of the Norman P. building preparing for an arraignment of a couple of losers who held up a mini-mart and evidently had never heard of security cameras. In the movies, criminals are either brilliant or glamorous. Don Corleone, Bonnie and Clyde, and their more recent millennial incarnations. In real life, the vast majority of criminals are flat-out stupid. That's why they become criminals, and that's why they get caught.

David Sullinger is an exception to the rule. He's smart because he can play stupid masterfully. He's smart because he's a murderer who won't be convicted. He's smart because he looks and sounds like a victim. I saw through him from the beginning, even when no one else did.

He's also lucky. His star witness was his squeaky-clean, pretty, college-student daughter, and my star witness was his drug-addled, defiant, high-school-continuation-dropout son.

When Lacey jumped to her father's support immediately after David's arrest, it became obvious from the get-go that the case wasn't ripe for prosecution. I told the district attorney not to bring this case right away, to marshal the evidence, to bide our time, because we'd eventually get something on David or the girl. Most trails go cold, sure, but a select few go hot. This one would've gone hot because David won't change his abusive ways. But pressure from the DA's feminist constituency to prosecute a wife killer meant more to her than the opinion of her chief assistant, who, unlike her, has tried a shitload of cases to a jury. So she pursued the case immediately. Then the feminists flip-flopped, and now they *support* a man who killed his wife. Why? Because of Jenna Blaylock and that damn battered-spouse defense. The feminists like that the defense usually benefits women, and they're using this trial to make some new law. So, as it turns out, the DA is twice fucked. She brought a bad case on the merits, and she lost public opinion.

I can't stand wife beaters. I've put plenty of motherfuckers behind bars for abusing their wives, and I'm proud of it. But abuse doesn't give a person a license to kill. We should be encouraging victims to rely on law enforcement, should be strengthening laws to protect the victims. What we shouldn't be doing is tolerating homicide.

Putting legal theory and my campaign platform aside, David Sullinger wasn't abused. He was the abuser.

I was against moving quickly, but once public opinion turned in David's favor, the district attorney assigned me to try the case. It was an obvious setup—assign Jack to the highly publicized loser because he's a threat to unseat the boss in the next election.

Still, I'm a good trial lawyer—better than good. Good enough to turn shit into Shinola, which I might've done in this case but for fuckups not of my making. Like when David Sullinger was rotting in jail where he belongs, unable to make bail, represented by the public defender after he couldn't afford a lawyer, because his murdered wife's assets were unavailable to him. That was cool with me, because you don't kill someone and use their money in your defense. Then Ms. Priss-pot Lacey Sullinger turned eighteen, and Judge Quinn-Gilbert lifted the freeze on Amanda's assets and released them to Lacey. The girl turned around and gave her father unlimited access to the money. How could Quinn-Gilbert let David Sullinger savor the fruits of his crime? Sullinger used the money to hire Jenna Blaylock, and the circus came to town, with Blaylock acting as combination ringmaster and eight-hundred-pound gorilla. She walked all over Nat Quinn-Gilbert and convinced her to include that "battered husband" language in the jury instruction—without any judicial precedent in our state. I do like that botched malice-aforethought instruction. Maybe the judge's mistake will seep into the brains of the jury. It should, because the judge was right the first time: Sullinger killed his wife with malice aforethought.

The judge hasn't been herself since her husband died. She and Jonathan were a real close couple. One Saturday night a few years back, my wife and I bumped into them at Downey's Grill, and they were sitting on the same side of a booth, sharing their food and holding hands. Kissing each other more than once. On the lips.

I noticed them and walked over. Wanda later scolded me for interrupting their private moment.

"Happy anniversary," I said to them.

The judge looked at me in amusement, and Jonathan had that wry, omniscient smile he was famous for. He was always three steps ahead of everyone. He should've been a judge, could've gone on the federal bench, but he didn't want it. "It's not our anniversary, Jack," he said in his stage actor's baritone.

I waited for him to tell me he was joking, that they were indeed celebrating their anniversary, and he finally said, "Our anniversary was three months ago, Jack. April fifteenth. We got married on tax day. We wanted something to be as inevitable as death and taxes." He made a show of kissing Judge Nat on the lips—there was tongue involved. Were they drunk? They'd had some wine, but I don't think they were over point-zero-eight.

When I excused myself, I saluted—a geek move that I make when I feel socially inept. Shit, was Wanda pissed at me when I got back to the table! Partly because I'd interrupted those geriatric love birds' private moment, partly because she'd seen me salute and she hates that, but mostly because our relationship wasn't like the Gilberts'. Whose is? Hell, at least Wanda and I aren't the Sullingers.

Yeah, it's a damn shame about Jonathan Gilbert. What the hell is an abdominal aortic aneurysm, anyway? How do you get one when watching a Chicago Cubs baseball game? I'm sorry for Natalie Gilbert's loss, but it was almost six months ago. Time to bury the dead and get your wits about you and not cause a jury to let a guilty man go free.

I blame Alicia and Cole. They say they want to move up in the DA's office, try the big cases, but their legal research skills—not up to snuff. Holy shit, no wonder they couldn't get a job at a big firm or in a big city. Jenna Blaylock's crew whipped our collective ass, especially with that Georgia Supreme Court opinion that validated a battered-spouse instruction. Alicia and Cole missed it. If the state legislature would only budget more for the salaries of county prosecutors, I wouldn't be stuck with less-than-stellar subordinates like that pair.

The news media, also known as the propaganda wing of the Jenna Blaylock defense team, reported each alleged cut, burn, bruise, insult, and expletive that Amanda Sullinger allegedly inflicted on her purportedly victimized husband. The public undoubtedly believes that she deserved to have her husband scalp her. The pisser is that the jury undoubtedly believes it, too.

Last night, my family waited on dinner for me. A nice gesture, because I didn't get home until a little before nine o'clock. It had been a bad day in court, with Judge Quinn-Gilbert approving the battered-spouse instruction. As we ate our Costco organic pumpkin ravioli, my son, Hunter, asked me if I truly believed David Sullinger was guilty. Everyone in his seventh-grade homeroom, including the teacher, thinks David is innocent, he said.

"As a lawyer for the district attorney's office, I'm an officer of the court," I said. "Not like the defense attorney, who's a hired gun. If I didn't believe David Sullinger is guilty, I'd drop the charges immediately. It's not about winning, Hunter. It's about justice." The right thing to say to a twelve-year-old, but a lie in part. It *is* about winning. Everything is. The system is rigged that way. I'm not a complete liar. David Sullinger *is* guilty of murder. Because of all the fuckups by others, he'll have the chance to kill again, and he won't pass it up. He's that type of killer—a psychopath who just can't stop himself and doesn't want to.

JUROR NO. 6

THE ARCHITECT

The jury deliberation room is, like the rest of the courthouse, decrepit. Jesus, the chairs are upholstered with a mustard-colored synthetic fabric that's permanently stained with coffee, soda, chewing gum, sebum, and who knows what else! The long, dark conference table conjures walnut but is, in fact, made of Formica and composite wood. In front of each chair is a spiral notebook, a Ticonderoga number 2.5 pencil, and a glass tumbler dotted with water spots. Just behind and to the left of the table's head are the restrooms. Binders containing the paper evidence are stacked on a credenza on the far side of the room.

"What a pit," I say to my new friend, the Housewife, but my voice is loud enough for everyone to hear. "Aren't they supposed to make the jurors comfortable? Why can't they put a window in these rooms?" My ex-husband, Ernesto, says I have no filter. He's right.

I like having no filter.

"No money," the Housewife says. "Just like we—"

"They could do *something*," I say. What I don't say is that I'm sure the judge and the prosecutor Cranston have windows in their offices.

I'm sure Jenna Blaylock has windows in her luxury suite at the Hotel Sepulveda. I'm not looking for grandeur, but I sure didn't think it would be this bad. It's much worse than that stuffy courtroom.

I did everything I could to get off this jury. I pleaded financial hardship. I run my own business and couldn't afford to be away for two weeks, I told the judge. (That had been the original estimate—two weeks. The trial has lasted nearly twice that, and we're still going.)

"There are quite a few people worse off than you, so don't complain," the judge said, although she took about six paragraphs to say it, so she could sound judicial and patient.

Then, during voir dire, Jenna Blaylock said to the whole panel, "Our Constitution provides that no person can be forced to testify against himself. This means David has the right not to take the witness stand, and you can't hold it against him. Would any of you hold it against David Sullinger if he decides to exercise his constitutional right not to testify?"

Perfect. My hand shot up. "I'd hold it against him."

Instead of excusing me, Blaylock asked more questions. Why would that woman—who isn't nearly as pretty as she appears on television and who's got a bad tattoo job on her eyebrows—want to keep someone who was biased against the defendant on the jury? Except that I'm not biased, or at least, not biased against a defendant who doesn't take the witness stand. That's his right. Fifth Amendment, as I recall. Yeah, I was lying to get out of jury duty. Who doesn't?

Damned if Blaylock didn't read my mind.

"Thank you for your candor," she said to me, flashing that TV smile. "You believe in our democracy and our Constitution, of course?"

"Of course," I said. Why did I say that? What else could I say? That I *didn't* believe in democracy? Sure, I wanted to avoid jury duty, but I didn't want to look like an idiot doing it. I felt my jaw clench and unclench rhythmically, a subconscious reaction when I become angry or flustered—so my ex-husband pointed out years ago during one of our quarrels. Well, I was quarreling, and he was observing my facial idiosyncrasies calmly, which was how he quarreled.

"Of course you believe in the Constitution," Blaylock said, her tone—what's the word, *unctuous*? Yeah, she was unctuous, but damn if it didn't work for her. Cranston, the DA, half stood, maybe to object, but he sat back down and fiddled with the knot of his tie, which was always loose and made him look like an exhausted pharmaceutical salesman rather than a credible attorney. Maybe if he'd stood all the way up and objected to Blaylock's questioning, I would've had the balls to stand up to her and wouldn't be sitting here now.

"And you understand that our constitutional rights are very important to a democracy?" Blaylock asked me.

"Yeah, sure I do," I said, trapped.

"So, as a juror, you'd follow the Constitution, wouldn't you?"

"Sure," I said. What a wimp. How stupid. Why didn't I add, *But if David refuses to testify, I'll still hold it against him; I can't help how I feel*?

Blaylock turned and went back to her table. David Sullinger was sitting there, wearing what became his signature doe-in-the-headlights expression. She rested her hand on Sullinger's shoulder. "And you'll give David Sullinger every chance, and assume he's innocent unless the prosecution proves him guilty?"

"Yes," I said meekly. I felt disgusted with myself, because I don't like meekness. Why didn't I say, *I despise meek people, and David Sullinger is obviously meek as a newborn lamb. Can I go now?*

THE HONORABLE
NATALIE QUINN-GILBERT

There's a knocking on my door, and I start. I almost never shut my door.

"Come in," I say.

The door opens, and my bailiff comes in. I admire Bradley. He's been through a lot yet keeps his dignity. Maintaining dignity was an especially difficult task for Bradley given the involvement in this case of his ex-partner—Beckermann was the deputy's name, I think.

"They're deliberating, Judge," he says. "Unless there's a note or a verdict, I'll let them go at five fifteen, just as you ordered."

I nod.

"Are you okay, Judge?"

"Yes, I'm fine. Thank you for asking."

He gives a grave nod and shuts the door almost tenderly.

I'm not fine. My husband's dead. We decided not to have children, made sure none of our friends assumed it was a fertility problem. We loved hiking, backpacking, traveling, and fine wine, and children interfere with hiking, backpacking, traveling, and fine wine. Children interfere with romance. Some of our friends whispered that we were selfish. Maybe so. We had careers and each other, had seen what children do to marriages (just look at the Sullingers). Now the same friends whisper, "We told you so. Don't you wish you had children to see you through this tragedy, to make life worth living, to fill the void?" They don't understand. There is no void. I don't want children. I want to feel my husband's arms around me.

What does anyone expect? I've been on the bench too long, the budget cuts are too high, my hands hurt from the arthritis, and those searing hemorrhoids leave me in dire pain after three hours in that hard swivel chair. My body is the shape and consistency of an overripe papaya. I'm tired but haven't given up, because Jonathan wouldn't want me to. I awake every morning expecting reinvigoration, anticipating a renewed spring in my psyche, but it never materializes.

No, Bradley, I'm not fine. I botched up a jury instruction in the worst possible way. Not only that, I might have made another, more significant error. All day yesterday, the parties argued over the jury instructions. It was grueling and tedious, more so because Jenna Blaylock was involved. We live in a small county, and the local lawyers all know each other, and they have to get along, because what goes around comes around. Blaylock isn't from here, so she doesn't have to be civil to anyone. After the trial, she'll go back to her law office in San Francisco and never set foot in this county again.

I left the toughest legal issue for last, thinking I'd wear the lawyers down so they'd more readily compromise. What I didn't bargain for was that the lawyers would wear *me* down. No, it was Blaylock who wore me down.

"It's not a self-defense instruction," Cranston insisted. "The People are cool with a self-defense instruction. Ms. Blaylock wants a battered-husband instruction. In our state—"

Blaylock rejoined, "After all those years of physical and mental abuse, David's psychological state is completely relevant to—"

"Amanda didn't attack *him*, didn't abuse *him*," Cranston said. "It was the other way—"

"Oh, she sure as hell did," Blaylock said.

I should have admonished her for using profanity, should have admonished them both for interrupting and arguing with each other rather than speaking to me. My head hurt—one of those migraines that split your skull like an ax. Unfortunate simile given the circumstances, but those headaches feel like that.

I was leaning toward ruling for Cranston, was inclined to let the case go to the jury only on self-defense, when Blaylock snapped a finger like a genie granting her own wish. Her paralegal handed her some papers.

"A short brief on the battered-spouse defense, Your Honor," Blaylock said. "Look particularly at the Georgia Supreme Court case."

"I object!" Cranston said, his already pasty face turning pastier.

Poor Jack. He'd been wearing his suit for hours, and he was so disheveled that he called to mind Jimmy Stewart at the end of his filibuster in *Mr. Smith Goes to Washington.* As cold as it was in the courtroom, he reeked of body odor. Blaylock looked as if she had just come out of a resort hotel beauty salon and spa.

I called a recess, read the defense counsel's legal brief, undertook my own computer search to verify the accuracy of it—Blaylock had hardly proved trustworthy during the trial—and ordered the lawyers back into chambers. Cranston begged for a chance to submit a written response, but I was done with it. He should have come prepared, as Blaylock had. In hindsight, maybe I was too harsh.

"We'll include the battered-spouse instruction," I said.

Cranston sprang out of his chair. "But, Your Honor—"

"Sit down, counsel," I said. "That is my ruling." What power there is in the judicial pronouncement! I swiveled my chair and turned away. I've rarely turned my back on a lawyer in my years on the bench. I'm not that kind of judge. Or wasn't. Cranston didn't deserve it.

As soon as they left, I closed my eyes. I was already overcome with what Jonathan called *judge's remorse*, which, oddly enough, seemed to dull my headache. I had erred on the side of the defendant, so it wasn't that my ruling might put an innocent person behind bars. On the contrary, it could result in a guilty man going free—the better alternative if you're going to screw something up. But what about Amanda Sullinger? I have an obligation to her, too. And to the citizens of the county. The postmortem photographs of Amanda are gruesome.

Did I decide the most important issue in the case in Jenna Blaylock's favor because of Jack Cranston's BO?

JUROR NO. 1

THE FOREPERSON

As soon as my sister and brother jurors sit down, I say, "I guess we should elect a foreperson." A take-charge kind of girl, that's me.

The Housewife and the Architect—Frick and Frack, the mean girls—glance at each other. They probably think I'm lobbying to be foreperson. I don't want to be foreperson. I just want to get things rolling. This has been a long trial, a really long trial.

My face flushes menopausal hot. With my fair complexion, which is pale from working in a windowless file room during the week and staying inside on the weekends to avoid more skin cancer, probably everyone can see my cheeks turn red. That's why they probably think I want to be foreperson, which I don't. My cheeks turn redder, probably, because they think I want the job, and they have it wrong. Maybe I'll say I'm having a hot flash. But I can't, not with the Clergyman and the Grandmother and the Express Messenger in here—too embarrassing.

If elected foreperson, I would serve.

"I nominate the Jury Consultant," says the Grandmother.

"Great idea," says the Student.

Wow. The Student agrees with the Grandmother even after the Grandmother was racist and called her *girl.* The hot flash gets hotter, even though I don't want to be foreperson. I never get picked for things like this. I'm not a popular girl. That's because I'm an assertive woman, and people don't like that, especially other women. Especially women like the Architect and the Housewife. On the second day of trial, I went to lunch at Subway, all alone, and the Architect and the Housewife were there, and they didn't invite me to sit with them. It's like I'm back in junior high, which they call middle school now. They won't pick me for jury foreperson. The popular kids always win, and I was never popular, never pretty like the Architect.

"I think the Jury Consultant is the perfect choice," I say brightly.

"It might not be a good idea, because of my job," says the Jury Consultant. "I don't want it to look like I'm controlling the deliberations—which won't happen, of course—but making me foreperson could make it seem like I am. Why don't you do it?"

My heart beats faster, my flashes flash hotter, because the Jury Consultant is looking at me. At least, I think she's looking at me, but I'm not sure, and I have a bad urge to look over my shoulder and check to see if someone's standing behind me, but who would that be, since all of us are sitting at the table?

"Oh, I'm . . ." I giggle, and my hands flutter on their own and cross over my chest because I'm a humble person. "Okay, but only if no one else wants to do it."

Everybody's quiet. The Architect wriggles in her chair, and for a second, I think she's going to volunteer. I know she's going to volunteer, so I say, "I guess if no one else wants to, I'll accept. I'm honored. I won't let you down."

"You're our new foreperson," says the Jury Consultant.

I really didn't care if I got it, but that'll show the Architect and the Housewife. I know those bitches didn't want me. I won't use my power against them like they would've done to me if they were the foreperson. I won't take their snubs personally.

"That's settled," says the Express Messenger. "Hopefully, we'll go this fast with everything else, Madam Foreperson."

Is that "Madam" part a dig? He's always doing digs at people.

I take stock around the table. The Grandmother is leaning forward, like she's trying to hear, but no one's saying anything. The Jury Consultant is writing something on her notepad. The Student looks nervous, poor girl—uh, I mean woman. But she is a girl because she's only twenty, younger than my son, so I'm not being racist. She's in college, and my son … maybe he'll go back to community college one day and get his associate of arts degree. (He lives in Arizona, working at a golf course as a caddy, hoping to get on the tour.) The Architect and the Housewife are sitting there, all snooty. The Clergyman is staring at me, picking at a thumbnail. How rude. He's a large man, probably six-four, 275 pounds. Every day, he wears a suit with no tie. If he wore a tie, he'd look like the lawyers. His belly hangs over his belt buckle. He disappears every day at lunch and during the breaks, so I haven't gotten to know him. Not that I know any of these people. But at least, I have a clue about them. Not about him. During voir dire, he seemed so nice and together and pious. He's a mystery now. I respect religious people, but there's something creepy about him, like you could see him being arrested as a serial killer or a pedophile or something like that. I know that's mean, but that's how I feel, and I'm an honest kind of girl. The Express Messenger is slumped in his chair, writing something on his notepad when nothing's happening. On second thought, he's doodling. I hope he isn't drawing insulting pictures of me. People have done that before, making fun of my kinky hair or my weight.

I pick up a pencil and tap it on the table three times to get their attention. "So I guess ... before we start, does anyone want some coffee?"

"If that's what you want to call it," says the Architect. "It smells like a burning tire."

"I'm going to get some coffee," I say. "Anyone else?"

No one accepts. I get up and pour the coffee into a styrene cup. I'm a little worried about that, because I've read that styrene causes cancer. They don't have Splenda here, only aspartame and refined sugar. I pick the sugar as the lesser of two evils. I'll ask the bailiff after court whether it's okay to bring in my own coffee, cup, and Splenda. Unless we reach a verdict today, but I doubt that, but if we reach a verdict, I won't bring coffee, because we won't be here. I've kept an open mind like Judge Quinn-Gilbert instructed, but I know how I'm going to vote. How are you not supposed to draw conclusions after four weeks? We're not birdbrains.

The Architect really embarrassed me that morning when me and her and the Jury Consultant were in the elevator coming up to the courtroom. It was only the three of us, so what harm was there when I asked the Jury Consultant, "Do you think there's still a chance David will plea-bargain?"

The Jury Consultant shrugged.

"It's inappropriate to discuss the case," said the Architect.

"I'm not talking about the case," I said. "I'm asking about something different. The Jury Consultant is the expert here."

"I'm no expert," said the Jury Consultant.

The elevator door opened right then, and the Architect walked out without waiting for us, her Jimmy Choo pumps tapping on the linoleum. Oh, my God, those shoes must've cost a thousand bucks. Her skirt was too short for court—too short, period. It was pleated, loose, and you could almost see her butt when she walked. Everyone knows she's been hitting on the bailiff. Then there was the day she wore that denim mini, crossing and uncrossing her legs when David's expert was testifying. I even think Cranston, the DA, was trying to look up her skirt—he sure lost points for that—and the Express Messenger was all over her during every break. Too bad for him, she sure shut him down fast. Still, how inappropriate. Who's she to tell me *I* was inappropriate? I should've sent a note to the judge about it.

"After you," said the Jury Consultant, who held the elevator door for me, and then we lined up, me first because I'm juror number one.

I take a sip of the coffee and burn my tongue, because they only have carcinogenic fake-dairy powder here, no real cream or milk to cool down the coffee, which tastes like charred toast dipped in scalding motor oil. I'll drink it all, because I'm not going to give the Architect the satisfaction. I wish they had a fridge and some ice cubes in the jury room.

"Moses and the burning coal," says the Clergyman.

"Excuse me?" I say.

"You burned your tongue," he says. "Are you all right?"

"I didn't burn ..." The blush-flash comes again. "Yeah. Fine."

"The hand of the angel," says the Clergyman.

I have to remember to Google that phrase when I get home. I hope he's not mocking me. Would a man of the cloth mock a girl like me?

The others in the room look away uncomfortably, all except the Grandmother, who strains to hear.

"It's kind of interesting that there's a big majority of women jurors," says the Student in a soft voice.

That's an off-the-wall thing to say. I think maybe she's just trying to change the subject, get us back on track.

"Hello to you, too," says the Express Messenger.

"It's just a coincidence," says the Grandmother. "One of those things."

"It's no coincidence; it's a big gamble," says the Architect. "The DA is betting that we women hate David because he's a man who admitted to killing his wife, and the defense is betting that we'll be less likely to convict, because we're not driven by testosterone."

"As if people are alike just because of gender," says the Student.

"Coming from the woman who just said it's interesting that there are so many women in here," says the Express Messenger.

"Yes, I said '*interesting*,'" says the Student. "I didn't say it was good or bad."

I'm not sure exactly what's going on. Do the Student and the Express Messenger have a thing going?

I raise my hand, wave slightly to get people's attention, then say, "To get started, why don't we—?"

"Isn't that what you do?" the Architect asks the Jury Consultant. "Predict what kind of people will convict and which will acquit? You probably know how I'm going to vote already."

"I work with probabilities based on demographics," says the Jury Consultant. "I'm not a psychic. During the past few weeks, I haven't even been a psychologist. I'm a juror."

"I didn't think they let people like you on juries," says the Architect.

"The metrics of jury selection have changed with the times," says the Jury Consultant. "Attorneys get on juries all the time these days. Trial lawyers are just looking for fair-minded people of any occupation."

The Architect half shrugs. She's rude.

I like the Jury Consultant. She's almost as pretty as the Architect, and she's definitely classier. She always wears business casual, a nice blouse and skirt or dark slacks. Nothing skanky like the other one.

"Can we get this show on the road?" says the Express Messenger.

"Sure. Yeah," I say. "So, I suppose the first order of business is to take a straw vote."

"I mean, like, shouldn't we talk about the evidence first, at least for a little bit?" asks the Student. "I mean after a four-week murder trial and all?"

"Yeah, no, I thought we should take a straw vote first, but we can talk first," I say. "We'll talk. Who'll get the ball rolling?"

"I will," says the Housewife. "Amanda Sullinger was a monster."

JUROR NO. 43

THE CLERGYMAN

More than a few still-incredulous trial witnesses testified that the Sullingers, albeit a superficially mismatched couple, appeared to have a happy marriage. I have learned in my business that sometimes the opaque curtain called perception camouflages the ghastliest nightmares.

"Amanda Sullinger was a monster," the Housewife says.

"Mentally ill," the Architect says.

Well, well. My prediction was mistaken. I had concluded that the Architect would lead, pulling the dowdy, repressed Housewife in tow. It is the other way around.

"First thing—and I'm embarrassed to talk about this," the Housewife says. "She seduced him when he was just a child."

She does not look embarrassed to talk about this.

"I wouldn't call him a child," the Express Messenger says. "He was seventeen. And from the evidence, we don't even know—"

"He was sixteen," the Housewife says.

The Express Messenger shakes his head. "David testified—"

"He testified sixteen," the Housewife says. She turns to the Architect. "Wasn't it sixteen?"

The Architect nods.

The Foreperson sits listening, tapping a pencil repeatedly on the table and creating an irritating metronomic sound. She stands and goes to the credenza, where the evidence binders are stacked. Her pear-shaped body and large behind confirm that she should not be wearing tight, white slacks. I had not anticipated that she would be foreperson. I predicted the Jury Consultant or the Architect or the Grandmother.

The Foreperson fumbles with the documents for quite a while, eventually sighing in confusion.

"Do you need help with something?" the Jury Consultant asks.

The Foreperson's face and neck turn splotchy, the patches appearing seriatim like a neon sign advertising her discomfiture. "I was just looking for the transcripts to see if David said he was sixteen or seventeen when he first had relations with Amanda."

"We don't have the transcripts in here," the Jury Consultant says. "If we want to hear testimony, it has to be read in open court in front of the judge and lawyers."

Her complexion transforming from pink to crimson, the Foreperson says, "I could press the—is it the green or red button for a question?"

"We don't need to do that," the Housewife says. "Sixteen or seventeen—what does it matter? He was a minor, she was in her late twenties—"

"*Mid*twenties," the Express Messenger says. "And sixteen or seventeen matters."

"It does *not* matter," the Housewife says. "He was a minor, she was an adult, and she was his teacher. In a position of power. That's the point."

"I agree that age doesn't matter," the Grandmother says. She conveys *sweet old lady*, but I see the lingering school vice principal. Sometimes her look is so sharp you feel like a student again. She puts both elbows on the table and gives that look to the Express Messenger. "I was a teacher. You do not *ever* sleep with your students. Even if you're a college professor and they're twenty-two-year-old seniors. It's an abuse of power."

"Does seventeen versus eighteen matter?" the Express messenger says. The man is persistent, if nothing else.

"Yeah, it does," the Foreperson says, playing the perfect foil. "An eighteen-year-old is an adult."

"That's just the law," the Express Messenger replies. "But a law doesn't change the truth about people. It's arbitrary. What's the difference between a kid who's seventeen years old at eleven-fifty-nine the night before his birthday and an eighteen-year-old sixty-one seconds later? Absolutely nothing. A year might or might not make a difference. David was full grown at sixteen, physically mature. He admitted that on cross-examination. The prosecution showed pictures. He looked like a grown man."

"To this day, he has the emotional maturity of a teenager," the Grandmother says. "What's your point?"

"My point is," the Express Messenger says, then lifts his eyes to the cottage-cheese ceiling for guidance, "I don't remember exactly what my point is. I forget because of all this ... Except there isn't much difference between a seventeen-year-old and an eighteen-year-old."

The Housewife glares contemptuously at the Express Messenger. "You realize you just agreed with my original point and contradicted what you said a few seconds ago, right?"

He thinks for a moment. "I didn't contradict … It's not inconsistent if you're talking about … A seventeen-year-old is just a tick of the second hand away from being an adult, but a sixteen-year-old is just a … Anyway."

The Housewife flutters her hand at him. "For your information, the two-minute difference between the seventeen-year-old and the eighteen-year-old matters not because it says something about the kid, but because it says something about the lack of judgment and warped moral compass of the adult who abuses him. Amanda raped a minor."

"I get it, but chill out," the Express Messenger says. "We just got in here. Jesus."

"I'm perfectly calm," the Housewife says, and she does sound calm. Overly assertive, but calm.

"We're off the point," the Architect says. "Can we get back on the point? Nothing I've heard changes the fact that Amanda was abusive. It's not just having sex with David when he was underage. That's just background showing how perverted she was."

The Student raises her hand tentatively.

"Yes!" the Foreperson says, apparently delighted to have a chance to exercise the power of her exalted office.

The Student pushes her eyeglasses up the bridge of her nose and says, "Does anyone believe Amanda's mother?"

Amanda Sullinger's mother, the prosecution's very first witness, testified that her daughter never seduced David, that David was a stalker. Supposedly, Amanda was insecure with men, was still a virgin at twenty-five, and, worn down and psychologically vulnerable, finally mistook David's insanity for romance. I did not believe the testimony and am surprised that the Student raised the issue. Perhaps she is acting only out of a sense of fairness. Perhaps she just believes she needs to participate.

"Do any of you think the mother was credible?" the Housewife asks.

"Sort of," the Student says.

No one else thinks the mother credible or, at least, confesses to thinking so. The Foreperson rises from her seat and pours herself another cup of coffee. The woman should not consume another drop of caffeine. She is as fidgety as a feral cat trapped in a one-car garage. We wait. She returns to her seat, sets her coffee cup down, picks up the pencil, and starts drumming it on the table. I do wish she would stop that. She looks up, sees me staring at her, and puts the pencil down. She's afraid of me. Good. That might come in handy later.

"I'd like to hear why you all don't think Amanda's mother was credible," the Student says. "Because I kind of feel sorry for her. I feel like she believed what she was saying."

"She not only lacked credibility, she was a brazen liar," the Housewife says, and though I concur, the undercurrent of stridency in her tone will not serve her well if these deliberations happen to continue for any length or deteriorate into controversy. "Why would Amanda let a kid stalk her through a year and a half of high school and for another year after that and then hook up with him? Amanda Sullinger was a lot of things, but she wasn't a fool. Which is exactly what Blaylock brought out on cross-examination when she ripped the mother to shreds. I was surprised at the DA. Calling the mother to the stand and encouraging her to spout such bullsh—" She glances at the Grandmother and then at me, as if I had not heard the word *bullshit* before. I have uttered the word countless times. "… I mean, such *drivel* proves what a bad case the prosecution has. The mother was a liar, arrogant. Both of her grandchildren hate her—maybe the only thing those kids agree on. No wonder her daughter turned out the way she did."

Several of the others nod.

This last I do not agree with, but I do not say it. I will not say it. Deuteronomy 24:16 says, "Fathers shall not be put to death for their sons, nor shall sons be put to death for their fathers; everyone shall be put to death for his own sin." You cannot blame the mother for who the daughter was. Amanda's mother lacks credibility because, like most loving parents in her position, she refuses to believe that her daughter was a demon. I do not say this, will not say this, to my sister and brother jurors. I will not say anything in this room unless I must. For I do not belong on this jury. My presence here is a sin of which I do not repent.

JUROR NO. 33

THE GRANDMOTHER

The heating system buzzes on, the first time in days. The heater whirs and rattles, like an inanimate object come to life but then immediately sent into its death throes. I adjust my hearing aids but can't shut out the ambient whine of that old machine. Oh, drat! I can't quite follow what the others are saying. The Housewife is doing most of the talking. She's a very bright girl, far brighter than I realized. I lean forward to read her lips, but …

"She … with her financial … David's power …" Beyond that, I comprehend not another word after she turns her head and addresses her friend, the Architect, and I can't read her lips.

The Housewife must have said that Amanda used her unequal financial status to dominate David. Or is she saying David used his less favorable status passive-aggressively to dominate Amanda, as the prosecution argued? I should ask. I would ask. But I see how they look at me. I don't know how to explain it. If they find out how severe my hearing loss is, they might remove me from the jury as incompetent, and I don't want to be removed from this jury. I don't want to be incompetent. My husband's incompetence impels me to stay, to make a difference, maybe for the last time in my life. Yes. The Housewife must be saying that Amanda used her economic powers as a psychological bludgeon against David. He couldn't have left her if he'd wanted to. He had no safety net. The defense attorney established that his parents had disowned him when he married Amanda, because they despised her. They both passed before there could be any reconciliation. His brother won't talk to him—didn't even bother to come to the trial, as far as I know. David depended on Amanda for his beer and butter.

But why couldn't David get a job of his own? That's what the prosecution kept hammering at. Why couldn't David get a job? I've asked myself that question many a time, and then I ask, does it matter?

The others must think I'm a horrible, uncaring person, abandoning my husband for so long. I'm the only living soul he still recognizes. He doesn't know the name or face of our daughter, the joy of his life, the object of my jealousy at times when I thought he put her needs over mine. The worst was when he bought her a brand-new Mini Cooper for her sixteenth birthday without consulting me, and there I was, driving that twenty-year-old Mercedes-Benz that had 188,000-some-odd miles on it. Great car in its day, but by then it was falling apart. Oh, I didn't speak to him for three weeks after and didn't have intimate relations with him for eight months. When my next birthday rolled around, I withdrew some of our retirement savings and bought myself a new Mercedes SUV the first year the model came out. I don't know how to explain it; it was an impulsive, imprudent thing to do, but it felt grand at the time. The car turned out to be a lemon. We sure could use that retirement money plus interest these days. Maybe I should have been more understanding.

My husband has a daughter by a previous marriage that lasted less than a year. He and his first wife were nineteen years old, and he got her in trouble and did the right thing. He moved to Minneapolis, where she'd been reared, and took a job working for his new father-in-law, who was an electrical contractor. His ex-wife cheated on him three months after they relocated, and when he found out about it, he left and came back to Sepulveda County. Though he never missed a child-support payment, he had nothing to do with his first child. She's a woman now, must be close to fifty, and still they have no relationship—all his fault. She has two kids and a good job. I wish it had been different for him. He must have felt so guilty about abandoning his first daughter that he compensated by becoming too infatuated with our daughter. I should have understood, shown more patience. Now, with his muddled, dying brain, he doesn't even recognize our daughter. He recognizes me.

He and I repaired things after our daughter moved out. *Repaired* is never as good as *undamaged*, but *repaired* is better than *Sullinger.*

"Do you want …?" the Student asks.

"Sorry, dear, say again?" I say.

"You're cold, aren't you. You can borrow my sweater."

The delightful girl pulls one arm out of her knit sweater, but I hold up a hand. "I'll be fine, sweetheart. The heat just came on. You're so considerate." I've read articles about millennials being unthinking and self-absorbed. Not this girl. I do worry that this trial will be traumatic for her. She's innocent at twenty—a trusting ingenue in the truest sense. Or she was when this trial started. Listening to the sordid testimony would take away anyone's innocence.

I watch my fellow jurors' mouths, strain to hear, turn my better ear toward the person speaking, but I miss most of it. Then, mercifully, the heater shuts down. The absence of ambient noise will allow me to hear what people are saying.

"At any hint of defiance, Amanda would become angry," the Housewife says. "Amanda used their children as leverage against David. Classic abuser."

"Blaylock used that word, *leverage*, all right," the Express Messenger says. "But what does it mean?" He tugs at the sleeve of his sport shirt. Although it sounds as if he's leaning toward conviction, I don't think the fellow has a point of view. I just think he likes to be the center of attention, just as he did in high school. Take this acting business. He announced to the jury panel that he was an actor, and at first Judge Quinn-Gilbert seemed very interested in his career, a wee bit starstruck, which surprised me because she's a judge—an esteemed position. But we're also small-town folks in this county, and she's lived here many years. Well, it turned out the Express Messenger's "acting" career amounts to working as an extra in two pictures and speaking three words in a Clint Eastwood movie seven years ago. He says he works as an express messenger only to fill the time while he's on "hiatus." He lives with his mother. I know I'm old-fashioned, but I don't think it's appropriate for a thirty-one-year-old man to be living with his mother. Why the lawyers left him on the jury, I don't know. This is an educated jury except for him and the Foreperson. Maybe they think him a cipher who won't influence us other jurors one way or another. Well, if he's a cipher, he's certainly an opinionated one.

"Let me be …"

Garbled. I missed it. The Housewife's eyes are gleeful. Why would they be gleeful? Perhaps I'm misreading her eyes. Glee, intensity, fear—how do the eyes show these in my world of muffled sounds?

"We heard Lacey testify that Amanda hit him with a coffeepot and broke his nose—in front of the children," the Housewife says. "Another time, Amanda got upset that her hamburger was underdone, accused him of trying to poison her, and pushed his hand down on the grill—in front of the children, who were what, eleven and ten at the time? She threw a steak knife at him once during dinner and claimed it was just a bad joke. And, of course, there's the tuna casserole incident."

I have the impression this is the first time in years that the Housewife has had the chance to speak to adults about adult matters and that she's not about to squander the opportunity. Raising three little ones, all under five, must be difficult. My husband and I had only the one girl, and that was hard enough.

"The tuna casserole," the Student says, "Do we really believe—?"

"Oh, we believe it," the Architect says. "David and Lacey—"

"Gave contradictory testimony," I say.

"Not contradictory," the Architect says. "Maybe ..."

"Inconsistent," I say. "That's a better word to explain it."

"The son denied it ever happened," the Foreperson says. "Of course, he's a liar."

"We should put a pin in that one," the Jury Consultant says. She's obviously holding back. It's quite apparent she doesn't want to be accused of manipulating this jury. Good for her. I do wonder what she's thinking. The most effective advocates talk—how do I explain it?—don't speak until after everyone else has. When I was younger, I followed that rule, but it's harder to do that now. Age is supposed to bring wisdom, but more often it brings impatience.

The Express Messenger turns and touches the Clergyman's shoulder as if they were long-lost pals, and says, "What do you think?"

The Clergyman tenses up. I tend to look at people's mouths because of my hearing loss, and I see the older man's jaw clench, as if he wants to smack the Express Messenger.

"I will give my opinion when and if I decide to do so," the Clergyman says. "Thank you for thinking of me." He speaks in a tone so soft and smooth that it's more intimidating than if he'd shouted. Even I heard him clearly. If there's such power in his whisper, how much more does he have in reserve? Although the Clergyman is at least twenty years older than the Express Messenger, he's also a much larger man. The Express Messenger raises a palm in surrender.

"David and Lacey's testimony about the tuna casserole incident is different, but it's not inconsistent," the Housewife says. "Not in a way that would undermine their credibility." When she begins talking about the specifics of that revolting incident, I'm tempted to take my hearing aids out.

CHRISTINA KELLEHER, CSR

Oh, how I wanted on *Sullinger.* Oh, I wanted on that case bad. If the cases aren't interesting, a court-reporting job sucks big-time. I used to work in LA and did some entertainment lawsuits, a bank-robbery trial in federal court, and a murder case involving two Persian cousins who hated each other—awesome. Nothing much happens here in Sepulveda County, and less happens in the courts—DUIs, landlord-tenant disputes, car repos gone wrong, scattered employment-discrimination cases, drug possession, personal injury, and more personal injury. Sometimes, rival motorcycle gangs get into it with each other, and that can heat things up, but mostly it's boredom. It's picturesque in these parts, sure. The high desert meets the lush foothills, all by a scenic river. I moved here four years ago, followed a guy who was sick of the LA traffic. We're no longer together. He's back in LA, working a good-paying job as a general contractor, which means *he* can now afford the exorbitant rent increases that happened soon after we left the city. I can barely make my rent here.

Boring days, boring nights. I just want to save up enough

money to get out of this town. When the possibility of a big-news, four-week trial came up, I saw the chance to make quite a bit of gwap. I lobbied hard to get on the case. I wish I hadn't. The nightmares aren't worth it. Oh, it wasn't the gore and violence—I'd seen stuff like that in other cases. It was all just so sad.

SUPERIOR COURT FOR THE COUNTY OF SEPULVEDA

	)
PEOPLE	) JURY TRIAL—DAY 22
v.	)
DAVID BENNETT SULLINGER	) Case No. 16-382
	)
	)

BEFORE: Hon. Natalie Quinn-Gilbert, Superior Court Judge

APPEARANCES: JOHN Y. CRANSTON, ESQ.
Assistant District Attorney,
Sepulveda County
On behalf of the People

JENNA MARIE BLAYLOCK, ESQ.
On behalf of the Defendant

TRANSCRIPT OF PROCEEDINGS

Reported by Christina Kelleher
Certified Shorthand Reporter

Direct examination of David Sullinger by Jenna Blaylock, counsel for the Defendant (excerpt):

Q. Mr. Sullinger, we've been talking about why, on the day of Amanda's death, you believed the use of force against her was necessary.

A. [The witness nods.]

Q. Is that a yes?

A. Yes.

Q. Was there an incident involving a tuna casserole?

A. Yeah, but Amanda wanted me to call it "tuna à la king." She thinks … thought it sounded classier.

[Laughter in the courtroom]

THE COURT: There will be no laughter, no reactions whatsoever from the spectators. Fair warning.

Q. What would have happened if you'd called the dish a tuna casserole?

A. She … she'd say things like I had no class, that I was born in a barn, that I was a pig. She'd say my fat gut proved I was a fat pig.

Q. At some time, did you have a confrontation about the tuna dish?

A. Yeah.

Q. A violent confrontation?

MR. CRANSTON: Objection. Argumentative.

MR. CRANSTON: Your Honor?

THE COURT: What is it, counsel?

MS. BLAYLOCK: Judge, are you—?

MR. CRANSTON: My objection, Your Honor. Argumentative.

THE COURT: Oh. Yes. The objection is overruled.

By Ms. Blaylock:

Q. At some point, when the kids were young, did you have a violent confrontation with Amanda over a tuna casserole?

A. [The witness nods.]

Q. You'll have to answer out loud, Mr. Sullinger.

A. Oh, sorry. I did it again. Yeah, it was violent. Very violent.

Q. When did this occur?

A. I don't exactly remember. I think Lacey was nine or ten and Dillon was seven or eight.

Q. About ten, eleven years ago?

A. [The witness nods.]

Q. Do you remember the confrontation well despite the passage of time?

A. Absolutely.

Q. Why?

A. Because it was horrible, painful, excruciating. But mostly, because my kids were in jeopardy.

Q. What happened?

A. I was in the kitchen cooking. I didn't think Amanda would be home for dinner. She had a late-evening showing of a town house to some prospective buyers. I didn't do the grocery shopping. I was supposed to do the grocery shopping. She made me promise in the morning that I would, but I … I guess I just got distracted doing other things. So, I took what we had in the house—a couple of cans of tuna, some cream-of-mushroom soup, peas, egg noodles, and whatnot—and whipped up tuna à la king and put it in the oven. It was Lacey's favorite.

Q. What happened next?

A. Just as I was taking the casserole out of the oven to cool, Amanda came home early. I could tell she was upset. Like I said before, you knew it because the muscles in her neck would be pulled tight like stretched twine, and her eyes would flash this intense nastiness that—

MR. CRANSTON: Move to strike as nonresponsive.

THE COURT: Overruled. Get to the point, Mr. Sullinger.

A. What I'm saying is that Amanda didn't look happy, to put it mildly. I learned later that her possible big deal to sell a luxury town house fell through that night. When she had that nasty look, I tried to walk on eggshells, act cordial but also stay out of her way. I said hello, and she didn't say anything. The kids were at the dinette table, waiting to eat. Amanda was carrying a used napkin or Kleenex, and she opened the trash can that we kept under the counter, to throw it away, and that's when she saw it.

Q. Saw what, David?

A. [Unintelligible]

Q. Please speak up, David.

A. The empty Campbell's cream-of-mushroom-soup cans.

Q. Was there a problem with that?

A. Oh, yeah. Amanda thought Lacey was getting fat. It wasn't true. Lacey was ten, just maturing like girls do before hitting puberty, so she looked pudgy, but she wasn't overweight. Even her pediatrician said she wasn't. Amanda wouldn't accept it. Amanda said Lacey had to diet, use low-fat products, no sugar. So when she saw the empty soup cans, she went ballistic.

Q. What do you mean "ballistic"?

A. Ballistic. Started screaming, calling me a fucking moron, said I was making Lacey a fat fucking pig like me, that I was a worthless slob, and she wouldn't let me make her kids pigs. Then she threw the empty soup can at me.

Q. Were you hurt?

A. No, I dodged it, which made her madder. She got in my face and was berating me.

Q. What did you do?

A. Nothing. When Amanda had one of her fits, the best thing to do was nothing.

Q. Like playing possum?

A. Absolutely not. If you showed weakness, it would get worse. If you showed strength, it would get worse. You had to pretend you didn't exist, and most of the time, even that didn't work.

Q. Did it work this time?

A. I thought maybe it would, but, but … but then Lacey got involved. I told the kids never to get involved, and before that they never really … But Lacey was getting older, and she … she went over to Amanda, yelled something like "Leave my daddy alone!" or something like that, and she tried to pull Amanda away. Amanda looked like she relaxed, had this weird, tight grin on her face, and she … she, you know, said, "You want to be a pig like your daddy? Fine with me." Then she grabbed Lacey by the hair—it was long then, down almost to her back—and jerked her toward the stove top. Lacey was screaming in pain, and Amanda with her free hand took off the lid on the casserole dish—it was still steaming hot—grabbed the serving spoon, dug into the food, and tried to force-feed it to Lacey, who was struggling and kicking and screaming.

Q. What did you do?

A. I … I … I …

Q. Take your time, David.

A. Sorry. Apologies to the court and jury. Sorry.

THE COURT: Do we need to take a recess, Mr. Sullinger?

A. No, Your Honor, I … Thank you.

MS. BLAYLOCK: Take your time, David.

A. I'm sorry. I still feel guilty after all these years. I was paralyzed at first. But eventually, I went over and pulled Amanda off Lacey, who ran out of the kitchen. Amanda shouted, "Get your fucking hands off me, you piece of shit!" So I backed away. I didn't want it to get physical. I never wanted to be physical. She backed away, too, and I thought it was over, and I turned slightly. I was going to check on Lacey, and I took a step or two, which meant that Amanda was behind me. Then there was this sudden heavy blow to the left side of my face, and I saw red flares like Fourth of July fireworks. I was dazed for a split second, then I screamed, because my face was scalding. Amanda had picked up the casserole dish and hit me with it in a way that caused the hot food to spill onto my face. Some of it got in my left eye. It was agonizing.

Q. Did you seek medical treatment?

A. Yes, I had to.

Q. What did you tell the doctors?

A. I made up a story that I was looking for a potholder in a lower drawer, that I left the hot casserole dish too close to the edge of the stove top, and I jostled something, and the dish fell and burned me. I had second-degree burns on my cheek. My forehead was cut, a lot of blood. I needed six stitches. Luckily, I didn't go blind in my left eye.

Q. Did the doctors believe your story?

A. They didn't say they disbelieved me. When a battered heterosexual male goes to the hospital and makes up a story, no one questions it. I'm not saying that to be homophobic. People always assume only men are violent."

MR. CRANSTON: Move to strike everything after the first sentence as irrelevant, improper opinion evidence.

THE COURT: Sustained. The jury will disregard the witness' statement about battered males.

Q. Was Lacey injured?

A. No, thank God. At least not physically.

Q. Where was your son, Dillon, all this time?

A. He was … Sorry. I promised myself I wouldn't do this again … You asked about Dillon. He was still sitting at the dinette table drinking his apple juice. He was perfectly calm. No crying, no shivering, no cowering. He might as well have been watching a kids' show on his DVD player.

Q. Did Amanda say anything after?

A. After I returned from the hospital? Yeah. She was crying, remorseful, said she loved me, couldn't live without me. But what scared me … she said if I left her she couldn't bear to keep living, would kill herself and take the kids with her.

Q. Did you have any reason to believe that she'd do such a thing, other than her words and violent actions?

A. Yes. Not long after Dillon was born, Amanda sold a house on the river to this couple from San Diego.

old at the time. They looked like such a happy family. The husband was much older than the wife—a second marriage. About six months after they bought the property, the husband killed the twins and himself with a shotgun that he supposedly kept for protection. The news reports said he thought she was cheating on him, but apparently … Anyway, Amanda and I were talking about the killing, and I said what kind of evil madman would murder his kids just to punish his wife? She said I was clueless, that I should realize that wasn't the reason he killed his twins at all, that he did it because he realized what a horrible world this is, and he wanted to spare them from suffering in such a horrible world. She said he did a noble thing.

Q. Did she specifically use the word "noble" to describe the murder-suicide?

A. That's exactly the word she used. "Noble."

MS. BLAYLOCK: I've finished this line of questioning, Your Honor. Maybe it's a good time to take our afternoon break.

RECESS TAKEN AT 2:42 P.M.

JUROR NO. 11
THE STUDENT

I feel like the adversary system doesn't work that well, because how are you supposed to make up your mind? You hear the DA's opening statement, and it seems like David has to be guilty. Right after that, you hear from the defense attorney, and you totally change your mind. Then you settle yourself down and try to wipe your conclusions out of your brain and try to follow the judge's instruction about keeping an open mind, and then the witnesses testify and direct examination goes one way and cross-examination the other, and you go from believing one side to believing the other. It's even more confusing now that we're in the jury room. How do you decide at all, much less make the right decision? I've continually tried to stay positive, to do the basics that the judge laid down for us. It's all so confusing. I keep telling myself not to trip. I'm the youngest in this room by ten years. Do I even belong here? I've been feeling like a grown-up for a while, but now I'm feeling like a teenager again.

Me and the Grandmother have bonded. She's awesome, reminds me of my own grandma, so cute. I'll try to follow her lead.

"Lacey contradicted her father," the Express Messenger says. "David testified that Dillon just sat at the kitchen table as if nothing happened. Lacey testified that Dillon was screaming and crying and covering his ears with his hands. Lacey also left out the part about her yelling and pulling at her mother. She just said that Amanda got angry about the mushroom soup and threw the casserole dish in David's face."

"That's not much of an inconsistency," the Housewife says. "It was a long time ago. Memories fade, especially a child's."

"Except that both David and Lacey said their memories of the day were vivid even after all these years," the Express Messenger says, nodding like he's some kind of King Solomon or something. "'Vivid.' Who uses that word?"

I don't like him. He tried to hit on me the third day of trial. He just came into my booth at Subway during lunch and sat across from me with no invite. That's when the Grandmother and I became friends. She rescued me by sitting down next to me and talking about English novels for the next twenty minutes. I took an English lit class last semester, and she used to teach English literature. We both love Middlemarch and aren't fans of Jane Austen, think she's overrated. As for the Express Messenger, he had no idea what we were talking about. The next day, he asked me out. Nope. Not this woman. I feel like guys these days don't have boundaries, have terrible radar. His radar is totally bad.

Over at the other end of the table, the Clergyman sits like some Mount Sepulveda, hands folded across his chest, eyes shut. Except for the occasional blink, I would've sworn he was asleep.

The Housewife says, "The fact that David and Lacey told slightly different stories—"

"Not that slight," the Grandmother says.

"Different stories, then—proves that they're *not* lying. If they were lying, their stories would be identical, because they would've gotten together on it."

"Not true," the Jury Consultant says.

The Housewife is about to respond, but the Architect places a hand on her wrist and stops her. I like the Housewife. But you know how sometimes a recording artist or an actor who you like a lot becomes overexposed, and then you don't like them as much anymore? I feel like that's what's happening with the Housewife, and we haven't even been in here very long.

The room is quiet. Even the Clergyman leans in toward the Jury Consultant.

"Here's what I think," the Jury Consultant says. "Poor liars get together and make up identical stories. Smart liars get together and decide how their stories will diverge—just enough not to sound like there's a conspiracy afoot, but not so much that they'll sound incredible."

"Are you saying that's what David and Lacey are? Smart liars?" I ask.

"Not really. Because the same kind of discrepancies can happen when people are telling the truth. You have to judge credibility in other ways."

"How?" I ask.

"Well, you—"

Before the Jury Consultant can finish, the Foreperson taps on the table three times. "Let's take a quick break and maybe we can talk about this witness credibility thing some more. I need more coffee. Does anyone want coffee?"

JUROR NO. 43

THE CLERGYMAN

Although these deliberations are hardly monotonous, it is that oscitant time of late afternoon when, with yawns and droopy eyelids and easy distractibility, the mind and body counsel cessation of labor, while cultural imperatives and institutional exigencies demand continued focus on the business at hand. The Foreperson pours herself another cup of coffee, although the liquid is undoubtedly tepid and charred; the glass pot crackles and sputters when lifted off the hot plate. The Architect pulls out a large bottle of reverse-osmosis bottled water and shares it with the Housewife, dividing it between two clear plastic cups. The Housewife gulps the water down as if desert parched, as she should be after her several long monologues. She sets the cup on the credenza and goes to the ladies' room, not so surreptitiously removing her cell phone from her purse and dialing, although making calls during deliberations is against the rules. The Express Messenger first tries to converse with the Architect and, after the preordained rebuff, approaches the Foreperson like a contrite Labrador retriever that got the worst of an encounter with a high-pressure lawn sprinkler.

He leans over and half whispers something in her ear that I cannot discern but which makes the Foreperson smile a genuine smile. I did not know he had it in him. The Student, the Grandmother, and the Jury Consultant remain at the table, talking about the Jury Consultant's love for this remote county, such that she is willing to travel to law offices and courthouses across the nation, always returning to Sepulveda. My not-inappropriate eavesdropping—they are speaking somewhat louder than normal so the Grandmother can hear—leads me to conclude that the Jury Consultant moved here six years ago to escape an ever more pressure-filled life in Portland, Oregon. And, of course, to escape the depressive rain.

With effort, I stand to stretch and activate my wobbly legs, creaky lumbar region, and frozen right shoulder. We will leave for the evening in about one hour if the judge keeps to her schedule, and I will return home to my medications for diabetes, high cholesterol, benign heart arrhythmia (if such a thing can ever be called benign), and hypertension. I will vow to diet and yet will overeat. I will vow to abstain yet will imbibe. I do sometimes wish I were affiliated with a more charismatic religion, that I were, for example, a Pentecostal or a Hasidic Jew, so that I might regard my ill health from a more mystical perspective.

JUDICIAL COUNCIL CRIMINAL JURY INSTRUCTION NO. 105

You alone must judge the credibility or believability of the witnesses. In deciding whether testimony is true and accurate, use your common sense and experience. You must judge the testimony of each witness by the same standards, setting aside any bias or prejudice you may have. You may believe all, part, or none of any witness' testimony. Consider the testimony of each witness and decide how much of it you believe.

In evaluating a witness' testimony, you may consider anything that reasonably tends to prove or disprove the truth or accuracy of that testimony. Among the factors that you may consider are the following:

- How well could the witness see, hear, or otherwise perceive the things about which the witness testified?
- How well was the witness able to remember and describe what happened?
- What was the witness' behavior while testifying?

- Did the witness understand the questions and answer them directly?
- Was the witness' testimony influenced by a factor such as bias or prejudice, a personal relationship with someone involved in the case, or a personal interest in how the case is decided?
- What was the witness' attitude about the case or about testifying?
- Did the witness make a statement in the past that is consistent or inconsistent with his or her testimony?
- How reasonable is the testimony when you consider all the other evidence in the case?
- Did other evidence prove or disprove any fact about which the witness testified?
- Did the witness admit to being untruthful?
- What is the witness' character for truthfulness?
- Has the witness been convicted of a felony?
- Has the witness engaged in (other) conduct that reflects on his or her believability?
- Was the witness promised immunity or leniency in exchange for his or her testimony?

Do not automatically reject testimony just because of inconsistencies or conflicts. Consider whether the differences are important. People sometimes honestly forget things or make mistakes about what they remember. Also, two people may witness the same event yet see or hear it differently.

If the evidence establishes that a witness' character for truthfulness has not been discussed among the people who know him or her, you may conclude from the lack of discussion that the witness's character for truthfulness is good.

If you do not believe a witness' testimony that he or she no longer remembers something, that testimony is inconsistent with the witness' earlier statement on that subject.

If you decide that a witness deliberately lied about something significant in this case, you should consider not believing anything that witness says. Or, if you think the witness lied about some things but told the truth about others, you may simply accept the part that you think is true and ignore the rest.

JUROR NO. 1

THE FOREPERSON

Our deliberations are going really good so far. Maybe I should try to get the Housewife to shut up a little more, but I figure she speaks for the Architect, so I'm giving her twice the amount of time. The Architect doesn't have a thing to say. I knew she was a bitch, but I never saw her as a ditz, especially with the job she has. Even now she's filing her fingernails with an emery board. How unsanitary. Does she have a hot date, or something? I want to call out, "Excuse me, are we boring you?" But that wouldn't be fitting for a jury foreperson to say.

The Express Messenger told me during the break I'm doing a good job. He actually said "great" job. I'm impressed with him. I never dreamed I would be, but he followed the trial pretty closely. I don't agree with all his points, especially not about teenage boys sleeping with older women being okay, but he's not afraid to take on the Housewife, and someone needs to take her on. If she keeps trying to dominate, I'll get her to shut up or we'll be here forever. What's the phrase? *Justice delayed is* ... something.

One sip of coffee to clear my palate, then we'll start, but my lips pucker from the burnt bitterness, and I half gag. I looked for grounds to make a fresh pot, but all they have left is decaf, and I don't drink decaf. The process they use to decaffeinate the coffee is carcinogenic. The Architect looks up from her self-manicure and smirks.

"Let's get going," I say, and tilt my head toward the Jury Consultant. "Like she said, our decision turns on witness credibility."

"To a certain extent," says the Jury Consultant. "Other evidence as well."

"To a certain extent," I say, nodding. I flutter a hand toward the Student, who reacts as if she wants to duck under the table. Before we got in the jury room, the Student was relaxed, but I guess she's one of those people who, no matter how social she is, gets nervous when she has to talk in front of crowds. I'm the other way around.

"Yeah, Lacey was totally credible," she says in a halting voice.

"We're talking about David's credibility," I say.

She places her hand to her mouth. "Oh, sorry, I ..."

"Don't be sorry," I say. She shouldn't be sorry.

"I can't lie, I wasn't that impressed with David," she says. "I feel like he was kind of ... slippery, you know? Even when he testified about the tuna casserole attack, he was always slipping in adjectives dissing Amanda—argumentative stuff. I mean, like, she deserved to be dissed and all, but still ..."

"David was an ineffective witness," says the Jury Consultant, nodding.

"You can say that again," says the Grandmother. "I understand a man crying under these circumstances, but that hysterical sobbing? Sometimes I wondered if he was feigning it."

"This trial was brutal on him and his kids," says the Housewife. "Many men would break down and—"

The Grandmother holds up her hand. "You've spoken for quite a long time already. Now it's time to let other people have a turn."

Her voice is surprisingly young for an old, deaf woman. I think it's the brittle tone more than the words that causes the Housewife to widen her eyes and jerk back slightly, like she's only just realized she's been stung by a bee.

"My husband has seen some tragedy in his life," says the Grandmother. "Up until the dementia, he never cried much at all. There's something else that troubles me. David shouted at the prosecutor during cross-examination. It made me wonder whether he *was* the abusive spouse."

"His testimony about what started the fight on the afternoon in question was credible," says the Housewife. I guess the bee sting healed over fast. "He asked what they were going to do for their wedding anniversary the following day, and she'd forgotten about their anniversary, and he was hurt and told her so, and as always she started spewing insults, and swore and him, and accused him of sleeping with Annalise Rauch—"

"Which he did," says the Jury Consultant.

"Yeah, but ... we'll get to that," says the Housewife. "My point is that it's all consistent. Amanda would go bonkers at the slightest provocation, and this time David stood up for himself, and she tried to kill him."

"Hard to believe a husband could care so much about a wedding anniversary after so many years of marriage," says the Express Messenger. "Especially an abused husband. Does your husband care that much about *your* wedding anniversary?"

"This isn't about me or my life," says the Housewife.

Which says to me that her husband doesn't care about their anniversary.

"A lot of men care about their wedding anniversaries," says the Architect, like the faithful Indian companion Tonto she is. "It's sexist to claim it's only wives who care. My ex-husband cared a lot. I wish I'd realized how nice that was."

"I'm not sexist," says the Express Messenger, who looks hurt. "I was raised by a single mom."

Who you still live with, I think. I glance around the room. I can tell that's what most of us are thinking.

"Anyway, David *looks* like a liar," says the Express Messenger.

"What does that even mean?" asks the Student.

"It means," says the Express Messenger, "that he looks like a liar."

"Just what does that look like?" says the Grandmother.

"Like Bill and Hillary Clinton," says the Express Messenger. "You know, always making up long answers, looking into the camera like they know everything, but telling lies."

"Oh, dear Lord," says the Grandmother.

The Clergyman, who for all I know has been in a coma all afternoon, comes to and lets out a deep belly snort that reminds me of this horny bull elephant I once saw on the Nat Geo channel. He calms down fast and sits back in his chair, folding his hands on the desk, closing his eyes, and acting like it never happened.

"I think we should focus on specifics, not speculation about whether people do or don't look like liars," says the Student. "There were a few times David contradicted himself or Lacey, like the tuna casserole thing, but his story was pretty solid, at least for me. So I feel like he was sort of credible, but not totally? That probably doesn't make any sense, but ... Sorry." She pauses. "I took this psychology-and-the-law class at my college last year."

"Yeah, I remember you talked about that during voir dire," I say.

"Anyway," says the Student, "I read this article saying lack of eye contact, arm crossing, picking or biting your nails, and, um, what else?—like, saying ums and uhs—is a sign of lying?" She realizes her mistake and covers her mouth with her hand to hide an embarrassed giggle. "Anyway, that's what the article said, and David did all those things."

"If that's true, almost everyone in this room is a liar," says the Housewife.

She's right. At the end of the table, the Clergyman is sitting with his arms crossed, as he's been doing almost the entire hour and a half we've been in here. He never makes eye contact with anyone. The Architect has stopped playing with her nails, but she's done it a lot. The Express Messenger is chewing on his nails. The Student says "um" a lot. What do I do? Do I do things like that? I don't think I do. I'm a calm kind of girl.

"Those supposed clues to lying are urban legends," says the Jury Consultant. "And, by the way, we're a mostly female jury, but another urban legend is that women are better at recognizing liars than men. The truth is, it's very difficult to tell through observation whether someone is lying. There are, however, other emotions that can go along with lying—fear, stress—and those do have expressions associated with them. A consultant named Cynthia Cohen calls them microexpressions: frowns, a raised voice, higher-pitched or faster speech, long answers. Changes from baseline behavior."

"I guess I should've said, 'David looks like a liar, sounds like a liar,'" says the Express Messenger, who's slouched down in his chair, sulking.

"We are all liars in the eyes of God," says the Clergyman, causing half of us to flinch.

"David was emotional, but who wouldn't be?" says the Housewife. "He's volatile, but Amanda shaped him like that ever since he was basically a child. His testimony was generally consistent, and Cranston hammered him on cross-examination for two days without undermining his credibility. As for these so-called signs of lying? I don't believe in convicting a man based on psychobabble and voodoo science."

"David Sullinger was *not* a good witness," says the Jury Consultant, shaking her head almost apologetically. "The shouting at the prosecution, the long answers, the slouching—I've seen hundreds, maybe thousands of witnesses during my career, and he just wasn't good."

"Voodoo science," says the Housewife.

"David admitted he lied about the casserole incident," says the Jury Consultant.

The Housewife almost jumps out of her chair, but the Architect subdues her with a touch on the wrist.

"He confessed to lying to the doctors in the hospital emergency room about how he got his burns," says the Jury Consultant.

"But that's what victims of spousal abuse do," says the Housewife. "They lie out of fear; they lie to protect the other spouse; they lie to protect the children."

"That might be true," says the Jury Consultant. "But do you realize you used the word 'lie' three times in one sentence to describe David Sullinger?"

The Housewife sits back and crosses her arms, her posture identical to the Architect's. Bitch bookends.

We spend the next ten minutes debating David Sullinger's credibility. I haven't weighed in, because, as jury foreperson, it's my job to be objective and let everyone have their say. Finally, whoever wants to talk has talked. There's no consensus. So I finally weigh in.

"I think David's credibility was *meh*," I say.

Every eye turns on me, like they're waiting for something more. I cross my arms. What more is there to say?

THE HONORABLE
NATALIE QUINN-GILBERT

Before this trial started, I read in the media that David Sullinger took a polygraph test. We judges can't allow the results of polygraph tests to come into evidence. The outcome of a polygraph test depends on the bias of the human being administering the test. So we leave credibility determinations to jurors. Juries have something that machines still lack: a sense of moral responsibility. My husband used to say that potential remorse is the sine qua non of doing the right thing.

Jonathan reveres—revered—Bob Dylan, whom he discovered in 1962 at age fourteen. There's a lyric from "Desolation Row": *They bring them to the factory where the heart-attack machine is strapped across their shoulders ...* Jonathan says—would say, *did* say—that the heart-attack machine was a polygraph machine, and I disagree—would disagree, did disagree—because that didn't make sense to me, and we'd have one of those silly debates that lawyers have, that spouses have, over the trivial and unprovable. Now I think I know what he means, what he meant: truth machines dehumanize and kill, just as heart attacks dehumanize and kill.

Jonathan said I became a judge because I was obsessed with discovering the truth. Jonathan says he didn't become a judge because he's concerned with stories. The best lawyers tell the best stories, based on the best facts and the best truths. Everyone seeks out the best stories, the best facts, and the best truths. Jonathan was a storyteller and a truth seeker. I am a judge.

The outcome of a polygraph test depends on the human administering the test. The outcome of a jury trial depends on the human overseeing the trial—and human biases differ, so outcomes differ. Judges can alter the truth. I alter the truth.

Jonathan's four loves are Natalie Quinn, trying cases, Bob Dylan, and the Chicago Cubs. Oh, and drawing and painting, so that's five. I have one love, and he's Roland Jonathan Gilbert.

If only Jonathan could have seen Dylan win the Nobel Prize. If only he could have seen the Cubs win the World Series.

JUROR NO. 52

THE EXPRESS MESSENGER / ACTOR

My mom can't get enough of the trial. It's awkward. She wants to talk about it, but I can't. Last night, she even woke me up in the garage where I sleep and asked me whether an article she found on the internet about the closing arguments was accurate.

"I can't talk about it, Mom." It sucks that I have to disappoint her.

"Oh, you know no juror ever follows that rule," she says, waving her hand at me dismissively.

My mom has never been on a jury, but lack of info has never stopped her from having an opinion. How the hell does she get out of jury duty? It's not like she has an important job. She manages a bowling alley. (She can still bowl in the 180s, even with fucked-up, arthritic knees.) She tells me she was a hustler when she was a teenager. Hustled suckers in the six bowling alleys located in Sepulveda County and never got caught. It's fifty-fifty whether she's making it up or telling the truth. Mom's a great bowler and a great storyteller.

This is the third jury I've been on. The only other people on this jury who've served as jurors before are the Grandmother and the Clergyman. The know-it-all Housewife hasn't even been on a jury. I know what I'm doing.

I only started living in my mother's garage when I came back from LA after my acting career hit a speed bump. The speed bump being that I turned thirty and lost my agent the next day. Man, those dudes must have ticklers that alert them when their unsuccessful clients hit thirty. At least I was better off than the actresses—for those poor girls, the tickler kicks in at twenty-four. Talk about sucking. At least I had an agent and got two entries in the Internet Movie Database. That makes my mom proud.

The judge didn't order us to say if we knew any of the other jurors, so I haven't told the Grandmother I attended her high school. The Grandmother either doesn't remember me or remembers me and doesn't want to embarrass me by acknowledging it. She scared me shitless back then. Now she's old and frail, and her hearing sucks. Time sucks. She also hates me—got the bailiff on my ass about using too many cuss words.

I do regret not acting in high school productions. It was harder for a boy to pursue drama back then. Sepulveda County was conservative, still is, and acting in student productions was gay. Yeah, I'm not proud of it, but I used that word back then. "It doesn't mean that; it's just an expression," I maintained when I got called to the Grandmother's office. That justification didn't fly with the Grandmother, and it especially didn't fly with my lesbian single mom, who's brave and worked her ass off all her life to provide for me and teach me right from wrong. The more ashamed I got, the more I protested my innocence to both my mom and the Grandmother. Why do we do stuff like that?

Anyway, I didn't get actor looks until senior year, when I grew four inches to five foot nine. Not tall; in the Tom Cruise range. Some people say I look like a younger, blonder Tom Cruise.

My father left when I was four years old. Went back to Buffalo, New York. I've seen him once since, when I was ten. Only when I got on this jury did my mom tell me that my dad, the fucking twisted turd, hit her. When she started going into more detail, I covered my ears like a six-year-old, and I said—no, I *shouted*, and I don't shout at my mom—that I couldn't talk about the case. Which was true, but mostly I didn't want to hear the details of the abuse, because I still remember it—or enough of it. My mom started crying, and I hugged her, and then she went to make chicken cacciatore for dinner, and a half hour later, she was fine. That was after the fourth day of trial, but it's stuck with me. I force myself to ignore my father's abuse of my mom. I'm a juror, so I have to ignore that shit so I can be fair. That's why I've been so hard on David's testimony—because I'm emotionally on his side, and I want to test my prejudices.

Now the Clergyman clears his throat and readjusts his position. The sound and movement startles me back to reality, because most of the time the man's a mute statue. How unfriendly the guy is! Oh, he'll say *hello, goodbye, excuse me*, and he'll chat about the weather and traffic, but that's about it. Yet, every Sunday, he preaches the word of God, where you have to be charismatic? Really? I've seen people like that in my acting class—no personality until they get on the stage or in front of a camera, and then they're fucking awesome. They can play anyone convincingly. They're like human sponges, and that's probably a good analogy, because sponges have nothing interesting about them intrinsically. It's what they soak up that matters. Maybe that's my problem as an actor. Maybe I'm so brimming with life that I can't soak up the lives of others. Or maybe my agent's right; maybe I don't have the talent to transform what I absorb into dramatic gold. It sucks when you want to be famous—not mega famous, just famous enough—and you can't be.

The messenger job is a pretty good one. I get to meet all kinds of different people, and that helps me hone my acting skills. When I was in Hollywood, I worked the wrong jobs, which may be why things didn't work out too good. Clerk at a baseball card shop; receptionist at an accounting firm; barista in Brentwood, where I met a lot of people but they were all rich. I just read about a news anchorman who quit his job to become an Uber driver because he wanted to meet people and hear their stories. Why didn't I become an Uber driver?

The Grandmother also hates me because I hit on the Student at Subway. I can't lie, I'm attracted to black women. It was an honest mistake. I knew the Student was in college, but I thought she was a few years older. She's a kid. I know I act like a kid, but I realize I'm not.

"Let's talk about Lacey," the Foreperson says.

"Absolutely," the Architect says. "She's the most important witness in the case. Believe her and you believe David, and if you believe David, then you gotta vote *not guilty.* If you all agree she was telling the truth—and how could you not?—then we can get out of here tonight."

Everyone nods—well, everyone except the Clergyman—but statues don't count.

The Foreperson checks her cell phone. "It's five minutes to five o'clock. Even if I agree with you, which I do, I don't think we can reach a verdict in time. We'll have to come back tomorrow."

I told the Foreperson during the last break I thought she was doing a good job. I lied because I wanted to make her feel good. She's doing a shitty job. She's allowed me and the Housewife to hijack the deliberations. My other juries picked really good foremen—I guess I should say forepeople, right?—and the other forepeople didn't allow bullshit to go on, made sure everyone participated. No one could talk too long, but no one could sit silently like the Clergyman. Yeah, I lied to make the Foreperson feel good. We're supposed to be judging credibility, and I just told a lie. We all lie, right? Anyway, I think if the Foreperson had done a better job, we could've gotten this done today, because I think we all believed Lacey, unless the Clergyman turns out to be a loose cannon. We could still get it done today. Ten minutes to talk, five minutes to vote, five seconds to push the red button on the wall, and we're done. I don't think the Foreperson wants to be done. More than anyone else in the room, she seems to be having fun.

This is not fun. A man's future is at stake.

"Who wants to talk about Lacey?" the Foreperson asks.

The Housewife raises her hand and starts talking without being called on. Of course she does.

CHRISTINA KELLEHER, CSR

I've transcribed the testimony of hundreds of witnesses. Always, I go into a kind of trance, and my mind leaves my body and becomes a cog of the stenotype machine, and the machine becomes me. Tina the Machine. My eyes are open, but vision exists only to read lips and process words. Have you ever heard a court reporter read back a question? We sound more automated than those eerie, nasal, vaguely Swedish-sounding electronic voices they used on early PCs. We give each word, each syllable, equal significance, which drains any emotional content that the speech might otherwise convey. We're trained to be objective, because we're cogs not only in the stenotype machine but also in the criminal-justice machine.

It was hard to be objective when transcribing Lacey Sullinger's testimony. She was one of the two most poised, confident, and appealing witnesses I've ever seen. My other best witness was a famous actor suing a fashion catalogue for ten million dollars for using his name and face. It later turned out that he was a big, fat liar.

SUPERIOR COURT FOR THE COUNTY OF SEPULVEDA

	)
PEOPLE	) JURY TRIAL—DAY 18
v.	)
DAVID BENNETT SULLINGER	) Case No. 16-382
	)
	)

BEFORE: Hon. Natalie Quinn-Gilbert, Superior Court Judge

APPEARANCES: JOHN Y. CRANSTON, ESQ.
Assistant District Attorney,
Sepulveda County
On behalf of the People

JENNA MARIE BLAYLOCK, ESQ.
On behalf of the Defendant

TRANSCRIPT OF PROCEEDINGS

Reported by Christina Kelleher
Certified Shorthand Reporter

Direct examination of Lacey Melinda Sullinger by Jenna Blaylock, counsel for the Defendant (excerpt):

Q. Lacey, please describe your educational background.

A. Of course. I went to the Sepulveda Academy from kindergarten through high school.

Q. That's a private school?

A. Yes.

Q. You seem embarrassed by it.

A. Not embarrassed, exactly. I … I just always wonder whether things would've been different if I'd gone to public school. I don't know why I say that. I guess I'm just grasping at straws. Anyway, Ms. Blaylock, you asked about my education. If you mean high school, I graduated with honors, finishing number four in my class. I played the clarinet in the school band. I was an editor of the school newspaper and also a member of the after-school computer and chess clubs. In the spring, I ran cross-country.

Q. That sounds like a very heavy workload. Was there a reason why you had so many activities?

A. My mother was very goal oriented. So when I told her I was going to do those activities, she was pleased. The real reason I signed up for those activities was so I wouldn't have to come home as early in the day.

Q. Why didn't you want to come home?

A. Because my mother was mentally ill. Abusive and violent, especially to my father, but also to my brother and me.

Q. Are you in college, Lacey?

A. Yes. I'm a sophomore at the University of Southern California.

Q. What's your major?

A. Psychology, with an emphasis in marriage and family counseling. I don't want other families to go through what my mother put ours through.

MR. CRANSTON: Objection. Move to strike the second sentence.

THE COURT: Sustained.

THE WITNESS: Oh, I'm sorry.

THE COURT: There's no need to apologize, Ms. Sullinger. Objections are part of the process.

THE WITNESS: Thank you, Your Honor.

Cross-examination of Lacey Melinda Sullinger by John Y. Cranston, attorney for the People (excerpt):

Q. Referring to your mother's alleged abuse—

A. Not alleged, Mr. Cranston. All too real.

Q. Ms. Sullinger, referring to your mother's alleged abuse, did you ever report it to a school counselor?

A. No, sir.

Q. To a teacher?

A. No, sir.

Q. To a friend?

A. I didn't have true friends, Mr. Cranston. My mother's behavior made that impossible.

Q. You had doctors, didn't you?

A. Yes. A pediatrician and, when I turned fifteen, a gynecologist. Oh, and an eye doctor and, of course, a dentist and an orthodontist.

Q. Thank you for being so comprehensive, Ms. Sullinger.

THE COURT: Watch the sarcastic tone, Mr. Cranston.

MR. CRANSTON: Your Honor, I … Ms. Sullinger, you didn't report your mother's alleged abuse to your pediatrician or gynecologist, did you?

A. No, I didn't.

Q. As far as you know, they didn't suspect abuse.

A. They testified in court that they didn't. But I could never understand how they couldn't figure it out, or at least ask … But that's not fair. My mother was a genius at hiding stuff.

Q. You mentioned that you had an orthodontist. He or she did a good job.

A. She, and thank you. Dr. Madison Powell. We called her Dr. Maddie.

Q. You liked Dr. Maddie?

A. Yeah, she was great.

Q. Did you have braces?

A. Top and bottom, plus a headgear, rubber bands. I hated it.

Q. Expensive?

A. I was eight or nine, so I didn't know then, but from an adult's perspective, absolutely.

Q. Did you need braces?

A. Yes. I had an overbite and a wide gap between my two front teeth. They show in photos from back then. Pretty severe. Of course, I didn't smile in most pictures. I had nothing much to smile about, with all the fighting.

THE COURT: Sustained.

MS. BLAYLOCK: Your Honor, I had no objection to the question. Is Your Honor—?

MR. CRANSTON: I was about to move to strike the commentary.

THE COURT: I just said sustained, counsel. Move on.

MR. CRANSTON: Just for clarification, Your Honor, did you sustain your own objection to the question or did you strike the witness' commentary?

THE COURT: Move on, counsel. Don't try my patience.

By Mr. Cranston:

Q. You needed to have your teeth straightened, did you not, Ms. Sullinger?

A. As I just told you, yes, sir. If I wanted to meet the standards of beauty in America.

Q. Who paid for your braces?

A. My parents.

Q. It was your mother who paid for your braces, wasn't it?

A. Respectfully, it was my parents, Mr. Cranston.

Q. Well, your mother was working and your father wasn't.

A. I don't remember my dad's job situation at the time. But it doesn't matter. I learned in a prelaw class that we live in a community-property state. Really, I knew that when I was probably nine years old. So my parents paid for my braces.

Q. Your mother didn't begrudge you the braces you needed?

A. No, she wanted me to have straight teeth. My looks were very important to her, which was why she was always shaming me for being fat.

Q. This was all paid for with income earned from her job as a real estate broker, correct?

A. Yes.

Q. And she also sent you to an expensive private school using money from her job as a real estate broker?

A. She did.

Q. Made sure you had nice clothes, good food, stayed healthy?

A. My dad made sure I stayed healthy, by making sure my mother didn't kill me.

MR. CRANSTON: Move to … No, withdraw that.

By Mr. Cranston:

Q. Did you go to school with a girl named Rachel Ruskin?

A. Yeah, like, Rachel was a school friend.

Q. I thought you testified earlier that you didn't have any friends.

A. I think I said *true* friends, sir.

Q. But you confided in Rachel Ruskin as if she was a true friend?

A. Not about my mother's abuse of me, my dad, and my brother.

Q. Didn't you tell a school classmate of yours named Rachel Ruskin that you wished your mother were dead, because you were in love with your father?

A. I never ... I might've told Rachel that I loved my ... She and her mother had this—

Q. You used the words "in love," didn't you? Said if he weren't your father—

MS. BLAYLOCK: Objection, Your Honor. Totally inappropriate and violates the court's order on a motion in limine.

MR. CRANSTON: The court's order only applies to the psychologist's—

MS. BLAYLOCK: I want a sidebar, Your Honor.

THE COURT: Before we—

MR. CRANSTON: We don't need a—

MS. BLAYLOCK: A sidebar. I insist that we—

THE COURT: Step back, Ms. Blaylock. Get out of the well.

MS. BLAYLOCK: I will not step—

MR. CRANSTON: Counsel's contemptuous—

[Colloquy unintelligible]

THE REPORTER: Please. I can't transcribe everybody talking at once.

THE COURT: The objection is sustained. Mr. Cranston, you shall drop this line of questioning. The jury wasn't supposed to hear this scandalous charge. You will—

MS. BLAYLOCK: Judge, with all due respect, your comment just now—

THE COURT: If you pursue this line of questioning again, I will sanction you, perhaps hold you in contempt. Members of the jury, Mr. Cranston has violated a court order. You are to disregard his questions and the witness' answers on this topic, and the supposed statement made to her classmate.

MS. BLAYLOCK: May we approach, Your Honor?

THE COURT: No, you may not.

MR. CRANSTON: I'd also request that we approach or take a—

THE COURT: Step back, counsel. Just all of you step back. Why won't everyone step back?

JUROR NO. 6

THE ARCHITECT

When the Foreperson suggests we talk about Lacey Sullinger, the Housewife thrusts her hand up in the air like those incredibly annoying, show-offy smart kids no one could stand in elementary school—or at any grade level, for that matter. She must've been a pain in the ass in her college seminars. No doubt she racked up the participation points.

I didn't see this side of her. When we met in the jury selection room a couple of hours before we were called down to Judge Quinn-Gilbert's courtroom, she seemed like a listener. I hate people who monopolize a conversation. She didn't do that when only the two of us were talking. I wish I could tell her that with her incessant arguing, she's fucking up, but we've been trapped in here all afternoon. I doubt I'll get the chance after we leave today. She's going to run home to those kids and that husband of hers.

I liked her because she was outgoing and because we were fellow prisoners trapped together in that musty central juror room. I have little in common with her, but I had nothing in common with those other people in there, or even these people in here. Am I supposed to hang with the Student? Nope. She's a kid, not to mention our different backgrounds. The Grandmother or the Foreperson? Give me a break. I tried to buddy up to the Jury Consultant. She and I have the most in common—we're both style-conscious, fortyish, divorced professional women, both attractive enough. But she's kind of aloof and is always working during breaks. Lucky her. My practice is slow, though the economy is better. How many public buildings can you construct in this underpopulated county? I'd love to leave and get a job in a larger city, find more interesting work, but you need connections. I don't have connections. Stayed in this goddamned place too long bumping my head against the glass ceiling, all the wounds self-inflicted.

Anyhow, the Housewife and I started hanging out, and she was such a good listener, wanted to hear about my life, my work, my men, and she revealed that her husband, Jared is his name, hasn't wanted to fuck her since their second kid was born—why after the *second* kid she didn't say, but I'd guess it's her weight—and I told her that I don't have any trouble getting fucked by different guys and occasionally—very occasionally—some girls. My ex-husband bored me. (In hindsight, I bored him, too, but he never said it, never acted on it as far as I know, which was mean of him. There's something mean-spirited about being the good guy in a marriage.) She was titillated, even curious, but she's not my type, because her weight is an issue for me, too. Aside from my sex life, she was interested in my job, complimentary, treated me like an artist, as if my kind of architecture is art. I let my guard down and showed her a couple of my paintings, riverscapes. She complimented them, effused over them, and said she has a friend who manages a gallery across town and she'd put in a word for me. I exhibited in a gallery once, rented space, and even my friends wouldn't buy a painting. Anyway, she showed me photos of her kids, as if they were her works of art—why do people do that?—and I effused in return, told her that the photos of her kids depict way more beautiful art than I've ever produced. It was the right thing to say, and those kids really are precious, especially the little three-year-old, who looks just like his mother. But children are not art, and deep down inside, she knows that, and it's killing her.

My ex-husband, Ernesto, is an architect, too, but he designs homes, has won some awards, has had his work appear in *Architectural Digest.* Unlike me, he loves his work. He never wanted to live in Sepulveda County but came here because this is where my job was. I resented him because he couldn't get me a job in a larger city, as if that were on him rather than on me. I resented him because he's more talented than I. I resented him because he demanded that we have kids. No, it was a plea, because he never *demanded* anything. I wish he had. Maybe if he'd demanded … It happened mostly with strangers on business trips—usually hot and a few times kinky, like with that couple I met at the public-building-design conference in New Orleans. I told the Housewife about that, and she was titillated, mesmerized. Amazing what intimate conversations you can have in a booth at a crowded Subway.

I blamed my ex for my guilt and then felt guilty about that. I told myself he knew, because how could he not? That assuaged some of my guilt, because I could brand him a fool, and a fool deserves what he gets, right? No, I didn't get caught. My resentment for him boiled over, and I blurted the truth out in frustration one day because I couldn't stand listening to him babble on about what a great mother I'd make. I couldn't stand lying to him anymore, didn't mean to hurt him. He's such a nice guy.

"I'm suffering, too, if that's any consolation," I said as he was packing his things, and, looking back, I marvel that I was so matter-of-fact about the whole thing. "The guilt's killing me."

"Your guilt isn't punishment," he replied. "It's your ticket for doing whatever the hell you please, no matter who it hurts." Those were the last words he spoke to me until the divorce mediation.

He has another wife now, his real wife, and they have a two-year-old son. They live in the San Diego area. Who would've thought that David Sullinger would remind me of him? Or does Amanda remind me of me?

Now that we're deliberating, the Housewife can't stop talking, isn't really listening, and I wonder whether I was just lowbrow entertainment for her and she's found a new way to amuse herself.

"As I said before, Lacey was the key witness," the Housewife says. "Entirely credible. So composed on the stand. If you believe her testimony about how David was a battered husband, we don't need to worry about the quality of David's testimony. There's reasonable doubt, so we should acquit."

"I echo that," I say, because she's right.

"Me, too," the Express Messenger and the Foreperson say in unison.

"I feel like Lacey was believable," the Student says. "Totally."

"As do I," the Grandmother says.

"She was a very effective witness," the Jury Consultant says.

We all look at the Clergyman. He stares straight ahead, then lifts his eyes to the ceiling.

"I'm in agreement about the quality of Lacey's testimony," he says. How can he whisper and speak loudly at the same time?

"Does this mean what I think it means?" the Foreperson says.

The room goes quiet.

There's a knock at the door, and I'm not the only juror who flinches. The bailiff pokes his head in and says, "It's five-fifteen. Time to send you all home."

"Ten more minutes?" the Foreperson says. "We're—"

"I'm afraid not," the bailiff says. "The judge has left for the day. You can't deliberate when she's not here. Go home; get a good night's sleep. Meet me outside of the courtroom. Nine tomorrow morning. Have a good evening, everyone."

"Oh, one more thing," the Foreperson says. "Would it be okay if tomorrow morning I bring my own coffee and some Splenda into the jury room? I'll share."

THE BAILIFF

BRADLEY KOBASHIGAWA

They file out. They all look tired except for Juror No. 1. She looks energized. She wants to stay longer.

"I'm the foreperson," she whispers to me gleefully as she passes. I wouldn't have guessed that. But I'm wrong a lot. Mick Redmond has a better record than I do, but he didn't predict this outcome. He thought the Jury Consultant or the Architect or the Clergyman. I do tell the Foreperson she can bring her own coffee cup and coffee and sugar substitute. She's worried they'll confiscate it at security. I'll alert them.

Jurors almost always look tired after the first day of deliberations. I get that. The lawyers and the jurors work the hardest during trial. The judge usually doesn't have as much to do in a jury trial except move things along and rule on objections. Mick says the judges in this courthouse, the not-so-good ones, see a jury trial as a mini vacation. Not Judge Quinn-Gilbert. She takes things to heart. For her, a jury trial is stressful. Mick says that seven or eight years ago, the judge worked so hard in a complicated six-week embezzlement trial that the day after the verdict, she had to be hospitalized for exhaustion and dehydration. It's not common knowledge around the courthouse. She cares too much, I think.

More worries. The judge left at a little before five o'clock. We didn't see her go, Mick or me. She just snuck out. I called down to lobby security. One of the deputies saw her exit the judge's elevator at 4:48 and walk to the parking lot. She didn't wave goodbye, he said. Judge Quinn-Gilbert always waves goodbye.

A judge isn't supposed to leave before the jury does. If Judge Quinn-Gilbert had stayed like she should have, I could've given the jury those extra ten minutes, probably more. Maybe David Sullinger would've gone free tonight. While it's only another eighteen hours, eighteen hours matter when you're on trial for murder.

I hope the judge didn't forget she has a jury out deliberating.

JUROR NO. 6

THE ARCHITECT

The Housewife does go for her cell phone as the bailiff escorts us out. A good little wife, reporting her whereabouts to her husband, though she'll be home in only twenty minutes.

The bailiff is holding open the door like a doorman for a Manhattan brownstone. As I pass, I reach out, give his left biceps a squeeze, and flash him a flirty smile. He half grins, half grimaces, and totally tenses up, which causes his perfect biceps to flex. I get that he has to act like he doesn't like it, but I know he likes it—a lot. Men aren't complicated. After the trial is over, I'll give him a call. As well as being gorgeous, he's nice, courteous, efficient. I think he's worried about our different income and education levels. That's a joke. My practice is struggling, and I'm not that smart. He'll come around.

I've never fucked an Asian man before.

Everyone else takes the elevator down. I head to the stairwell. This trial has played havoc with my workout schedule, and I need to stay in shape.

Just as I'm about to open the door to the stairwell, I hear, "Hey, wait up!"

The Housewife waves and comes over. "How about getting a drink?" she asks. "A girls' night out to celebrate the impending end of this marathon?"

"Don't you have to get home to Jared and the kids?"

"To hell with that."

Uh-oh, a domestic quarrel. Not my problem. "You know, I think I'll pass," I say. "I want to get to sleep early and have my mind clear for tomorrow."

"Tomorrow won't be ..." She lowers her eyes and nods her head slightly, wounded. Whatever she might or might not be, she's perceptive.

On any prior night during the trial, I would have said yes, because what else do I have to do at night except watch quirky original programming on Amazon or Netflix, pass the time on Twitter and Instagram, search for guys on dating sites, or hang out with my interchangeable friends? Oh, and drink too much sauvignon blanc? I would have said yes because her tales of diaper changes, autism-inducing childhood immunizations, and quests for admission into prestigious preschools still entertain me. I would have said yes just because. But after her performance today, the thought of spending time alone with her now makes me sick to my stomach.

The Housewife won't take the stairs, because she thinks the courthouse stairwells are dangerous, though the place is crawling with sheriff's deputies. I change my mind and don't take the stairs, either, because how much more of a shit can I be? We make small talk in those faux-friendly, high-pitched tones that women use when there's tension between them. I even hug her goodbye before she gets into her car.

"See you tomorrow," we both say.

"It's been so great," we both say.

"It isn't over quite yet," she says, her smile broader than I've ever seen it.

God, I'll be glad to get back to real life tomorrow.

I drive out of the parking lot, but instead of turning left down Lake Street, I make a right, drive a mile, and head up into the foothills below the Capistrano Mountains. Most of the county is flat and semiarid, but because it's winter, the higher elevations are lush with chaparral—greasewood, red-bark manzanita, and scrub oak. My ex told me you can eat manzanita berries, that the Native Americans used the leaves as toothbrushes, and that the leaves can cure UTIs. I replied that I'd remember his advice next time there's a cranberry juice shortage. My ex knows trivia like that. It used to make me bonkers. Why did it?

I head in the direction of the Sullingers' house, which we toured as part of the trial. No, this is not a case of a juror returning to the scene of the crime. I want to pass by a house my ex designed. It just happens to be three blocks from where the Sullingers live. It's my favorite of all his homes. He combined California case-study design of the 1950s—steel, glass, and modular boxes—with postmodernist elements that include a roof made of sedum plants and a wall constructed with recycled water bottles to provide insulation. When he showed me the first mockups, I thought he was crazy. I was also envious of his talent and creativity. Envy isn't always an entirely negative emotion. If turned inward, it can spur you to improve. Turned outward, it causes resentment. I turned my envy outward. I could spend the rest of the evening trying to psychoanalyze why I want to see the house, but I'm not going to do that. I'm not an introspective person and don't want to be. I just happen to be in the mood to see the house; that's all.

The winding road up the mountain has quite a few cars on it—the county's elite returning home. My ex and I talked about moving up here, but it never happened. He's not the greatest driver, and he's often distracted (or was when married to me), and I feared he'd have an accident on the poorly lit mountain road.

Finally, I reach the bluffs, navigate the narrow streets, and drive up to my ex-husband's tour de force. The home is lambent, even at night with the interior lights off, yet still private—a brilliant postmodernist touch. I park the car and stand outside in the open air to get a better look. It's chilly, in the midforties. I'm wearing a light sweater, so the wind knifes through me. I look up at the sky, speckled with stars so bright that it seems as if my ex designed the luminous structure as an earthly complement to the heavens.

Finally, a subarctic gust sends me back into my car. I start the engine, and for the second time I give in to an impulse, this one easier to explain. A few blocks later, I'm on Bedford Road, rolling at a crawl toward the Sullingers' home. There's nothing wrong with what I'm about to do. At least, I don't think there is. We walked through the house during trial, after all. We live in the community.

David still lives there, out on the bond that Lacey posted once she turned eighteen, took control of Amanda's money, got her father out of jail, and hired Jenna Blaylock. Those facts were all over the local media months before we could imagine we'd be jurors, so there's no harm in knowing about that.

I stop the car, set the parking brake, and leave the engine idling for a quick getaway. Jesus, if David or Lacey sees me, I don't know what I'll do. Probably get thrown off the jury for being a weirdo stalker. Funny that I don't want off the jury anymore.

The lights are on in the back of the house. Are they in there now? What are they doing? Cooking dinner? Something dark and perverted and twisted, as the prosecutor implied before the judge shouted at him? I wonder how Lacey would have answered Cranston's questions. I know what he meant to bring out. What did Lacey tell her friend? The answer to that question could have changed everything.

Don't speculate, I tell myself. Disregard the questions. Do the right thing. I've spent my adulthood telling myself to do the right thing.

I close my eyes and reimagine the killing, and the chill that goes through me rivals the one I felt while standing in the cold. During trial, just walking into the house was scary, and walking into that kitchen was horrifying. There was still a stain from Amanda's blood on the untreated granite countertop. Who would want to live in a house where a brutal murder happened? More importantly, what husband would want to live in the house where he killed his wife? And what daughter would?

THE BLOGGER

KELSI CUNNINGHAM

David Sullinger is NOT GUILTY. No, David Sullinger is INNOCENT! Some of my feminist friends and colleagues and readers think a battered-husband defense is bullshit. I disagree. To be gender-blind, you must acknowledge that a woman has the power to abuse a man. So I've written in my blog posts and articles. In fact, I've painted David as far more sympathetic than he really is. He was rather sniveling on the stand, and he did, after all, split his wife's skull with an ax. But if David prevails in his defense, battered *women* will have a better shot in future trials, and that would be an awesome consequence. I'm all in on David.

My reportage is hardly objective, but objectivity is pointless in this era of limitless information. The public meets objective news reports with charges of bias, anyway. Face it, the *New York Times*, the *Washington Post*, the network news, and CNN are fucked. Twitter fucked them. Facebook, Instagram, Snapchat fucked them. Alt-right websites have fucked them. WikiLeaks and the Russians have double-fucked them. So if you're me, why not write a slanted article that might just influence readers?

That's exactly what I've done. Sure, my stories focus on the Sullinger family's dirty little secrets at the expense of reporting the dry facts unfolding at the trial, but unlike the mainstream reporters, who behave like human recording devices, I have a perspective. Well, I should, because I work for a tabloid. The purpose of a tabloid is to entertain and motivate. Objectivity is neither entertaining nor motivating.

Until my sophomore year in college, I never considered becoming a reporter, and I'm not a reporter now. I majored in premed, documentary filmmaking, and philosophical theories of sexuality. Then, one day, my smart-ass roommate, Lola, said, "You're a decent writer, an alpha female, and a gossip. Why don't you major in tabloid journalism?"

"What an awesome idea," I replied.

Naturally, I didn't major in any type of journalism, which, as a profession, was dying then and has died more since. The internet was killing iconic newspapers and magazines, which were folding all the time. Why pay a subscription when you can get your news for free? What I did was join my college newspaper, the *Westholme College Weekly*, reporting on school sports, music, and drama and writing about diverse, mundane topics in a blog called the *Westholme Wonk.* Not scintillating fun, but better than premed or theories of sexuality. Then I discovered that the college's married athletic director / football coach was having an affair with one of his female assistants. Sleazy enough, but he had hired her after they started sleeping together. He'd kept that secret from the administration, of course. Who would admit that he put his mistress on the payroll? When I vetted the story with the managing editor, the gutless second-semester senior panicked and called our spineless faculty advisor, who panicked and emailed the school president, the big pussy, who, in a panic, ordered the story killed. I published it anyway. That's the beauty of cyberspace. All you have to do is click a couple of keys and promote the story on social media, and presto—you're published *and* disseminated. By the time the school authorities took the story down thirty minutes later, the mainstream media had picked it up, and I was a full-fledged cyberjournalist. Not long after, I started working for a successful online tabloid. I wanted to cover *Sullinger.* They didn't think the trial was big enough, but I was right and they were wrong—we have homicide, adultery, spousal abuse, sibling rivalry reminiscent of Cain and Abel, hints of incest, a celebrity defense attorney, a bumbling prosecutor, a possibly mentally impaired judge. Millions of views on our website. What could be better?

I'm the perfect woman for the job, by the way. I write well, I'm not afraid to confront people, I have a flexible moral compass when it comes to lying, and as a little kid, I enjoyed peeping into the neighbors' windows. True story.

The other media members left the courthouse after the judge sent the jury into the deliberation room, certain the jurors wouldn't reach a verdict for days. After all, it had been a four-week trial. To come back in less than two hours would have been disrespectful of the process, and my colleagues didn't think this jury would disregard the process. I wasn't sure about that, so I hung around. My colleagues were right, damn it—no verdict today. But I saw many of the jurors walking out, and I think they're close. I haven't been doing this for very long, but I have an instinct for these things.

As I walk across the parking lot, I notice a woman fumbling with her car keys. Holy crap, it's Judge Quinn-Gilbert! Without her clerk or bailiff to block my access! I start walking in her direction. The infinitesimal odds of her granting an interview don't deter me. The way I approach interviews is best summed up in a joke a sexist classmate of mine told in college. Two guys walk into a popular nightclub. Guy number one sidles up to a beautiful woman and asks, "Wanna go back to my place and fuck?" The woman slaps his face. The same guy walks up to a second beautiful woman, then a third, asks each the same question, and gets two more slaps. Guy number two says, "Wow, I bet you get your face slapped often with that line." Guy number one replies, "Nine times out of ten."

Before I take five steps toward Quinn-Gilbert, she's inside her car, and the brake lights are illuminated. To my surprise, she drives a Jeep. I figured her for a Mercedes or Lexus kind of woman or, if she wants to buy American, a Cadillac. Hers is a Jeep Wrangler Rubicon, if I'm not mistaken—an off-roading car. She's closer to the entrance than I, because she gets to park in the judges-only zone. I sprint for my rented Toyota Corolla about ten rows down. Good thing I got to court earlier than anyone else and found a decent parking space. I might still be able to catch Her Honor. Yes, I'm going to follow a superior-court judge home and ambush-interview her. Might be a violation of journalistic ethics, but as I said before, I'm not a journalist.

When I get out of the parking lot, I spy the judge's car about a block ahead of me. I don't know this part of the world at all, haven't had occasion to visit Sepulveda County (fortunately), and I'm not sure where the judge lives or how she's going to get there. These one-way streets are a hazard because they're not consistent—there can be two in a row going the same direction, followed by a two-way and then a one-way going the other way. What the fuck, city planners!

She drives not up into the hills, where the Sullinger house is located, but to a quiet street lined with 1920s gingerbread, Cape Cod, and Tudor-style homes. Small-potatoes rich. I probably pay three times more in rent for my apartment in New York than the judge pays on her mortgage. *Big fish, small pond*—that's Judge Quinn-Gilbert. Although that wasn't true of her late husband. He was a superstar, hired to try large cases everywhere. I researched it, and they had houses in Park City and La Jolla and an apartment in midtown Manhattan. He must have left the judge in good financial shape. Maybe she's a bigger fish than I thought.

She makes a left turn into her driveway and stops, leaving the engine running. Nice house! She seems to be fumbling for something—oh, the garage door opener—and I have time to park, get out of my car, and run over and rap on the driver's-side window. She doesn't flinch. Fuck, if someone sneaked up on me like that in the dark and knocked on my window, I would've shattered the moonroof with my head, pissed my pants, started honking, and tried to escape. The judge rolls down her window. Is she bat-shit crazy, or has she reacted this calmly because this is a small town and people are trusting?

"May I help you?" she asks, and while there's no smile in the question, there's no concern in it, either.

She doesn't recognize me! I'm mildly offended because I've been sitting in the courtroom every day for the past month, but I'm also thinking, *Yass, this gives me some options!*

"Judge Quinn, so sorry to disturb you at home," I improvise, making my voice tremulous and calling her by her maiden name to make her think I'm a clueless, low-level ditz. "I'm a messenger working for the law firm of Richardson & Pierce." That's the county's largest firm, which isn't so large and which I know only because one of their lawyers originally represented David Sullinger until he—or, more correctly, his daughter—hired Jenna Blaylock. "We have a—whaddya call it—an emergency motion. A client was put in jail without probable cause, and the police refuse to bring her before a commissioner or a … They say there's no judge available. They wanted to see if I could find a judge available while they finish up the papers. It's after hours. If you'd be available, I could call them and they could bring the papers up." I hold up my cell phone and surreptitiously press the record icon. "I'm supposed to call when I find somebody—a judge, I mean." I cobble this story together based on the facts of some lawsuit my attorney mother handled back in the 1980s. She told my brother and me about that case many times, not that I paid attention. One reason I didn't go to law school is that my mother wanted me to follow in her footsteps.

The judge regards me with concerned eyes, the Irish-green irises gleaming in the darkness. "I'm not sure I understand. Why don't they go to the duty judge?"

"Oh, I don't know anything about that," I say meekly. "They just told me to find a judge, and I saw you pulling out of the parking lot. I've delivered a lot of papers to your clerk, Mr. Redmond."

"I'm not the duty judge tonight. I think its Judge …" She puts an index finger on her cheek and tilts her head as she thinks—an endearing, childlike gesture so endearing and childlike that I feel a wave of guilt about deceiving her. Usually, I don't feel guilty till afterward—not that guilt would stop me.

"Why didn't someone call ahead?" she asks.

"The duty judge? I wouldn't—"

"No. Call ahead."

"I'm sorry, ma'am, I don't know what you mean." I actually don't know what she means. I call her *ma'am* to show a lack of sophistication. Only someone inexperienced in the law would address her as anything other than *Judge*.

"Come inside, and I'll check the internal court website for you," she says. "Tell you who the duty judge is."

"Oh, you don't have to do that. We could use the browser on my cell phone. Just tell me the link." I'm taking a risk, but playing hard-to-get promotes trust. I fake a shiver and wrap my hands around my chest. "Woo, it's cold." It is chilly, but I'm not cold. This game, the chase, keeps me warm.

"No, my eyes and fingers won't …" the judge says, shaking her head. "It's easier for me to search on my computer. And you're cold. Come inside."

How nice of her. How *weird* of her. How foolish of her. Most judges would tell me to tell my bosses to get their act together. Then they'd order me off their property.

She opens the front door, sets down her briefcase—the old-fashioned square leather kind, all scuffed, with tarnished brass hardware—disarms the security system, and leads me into what looks like a study. Inside, the house is stylish—traditional, like what you'd expect from a judge—but also cozy. Inconsistently, there are nontraditional paintings on the wall. Abstract and surrealistic is how I'd describe them. One in particular strikes me as odd and rather disturbing: a painting of a courthouse foundering on a rough ocean, with some kind of colossal creature—a shark or whale or sea serpent—rising high out of the water and hovering over the building. The creature's jaws are open wide, poised to swallow the courthouse whole. But it's not the subject matter that makes the painting eerie; it's the color, or lack of color. The entire painting is rendered in shades of gray, except for the creature's blank-slate, dark-blue predatory eyes, which stare directly out at the observer.

"Oh, what nice art you have!" I say.

"My husband's work. He's … he was very talented."

"Was he a professional artist?"

"A trial lawyer. A great one."

We go into the study, and she sits down in front of an antique rolltop desk. The shelves are lined with books—mostly legal treatises, I think, but also some classic literature, nonfiction, and bestselling commercial fiction of years gone by. There are framed snapshots of the judge and her husband in their younger days, plus some professionally rendered photographs of the judge with dignitaries, including the former governor. She was never a beautiful woman. Her husband was a very handsome man—a *dashing* man.

"Cool desk," I say. "Is it a real antique?"

"From the 1880s, a lawyer's office. Quartersawn oak, or so Jonathan would tell me."

"Cool. So my bosses say that you're the judge who has that murder case everybody's talking about. Where the husband murdered the wife in self-defense?" She's logging on to her computer. I try to see her password without being obvious, but she types too fast. I could make out a "c" and an "o" and maybe an asterisk, but that's about it. Damn. And yes, I'm willing to hack into her computer.

"Sullinger. Yes. I have a jury out."

I glance down at my phone. The voice recorder is still going. The recording will never become public, but I'll use it to convince my bosses that I didn't make this interview up.

"Yeah, that's what one of my bosses was saying. I read about the trial on the internet. I think he killed her in self-defense. I hope they let him go free."

"Oh, it's a very sad case," she says, her back to me, eyes on the monitor. I stare at her hair: drab auburn over silver-gray roots, short and layered. It's the classic cut of the older professional woman—dowdy, though her "stylist" undoubtedly maintains otherwise.

Her shoulders are rounded from years of sitting, and her back is soft with postmenopausal flab.

"Very sad," she says. "Difficult legal issues. Even more difficult testimony to listen to. Sometimes, I wonder ..." She pauses to type. "David Sullinger is such a large man, and Amanda was so petite." *Type, type, type.* "I gave that battered-husband instruction because Jenna Blaylock handed me a very well-written legal brief." *Type, type, type.* "It was so late, and the prosecutor didn't do his homework, but maybe I should've let him file a response, but ..." *Type, type, type, type, type.* "Okay, here you go. Tell the lawyers at your law firm that the duty judge is Judge Barnes."

God, I wish she'd keep on rambling, but I have enough for a great story, especially in the tabloid world: *Judge Admits Error in Wife-Killer's Trial! Judge Doubts Wife-Killer's Story!* Sure, I've maintained in my stories that David is innocent, but who cares? I now have something better: an exclusive with the judge, who says he's guilty, who admits she fucked up. She'll claim I'm overstating? Let her sue. This is awesome!

She peeks back over her shoulder at me. "Which lawyer at your firm is handling this matter?"

This is a small county with a small legal community, and I'm betting she knows most of the lawyers at the firm. "Sabrina

Goldman," I say, pulling the name out of a location in my ass that I didn't know existed. "She's a new associate. A … a lateral from Gibson's Los Angeles office."

The judge gives me an odd look, and why not? I just broke character. A stupid messenger girl knowing about lateral hires? About a huge LA-based BigLaw firm?

She swivels in her chair and faces me. "Just tell her to call the duty judge."

My momentary apprehension dissolves. "Absolutely, Judge. Thank you *so* much." I reach out and shake her hand, then hurry toward the front entrance like a thief fleeing with the stolen loot. But I'm no thief; I'm the purveyor of truth. I open the door only to come face-to-face with Mick Redmond, that scary courtroom clerk for the Honorable Natalie Quinn-Gilbert.

THE COURTROOM CLERK

MICK REDMOND

The judge and I have a tradition: if the jury deliberates more than one afternoon, she and I bake the jurors cupcakes for the next morning. Arms laden with bags of baking ingredients, I climb the steps to the judge's front porch. The front door swings open, and I come face to face not with the judge, but with that tabloid reporter, Kelsi Cunningham.

Have you ever seen an injured boxer smile at the opponent in a futile attempt to hide the fear and pain? That's how Cunningham is smirking at me now, the arrogant, frightened little bitch. Yes, harsh words, but not harsh enough for the little bitch.

When she takes a step forward to leave, I drop my grocery bags, take a step forward myself, and put my hands on the door-jambs to block her way. I can be intimidating when I choose to be. I was an army corporal during the first Iraq war. It was the era before "Don't ask, don't tell," so I lied.

"What the fuck are you doing here?" I ask.

"That's none of your business, but if you must know, the judge invited me in. Now, if you'll excuse me ..."

It's all bravado.

"You're not going anywhere yet," I say. Then I notice the cell phone in her hand and grab it.

"Hey, what the fuck, man! That hurt!" She countergrabs at the phone but not very seriously.

"Mick, what's this?" The judge is standing at the entrance to her study, hands on hips.

"Judge, don't you know who this is?" I say.

"She's a messenger from a law firm."

"She's a reporter," I say. "A tabloid writer. Her name's Kelsi Cunningham. Judge, she's been in court every day since the trial started. How could you not have recognized her? She has a ring in her nose and tattoos." I try to hide my frustration from my beloved boss, to whom I've never said a harsh word. She's one of the few people who have that distinction.

The judge stands erect, straightens her gray woolen jacket by pulling at the hem with both hands, and walks over. "I didn't recognize her, Mick, because I don't pay attention to the media or the spectators or even family members of the defendant or anyone in the gallery. I pay attention to the attorneys and the witnesses, and I rule on objections, and I ask questions for clarification, and I make sure the jurors are comfortable and listening. That's why I didn't know who she is. She's insignificant to me."

This is the cocksure, confident Judge Quinn-Gilbert I know. I glance down at Cunningham's cell phone. It's on the *voice recording* app. Shit. I hit the *play* button.

> "Yeah, that's what one of my bosses was saying. I think he killed her in self-defense. I hope they let him go free …"

> "Oh, It's a very sad case. Very sad. Difficult legal issues. Even more difficult testimony to listen to. Sometimes, I wonder ... David Sullinger is such a large man, and Amanda was so petite. I gave that battered-husband instruction because Jenna Blaylock handed me a very well-written legal brief. It was so late, and the prosecutor didn't do his homework, but maybe I should've let him file a response, but ... Okay, here you go. Tell the lawyers at your law firm that the duty judge is Judge Barnes."

"You're despicable," I say, and make a move to erase the recording.

"I'll fucking have you arrested for false imprisonment and destruction of property," Cunningham shrieks, grabbing at the phone so ferociously, she scratches my arm with her fingernail.

I take a step forward, nudge her with my body, and shut the door behind me so she can't make a break for it. "You're a fucking child trying to play in the grown-ups' league. You're not ready."

"Return her cell phone, Mick," the judge says in a quiet, almost amused tone.

"But, judge, she's going to put this garbage on the internet, embarrass you, maybe cause a mistrial."

"She won't do any such thing," the judge says. "Do you remember that divorce case we had three years ago? *In re Marriage of Gulliver*?"

The dimmer switches in my brain are turned up, and I get it. "I do, Judge. That was the case where the husband recorded a conversation with the wife's best friend without consent? He served three months in jail, if I'm not mistaken." I hand the phone back to Cunningham, who takes it, her expression that of a frightened yet curious cat.

"You're not from this jurisdiction, I take it," the judge says to Cunningham.

"She's from New York, Judge," I say.

"You obviously don't know about Criminal Code section 632," the judge says. "The statute that makes it a crime to record a conversation without the other person's consent. Punishable by up to one year in prison and a fine of twenty-five hundred dollars. How do you think a superior court judge is going to react when you're being sentenced for illegally recording another superior court judge?"

Cunningham flaps her jaw, but the judge stops any words, saying, "And please don't insult my intelligence by spouting platitudes about freedom of the press. I suspect that if your behavior becomes public, your website, or whoever employs you, will summarily fire you to avoid becoming the target of a criminal prosecution itself. You might never find media employment again."

Cunningham shuts her eyes and sucks in her lower lip.

"You know, I saw my little nephew suck on his lip like that when his mother took away his pacifier," I say. "He also pooped his pants a few times, though he'd been potty trained. Are you feeling the same way?"

"That's enough, Mick," the judge says, holding up her hand and glaring at Cunningham with those eyes that have made even the most hardened criminals cower.

Cunningham's body droops in submission. There's comfort in admitting defeat. "What do you want me to do?"

"You're going to email my clerk that recording so we have proof that you made it," the judge says. "Then you're going to hand your phone back to Mick, and he's going to delete the recording."

"As well as the sent email with the attachment," I add.

"Mick is much more technologically savvy than I am," the judge says, which wasn't true until three or four months ago.

Cunningham nods wearily, her lips now puckered like an old crone's. The email is sent to my phone; the recording is obliterated from hers—I make sure of that. I hand her back the phone, open the front door, bow, and gesture for her to leave with a sweep of the arm worthy of the best fairy-tale footman.

"I'll see you in court, Ms. Cunningham," the judge says.

The little twit looks at the judge in bewilderment.

"I mean, I'll see you when the *Sullinger* jury comes back. Far be it from me to impinge on the First Amendment guarantee of freedom of the press."

When the door closes, the judge lets out a long sigh. "You saved me on that one, Mick. Thank you."

"Thank the cupcake tradition, Judge. Which reminds me, I brought ingredients for maple bacon."

She blanches slightly. "Mick, I don't know. Jonathan didn't ..."

Jonathan didn't like her to use pork in cupcakes. He thought it disrespectful to observant Jews and Muslims who might be on the jury. Unbecoming of a judge. That's exactly why I suggested these. She's got to start to let go somehow.

"Oh, he didn't really mind," I say. "You know him. He was always lawyering, and with the cupcakes he was just doing some pastry lawyering. Anyway, I made a batch for Eric last week. He ate so many, he's gone to the gym every day since. My little nephew loves them, too, the little sugar junkie, and he ordinarily won't eat bacon."

She thinks for a moment and nods her head as if making a momentous decision. Maybe it is momentous for her. "Let's do it," she says. "I've got to change my clothes first."

After she leaves the room, I pick up my bags of goodies, go into the kitchen, and set up. It's a true cook's kitchen with a large island, two ovens, and—best of all—plenty of counter space. An easy kitchen for two cooks to work in, which is how it was designed. The Gilberts loved to cook together, even took cooking classes at Langlois in New Orleans and at Le Cordon Bleu.

A few minutes later, the judge comes out, smiling broadly. But her eyes are a shimmering red, a tip-off that she's been crying.

We start making the cupcakes, and just as we finish blending the batter, she says in a resolute tone, "I am not losing it, Mick."

"Of course not, Judge." It's the right thing to say, but we both know that if she were sure, she wouldn't have made the statement. I do feel a whole lot better after watching how she handled Cunningham.

THE PROSECUTOR

JACK CRANSTON

They didn't come back with a verdict today, and that's a good sign, because it's easier for a jury to rush an acquittal than to cavalierly find a man guilty.

Nope, it's a bad sign, because he murdered her, and all they need to decide is whether he acted in self-defense, and he didn't, because he could've just taken the knife from her and run away, just as he took the ax from her.

No, the fact that they're still out doesn't mean anything at all, because they've only been out a couple of hours, and the trial lasted a month.

"Hey, Bauer!" I shout to one of the other assistant DAs, the only person who's worked in the office nearly as long as I have. "What do you make of no verdict yet?"

"It means nothing. They've been out two hours," he says, walking by without even a "congratulations" or a "job well done." Is he competitive, or does he believe I'm not deserving of a "job well done"?

The cops couldn't explain why Amanda bought that ax, which

means I couldn't explain why Amanda bought that ax. That's the Achilles' heel of my case, that goddamn ax. There has to be some explanation other than that she was buying a murder weapon with the intent to kill her husband. I urged the sheriff to request help from a big-city police department, but no, he wouldn't do it—ego. So he lets Detective Beckermann botch things up. Damn the sheriff. Damn Beckermann. Damn that ax. Damn that Dillon Sullinger, who testified exactly the way I wanted him to but looked and sounded as if he's the one who belongs in the state penitentiary. The impudent little prick didn't even bother to wear a sport coat to court when he testified, even after I told him to. Hell, I would have settled for a T-shirt without the holes. He was honest, though, and Lacey … well, I don't know what to make of Lacey, because she was a terrific witness. I hate to say it, but she was a terrific witness.

Even after all this time, my wife is still pissed at me for trying to raise that incest issue during Lacey's cross, all the more pissed because Hunter overheard us debating—oh, let's be honest, *arguing*—about the issue, and he asked what incest is. I thought twelve-year-olds learned everything about everything from the internet these days. Oops.

The thing is, I'm convinced there's something hinky about David and Lacey's relationship and that it was a proper area of cross-examination.

I blame Alicia and Cole. If I just had better associates helping me …

"You want to get a drink at La Fiesta's? Celebrate the end of a long, notable trial?"

It's Bauer, with Alicia and Cole in tow, standing in my doorway. What does he mean *drink to the end of a long trial*? Why not drink to a job well done? And why isn't the district attorney joining us? She's probably elsewhere, celebrating the demise of her political opponent, Jack Cranston. Well, I haven't given up, even though everyone else has.

"Drinks are on me," I say.

They all doth protest, but not too much.

I push myself up out of my desk chair and grab my coat, and it's all I can do to put it on. Oh, adrenaline, where are you when I need you? Grungy. My coat is grungy. I didn't have a chance to make it to the dry cleaners during the last two weeks of trial, and I don't have fourteen suits to wear. More like four, which I recycled. After the incest debate, I didn't want to ask my wife to take care of my laundry. I was an English major, you know. Still read Shakespeare when I get a chance. David Sullinger reminds me of a kind of wimpy Macbeth who turned on Lady Macbeth. Maybe some avant-garde producer will do an adaption like that someday. *The Tragedy of Macbeth: The Battered Husband.* Or is Sullinger more like Richard III? An ax, an ax, my kingdom for an ax.

"Congratulations on a job well done," Bauer says.

"These two deserve most of the credit," I say, patting Alicia, then Cole, on the shoulder. "They worked their asses off."

JUROR NO. 52

THE EXPRESS MESSENGER / ACTOR

"So are you going to reach a verdict soon?"

"I can't talk about it, Mom. How many times . . .? I'm watching the game. Wanna watch with me? Warriors verse Clippers."

"Oh, come on. Your generation is so ... When I was your age, we weren't so afraid of authority. We marched in favor of civil rights in the South and protested the Vietnam War. And we invented feminism."

"You're not old enough for the civil rights movement. And, I'm not afraid. I'm just doing the right thing. Following the law, and stuff."

"Who's winning?"

"The Warriors, but the Clippers have—"

"No, who's winning in the jury room."

"Jesus, Mom."

"Don't say 'Jesus.' You know I don't—"

"Okay. Sorry. I'm watching the game."

"Will the trial be over tomorrow?"

"I can't talk about it."

"This week?"

"I just can't."

"I bet the Jody Arias jury talked to their mothers … or family."

"Who's—?"

"Don't you watch the news? Well, I guess you were a kid. Well, not a kid, but three, four years younger. You're still a kid. You should watch the news if you want to be an actor. And read the news. She was the girl who killed her boyfriend, stabbed him fifty times or so, shot him to make sure he was dead, and claimed self-defense because he made her do anal sex, but really she was just nuts. They convicted her. Life imprisonment, not the death penalty."

"Jesus, Mom."

"Don't say 'Jesus,' and don't cover your ears when I talk to you."

"If you're going to talk about … I'm going to bed soon, so maybe you'll let me get some sleep. I have to be in court first thing."

"Okay, yeah, get some sleep. That Jody Arias reminds me of that David Sullinger. Stabbing. Or, in your case, axing, but same thing. Self-defense claim. No shooting with Sullinger, I'll grant you, not that it makes a difference. Dead is dead."

"Jesus, Mom."

"Kiss your mom good night."

THE PARALEGAL

SAUL MEADE

A paradox: those who speak best for the downtrodden eventually become rich, famous, privileged, worshipped, all of the above—and, as a consequence, more adored by the downtrodden. The legendary rock singer with the private jet still sings about his hardscrabble Pittsburgh neighborhood. Electioneering from her luxurious brownstone on the Upper West Side, the still-beautiful, still-working, award-winning actress urges everyone to vote radical-progressive. The billionaire corporate mogul dabbles in politics and snake-charms the working class. Even Mother Teresa became something of a rock star. How else can you explain her expedited sainthood?

Just so with defense attorney Jenna Blaylock, though on a much smaller scale, because, after all, even the most prominent attorneys have a fame ceiling. Athletes, entertainers, and artists entertain and edify. Lawyers can't do that. How many remember Clarence Darrow and Daniel Webster these days? And no, Abraham Lincoln doesn't count. In any event, Jenna started as a socially conscious public defender in Chicago, won a high-profile trial for an accused cop killer, earned a gig on cable TV because she was smart, articulate, and a pretty blond, and soon went into private practice, taking on one of two types of clients: the rich and the notorious and, if she was lucky, both at once.

In Jenna's seventeen-year career, she's never lost a case. If you don't believe it, just take a look at her website, which I designed. When she does lose, she claims that she had nothing to do with the case, that her cocounsel took the lead. Legal insiders know the truth, but the truth can't trump a well-designed website and exposure on national television. Unblemished record or not, Jenna is a superb trial lawyer, and I should know—I've worked for her since the beginning.

Two hours after the Sullinger jury left for the evening, our defense team sits in the town's best restaurant (mediocre food, excellent cocktails). Our group comprises a junior partner—who's a partner in name only, because she doesn't share in firm profits—a second-year associate, and me, her paralegal.

"To another victory," Jenna says, raising her martini glass.

Everyone but me raises a glass in response. When Jenna sees this, she sets her glass back down, as do the others.

"What's the problem now, Saul?" she says, her tone portending the approach of an arctic cold snap.

"You know exactly what the problem is," I say. "The jury is still out, to coin a phrase."

"We're celebrating because we've got it won," Jenna says, biting her martini olive with such hostility that the pimento falls onto the table. "The daughter won it for us—slam dunk. I have a fund-raiser in Boston day after tomorrow, and after the jury comes back, I want to get a reasonably early flight. You can't expect me to take a red-eye back east just so I can have a dinner in *this* town." She picks the pimento off the table and pops it into her mouth. "No more of your negativity, Saul. Buzzkill. You do this every time we have a trial, and I always win."

"I just don't want us to jinx it," I say—a quarrelsome statement because, as Jenna learned long ago, I'm not superstitious.

"Trials are resolved based on the lawyer's ability, not superstition," she says. "And next trial, shine your shoes before you walk into court. They're all scuffed. And you don't wear brown shoes with a charcoal-gray suit."

"I didn't think trials were decided by fashion choices," I say. "I thought they're resolved based on truth and justice."

"You forgot to add 'the American way,'" Blaylock says. "And yes, fashion matters. Don't you think the jury noticed Cranston's ill-fitting suits?"

The nonpartner-partner and the associate chuckle.

She looks at the two lawyers at the table as if they were jurors. "No, trials don't remotely involve the values of Superman. Sure, guilt and innocence matter, but only because some people are so guilty that you can't spin the facts any other way. I don't take those kinds of cases anymore. I had more than my fair share when I was a public defender—although, even on those tough cases, I worked magic."

"How humble of you," I say.

"Cases are won by spinning facts, appealing to prejudices—"

"Prejudices?" I say. "I've never heard you admit quite so blatantly—"

"Yes, prejudices. We're all friends here. We are friends, aren't we, Saul?"

I lift my wineglass, although I'm not feeling very friendly now. We've all had too much to drink.

"Yes, in advocacy, you appeal to prejudices, spin the facts when possible, quibble, deflect, distract. You challenge the credibility of the most credible witnesses, which is an easy thing to do. No one can know everything—which you use against them, and you also take what they know, and use *that* against them. You demonize the victim, because most victims can be demonized. God knows Amanda Sullinger could be demonized. She demonized herself. And then you use your God-given talents to charm the jury, to make your opponent look plodding and untrustworthy, whether he's trustworthy or not. I have to admit it—Jack Cranston is a pretty straight shooter as prosecutors go, and he's not a bad trial lawyer. I just made him *look* incompetent." She sits back in the booth, takes a self-satisfied sip of her drink, and raises her glass again. "Here's to winning."

The others drink, but I just swirl my glass and stare into it, as if the answers to unanswerable questions could be discerned by reading the pattern of sediment at the bottom of a glass of pinot noir. *Haven't you learned, Jenna, that sometimes the star can get too big for the show, that the jurors might begin to attribute their initial belief in David's innocence not to the truth but to a masterful Vegas-worthy magic trick, and if that happens, the cause is lost?*

"What's wrong now?" Jenna asks when she notices I didn't participate in her toast.

"Why aren't we drinking to David Sullinger's freedom?" I say. "Or to justice?"

She shrugs. "Sure, why not? Here's to justice for David Sullinger." She touches the rim of the glass to her lips but doesn't drink this time.

"We'll continue this discussion later," I say.

"No. We won't."

That ends the conversation. Once upon a time, she would have listened.

"Whatever you say, boss."

The associate chortles, then clamps a hand to his mouth in mortification. Jenna ignores him, which is the worst possible reaction one can get from her. Better that she scream at him.

Jenna Blaylock and I fell in love three months after she hired me. She'd just left the Chicago public defender's office and started her private practice, the Law Offices of Jenna M. Blaylock, Criminal Defense. A life-altering event and a huge risk for a young lawyer who'd never worked at a firm, never operated a business.

I, too, had made a recent life change. A year earlier, I'd given up on my seven-year attempt—I won't dignify it by calling it a quest—to finish my doctoral dissertation, supposedly an analysis of postmodernist literary criticism and its relevance to the criminal justice system, but in fact a hodgepodge of arcane theories and suppositions that became so byzantine even I couldn't understand them. Something about Jacques Derrida, Sir Edward Coke, and Antonin Scalia meet *My Cousin Vinnie.* Not that the inability to understand your own work disqualifies you from publication.

My parents had stopped helping me financially with grad school two years earlier, and since then I'd worked as a legal secretary and then a paralegal to help defray the costs of daily existence. I knew I was doing a good job when the law firm offered to pay my way through law school, with a promise of employment when I passed the bar. My parents urged me, and later begged me, to accept the offer and follow in my mother's footsteps. (She's a litigator who runs her own boutique employment-law firm.) Then, perhaps, if I wanted to return to academia, I'd follow in my father's footsteps and become a law professor. I declined. I was not going to attend school for another three seconds, much less three years, and I wasn't going to subject myself to the absurd pressure that BigLaw attorneys, and particularly BigLaw associates, must endure. I'd rather keep paying off the student loans.

There were no hard feelings on the part of the law firm, which just gave a corporate shrug, changed my job title from "paralegal" to "senior analyst," and raised my billing rate a hundred and fifty dollars per hour. I functioned as a de facto associate. Indeed, my annual job reviewers said I was better than most associates, smarter than most partners. I didn't want to feel better or smarter than anyone. I just wanted to leave the office at a decent hour, go home, read fantasy and horror novels, watch edgy internet-television programs, and play in my twice-a-week hockey league. I wanted to avoid any involvement in law firm politics, because as a graduate student, I'd nearly been devoured by university politics. Most of all, I didn't want to be judged. A senior analyst at a law firm isn't judged but, rather, is the object of a condescending admiration.

I was happy at the law firm, but that didn't stop me from answering an internet notice announcing that a criminal defense attorney who had recently opened an office was looking to hire a paralegal—someone creative, hardworking, willing to take the initiative, good with people, and in possession of a social conscience. My decision to interview was the result of a kind of academic curiosity, an inquiry into what makes a celebrity lawyer tick. Jenna had appeared on cable news shows as a pundit on high-profile criminal cases, and I ... To be honest, I wanted to find out whether she was as beautiful and caustic in person as she was on TV.

The answer was yes and no. *Yes*, she was beautiful, and still is. More so now, because she's truly a woman and not partly a child.

No, she wasn't the tough chick of the small screen and the internet but, rather, a scared young lawyer who had heretofore relied on the security net of a government job and was now staking success in private practice on a growing reputation she didn't fully believe she deserved. She'd ended up at the public defender's office because she had washed out at a large law firm. She needed help with legal writing and theory, and my credentials impressed her mightily. Oh, she didn't say that in so many words, but I perceived it.

"I'll start in two weeks," I said when she offered me the job. I was ensconced in her office suite in a week. What can I say? I found her intriguing.

As it turned out, it was the perfect symbiosis. I'm a writer and she's a talker. I'm a thinker and she's a doer. I'm an introvert and she can charm, manipulate, and persuade like no one I've ever met.

So many relationships develop out of necessity and the desire to avoid isolation. We fought our first legal battles virtually alone. We married the year after she hired me. There was something old-fashioned about her desire for a wedding, though marriage didn't seem necessary. At first, we behaved as equal partners, handling ever more lucrative criminal cases, but also a fair share of cases for indigents and the wrongfully accused. The pro bono work stopped as Jenna became more successful and the firm grew from just the two of us to a dozen attorneys and a large support staff. She's received numerous offers from prominent law firms desperate to acquire the incomparable Jenna Blaylock and has rejected each offer out of hand. She wants to be her own boss. She wants to be the star. Fine with me—I want to be neither a boss nor a star.

One day about a year ago, she asked me, "Why don't you reconsider law school? You're smarter than anyone I know, and you already function as a lawyer. You and I, we're not BigLaw, so things are different than before." It was phrased as a compliment, but it was a message: in his present incarnation, Saul Meade is no longer worthy of Jenna Blaylock.

Of course I didn't go to law school, and of course she was disappointed in me.

Yet the marriage endures. We still work well together. This Sullinger trial is an example. But more and more, she treats me like an employee, and not only while we're working.

I didn't want her to take this Sullinger case. We were too busy, the town is too remote, the law is too ambiguous, and the facts are too horrifying.

"That's why I'm going to take it," Jenna said. "If I get him off, they'll write about this case for decades to come."

Now, while the attorneys at the victory table dissect the trial and praise Jenna for her brilliance, I'm seized with remorse that I've spoiled her moment in the sun. So much remorse lately. I chug down my wine and, without waiting for the server, pour myself another glass. We've both had too much to drink. That's become a habit lately, in the name of victory celebrations and wine connoisseurship.

She lifts her glass again. "You all did a terrific job on this trial. Here's to my loyal staff." The reference to "staff" is more offensive to the lawyers at the table than it is to me, but they're just collateral damage.

I never told her the real reason I didn't want her to represent David Sullinger: The case would involve dissecting the Sullingers' horrific relationship, and I feared that picking through the doomed couple's matrimonial carrion would not only subject us to the stench of their marriage but also expose something putrid about our own. I was right.

JUROR NO. 33

THE GRANDMOTHER

The Student helps me down the courthouse steps, and when I take out my cell phone to call a cab—I haven't driven in eighteen months, since the last fender bender—she uses her phone to call an Uber. Except that she doesn't call; she touches an app.

"My daughter has been trying to get me to use Uber," I say. "But I still have my flip phone, and that's enough technology for me. I never thought I'd turn out to be an old fogy, but it happens to the best of us."

"Hmm. I feel like your daughter's right. There's so much you can do with a smartphone, whichever brand you get. Not only calling for Ubers, but searching the web to get information …" She turns her head away for a moment. "Text, insta … wake up …"

I fiddle with my hearing aid and cup my hand behind my left ear. "Texting instant *what*?"

"You can use a phone for texting friends, Instagram, setting alarms to wake up to," she says slowly and loudly.

"Oh, yes. I have a clock radio for that. You sound like my

daughter. She's been trying to get me to replace my old flip phone with one of those newfangled phones with a touch screen."

"Smartphones aren't that new anymore."

"Be that as it may, I've resisted. Too many people in restaurants, on buses, walking on the streets—all these people have their eyes on their smartphones and not on what's around them. The Housewife and the Jury Consultant and the Express Messenger grab their cell phones the moment they're able. How do I explain it? Addiction. You know, several months ago, I went to dinner with my daughter, my son-in-law, and my adorable five-year-old granddaughter—the light of my life, by the way. Do you know that my daughter and son-in-law had their heads buried in their phones? It sounds nuts, but I suspect they were texting messages to each other."

"That actually happens. Two friends sitting at the same table and Snapchatting."

"I just don't understand. I get the sense that with all this cell phone use, people are invading their own privacy."

"I feel like technology really has advanced our lives."

"Children used to play. Did you play, or are you too young?"

"I played. Also watched too many DVDs."

"When I went to dinner with my family, my granddaughter had some sort of device that resembled a cell phone. They don't give cell phones to five-year-olds, do they?"

"Not yet. But there are gadgets for kids."

"Yes, she was playing a game on it while her parents texted. I finally banged my hand on the table to get everyone's attention—an old technique I used when I taught school. Abrupt, but effective. The adults both apologized ... and stuck their noses back in their phones five minutes later."

The wind picks up. The poor girl is wearing only a light sweater.

"You go on home," I say. "I'm keeping you."

"No, you're good."

It's nice to know someone thinks I'm good. "Do the Uber drivers take both cash and credit cards?" I ask.

"They just charge my credit card when I use the app … well, my father's credit card. Already taken care of."

I reach into my purse and offer her a twenty-dollar bill.

"No, no, my father would insist that I treat you."

"Well, I also insist, and I'm a grandmother, so I outrank him." I can't let her pay for this. I still have my pride.

We stare at each other in one of those awkward impasses where each party is trying to be so polite and helpful that both parties might end up insulted.

"You're so sweet," she says. "How about this? You can buy me lunch at the break tomorrow. The ride won't cost twenty dollars. Probably half that."

"If we're still deliberating by lunchtime, it's a bargain."

"Well, if we're not, you can buy me a farewell coffee."

"It's still a bargain."

"Awesome." She inhales. "Do you actually think we'll be done by lunch? Because I'm worried that … Oh, don't answer that."

I'm not sure of the rules, either.

"It's just that I saw the ESPN documentary on the O. J. Simpson trial, and then I watched the series from the guy who made the *Glee* TV show. African Americans on that jury got such a bad name for rushing to judgment. To be honest, it kind of embarrassed me."

"A different time," I say, though I don't disagree with her. In fact, I agree with her wholeheartedly about the Simpson jury. He was acquitted because of reverse racism.

The Uber arrives quickly. Bravo technology, because it's chilly outside. The Student helps me into the car while the driver puts my cane in the trunk. She looks at me as if she's about to cry, then gives me a gentle hug.

"Maybe you can visit me after it's over," I say.

"Absolutely."

We both know we'll never intentionally see each other again, and that's too bad. I suspect it's like a close-knit group of soldiers after the war ends.

I can't really explain it, but it's odd how, of all the jurors, the Student is closest to me. She seems the least likely of allies. She's the youngest on the jury, while I'm the eldest. She's black, while I'm a WASP through and through. She's a technological whiz, while I'm a Luddite. I know who Rosalind Russell is, and she doesn't. On the surface, the other jurors are more like me. The Clergyman is younger than I, but closest in age and also apparently reserved and proper. Yet the man has the personality of a poached salmon. The Jury Consultant, Architect, and Housewife all have backgrounds much more similar to mine, yet we seem to have nothing in common. I'm neither a divorced professional woman on the prowl nor a mother with mewling little kids. The Express Messenger hasn't matured a whit since he was a student at my high school. The Foreperson … Let me amend what I said. I have more in common with the Student than I have with the Foreperson, who got chosen for that job out of pity.

The Student and I do have something in common. We're both minorities. I've only lately become such—I've gotten old. It's the qualitative, not the chronological, aging that matters. I have the ills of a woman ten years my senior. The hearing loss, the arthritis in the hips and knees. Not all seventy-eight-year-old women become afflicted with such ailments, but I'm one of the unlucky ones. My son-in-law's mother is eighty-two, and she's complaining that her tennis game has suffered because she got shin splints from jogging.

The Uber driver drops me in front of my house. The moment I walk inside, my husband's attendant, a sweet Filipina, says, "He wants to dance."

"I'm sorry, Ligaya," I say. I'm sorry because my husband wants to dance with me, but when I'm not around, any woman will do. A moment later, he comes out of the bedroom wearing a big smile and waltzes with an invisible partner, his eyes twinkling like a bewildered toddler's. But unlike a toddler, whose bewilderment is the precursor to clarity, my husband will never see anything clearly again.

Now he starts humming "Moon River" and beckons me over. We had our troubles, but one step in healing our marriage was a ballroom dancing class he insisted we take—which amused me, because before then, he had two left feet. We both loved to dance. I can barely manage it these days with my aches and pains, but he still moves nimbly. This love of the dance is an artifact of who he was, a reminder that elements of his essential personality endure for now. We're quite a complementary pair. At eighty-one, he remains physically strong, while at seventy-eight, my body is failing. His mind has deteriorated into dementia's dross, while mine sees our tragedy in cruel clarity. Still humming, he approaches me and bows. I curtsy, and he takes me in his arms, the part of his brain that remembers gentleness still intact. We dance.

JUROR NO. 1

THE FOREPERSON

Sinatra jumps in my lap, making me make a typo.

"Oooh, you naughty boy, Sin-Sin! Ooh, you naughty kitty!"

Sinatra meows. I named him Sinatra because he's part Siamese and he has blue eyes. He was five when I got him—old—so he's Old Blue Eyes, meaning Sinatra, get it? Everything was wrong with him when I got him: a UTI, fleas, worms—yuck!—you name it, but I nursed him back to health. My tabby, Melody, loves him. My black kitten, Teddy, doesn't like Sin-Sin. It's Teddy's fault. He's an adolescent, annoying, always wanting to play, and Sinatra has no patience for it.

Phew. Tomorrow morning, it'll all be over. Phew! Hard to believe. Phew. Why am I feeling sad? But it's kind of sad. I've done public service, done good. Day after tomorrow, it's back to work at the insurance agency. Not much public service in the records department. Maybe I'll look for another job in an animal shelter or something. I could start that pet-sitting business I've always talked about. The problem with that is, I doubt I can get the permits, and my son says no, the house already stinks of cat pee.

He doesn't live here, so what business is it of his? It'll be tough. Real tough. Who wants to hire a fifty-six-year-old with only two years of community college? It won't be enough that I'm good with animals. Maybe I should learn QuickBooks. I'll learn QuickBooks and work as a bookkeeper, maybe for a vet or in a shelter. If I had the money to quit my job and go back to school, I could become an architect. I have a better eye than her.

The folks at work are going to want to hear all about it. I'll be a rock star. I'm the jury foreperson in the Sullinger case. If any of the guys get into the sex part, I won't tolerate it. I'll report them to HR.

Are we doing right by Amanda? The trial lasted so long, and to only be out a day, less than a day? Us jurors must take the process seriously. That's what the judge instructed. Are we doing that? I hope so. Maybe this isn't a hard case. Two words make this an easy case: Lacey Sullinger.

"You be a good boy," I say to Sinatra, who starts purring. I hit the backspace key, delete Sinatra's typo, and retype my name in the search box. I'm curious about my brother and sister jurors. Yeah, the judge said to stay off the internet, but we're human, right? Anyway, I'm not looking at articles about the case or anything, just stuff about the other jurors.

The results come up. I don't have more than a page of search results about me, and they just mention my address, age, relatives. Phone book stuff. I guess that's because us jurors are anonymous and our names aren't linked with the trial yet. I'm Juror No. 1. You'd think the reporters would discover our names. But maybe they don't print our info out of ethics. After the trial, I'll give some interviews and let them use my name; then I bet I'll have thousands of Google hits. What's the harm in giving the reporters my name? We're letting David go free, so he's not going to come and kill me, right? Then again, his crazy son, Dillon ... I'll cross that bridge tomorrow.

Nothing much comes up about the Grandmother except, a long time ago, she won some awards for teaching. The Architect doesn't have that many more hits than me, just testimony in front of planning commissions of small cities and towns. Most of them I haven't heard of. There's a reference to her ex-husband, who's a real famous architect, not like her. The Housewife has quite a few hits, believe it or not, like alumni events for her college and volunteering for her kids' preschool and some charity stuff for soldiers overseas. Her husband is a computer software developer or something. The Student has her school events and social media page listed, but that's it. From reading this stuff, she's just a kid. Sexy pictures of her friends, big group hugs with others in her dorm, all the boring stuff that college kids do. But how would I know, because I didn't do them and my son refuses to try college.

The Jury Consultant has the most Google hits, because she's dealt with a ton of trials. Not much about her personally, except on her web page. PhD, the most educated of the bunch.

The search of the Express Messenger returns the phone book info plus his two movie appearances on IMDB, but other than that, he's like me, nothing special.

Last, I search the Clergyman. Everyone introduced themselves with first and last names when we were first empaneled, so finding out stuff about them was easy. The Clergyman only gave his first name. But I'm a creative girl, so I type in his first name and "Methodist minister" and "Sepulveda County" in the search box, scan the results, and *voila!* as the French say. He had a big fight with the Methodist hierarchy over gay rights. He's pro same-sex marriage. Good for him. I would've thought the opposite just by looking at him.

"Wowie, Sin-Sin, the Clergyman's Google presence beats everyone! Hundreds of hits. Who knew, big old, sweet old kitty cat?"

Sinatra shuts his eyes for a moment and purrs again.

"I hope nobody catches Mama doing this. I don't think it's illegal, because Mama is an honest foreperson."

Sinatra looks up at me, demanding a caress. "You're such a needy kitty," I say as I stroke his cheek.

"Why didn't this stuff about the minister come out in voir dire, Sinatra?"

My kitty has no better answer than I do. I guess, the lawyers didn't ask the right questions, though they did with the rest of us.

"He's quite the political activist," I say. "Environment, children's rights, interracial harmony, charities, and the pro-gay stuff. Why didn't that come out? Maybe it did and I wasn't paying attention at that moment. But I was paying attention, because I wanted to get on the jury, and good jurors pay attention. I had to sweat it out because I was first in the box. Juror number one." I stroke the cat behind the ear. "Just like you're kitty number one."

There are quite a few photos of the Clergyman doing his thing. Planting trees in a new park in the inner city. Schmoozing at some fund-raisers. Flashing broad smiles, which he hasn't done once as a juror.

"Is this the same guy, Sinatra? Or did we get his evil twin?"

Then I see the next image and want to pee my pants. I zoom in to make the photo bigger. Do the lawyers know about this? Does the judge? They can't know, or …

I hit the print button and hop out of my chair. Poor Sinatra flies into the air and onto the floor. He looks at me like I betrayed him.

I pick him up and rub my face against his. "I'm so sorry, Sinny. Mama just discovered something important. At least, I think so." Carrying him in my arms, I go over to the printer and grab the page. The photo is just as unbelievable in hard copy as it is on the screen. More so. I'm hit with a weird feeling in my chest, and I know why. There's something about holding the truth in your hands, actually touching it.

THE PARALEGAL

SAUL MEADE

Jenna and I don't speak on the ride back to the Sepulveda Deluxe Suites, a three-diamond-rated hotel, best in the county. Always put on a good face for the limo driver to keep those passenger ratings up. The nonpartner-partner and the associate are staying at a two-diamond downtown near the courthouse, where we also rented a suite we use for a war room. The area is an unnerving combination of rundown and deserted, with a high crime rate. Every time they go back there late at night, I worry about them. Not that I feel much safer in our area, with all the kooks who stalk Jenna, but at least we have a river view.

As soon as we get inside the room, Jenna says, "I'm going to pack."

She's probably making the right decision. A defense verdict, and we're out of here tomorrow.

Jenna likes to pack in private, so I go into the living area and mindlessly check the national news on my cell phone. Nothing encouraging there.

One reason I stopped pursuing my PhD was how it was

affecting my worldview. I love literature, and yet, the theory in which I was steeped started from the premise that there is no literature but only the reader's interpretation of it, which is unstable. If that's true, then there's no Holy Bible, no Constitution—in other words, no fixed laws of God or man. Those conclusions were fine with me; they reflected my progressive view of the world and politics. But then I came to a troubling realization: if our interpretation of texts is subjective, maybe our impressions of other people are as well. Which would mean that "real" human beings are no more real than characters in books. Look at David and Amanda Sullinger. Their public lives were interpreted one way and their private lives quite another. Which was true? Both? Neither? Even their children don't agree. Which leads me to ask, Did I make up Jenna Blaylock, or at least the Jenna Blaylock that I loved? Did *she* make *me* up? Do our separate stories no longer converge?

I don't want the people I love to be stories, dammit. I don't want my life to be nothing more than theory.

Jenna comes into the room. She's dressed in her designer cotton blouse from court, her bra, and nothing at all from the waist down. After so many years of marriage, this doesn't mean a thing. It's just the way she feels comfortable. In the early days, I found the contrast between the fully clothed top and the nude bottom raw and enticing. These days, I can't allow that, because she doesn't allow it. Another reinterpretation of each other.

"What are you doing?" she asks.

"Looking at my cell phone."

"Are you mad at me?"

"Why would I be?" This answer is, in a nutshell, indicative of one of our problems: Jenna uses questions to attack; I use them to deflect.

"I'm sorry I treated you that way, Saul. I don't know why I do it. It's just that all the pressure, all the obligations, too much to drink ... I've got to stop drinking so much. You know I couldn't have done it without you. I can't do any of it without you, you're so brilliant. I need you, Saul."

My ego is still big enough to believe the last part. I want to ask, *Is that why you keep me around? Because I'm good at legal research and writing?* I've asked as much in my more vulnerable moments. At this moment, I'm not feeling vulnerable.

She leans back on the doorsill and crosses her private-trainer-shapely legs, and I try not to stare. Jesus, she's been my wife for years, and I try not to stare.

"Do you truly believe the jury could convict?" she asks. Her eyes are half shut, her lips pressed together in what might be a tight smile or a mild grimace, or a pensive look, as if she's seriously considering the possibility of losing.

"I think you have it won," I say truthfully. "Ninety-nine point nine-nine percent. Sorry I spoiled our dinner."

"Just ninety-nine point nine-nine percent? Not a hundred?" The sly smile and the melodious lilt convey that I gave the right answer. Then "Are you staring at my pussy?"

These words could be an observation, an accusation, or an invitation. So here it is: My abandoned field of endeavor practically applied in all its Derridean, Foucauldian, Kristevaean glory to whether I should make a move. My half-nude wife is an ambiguous text whose meaning depends on the listener's (meaning *my*) subjective response. In recent years, I haven't been very good at making meaning between Jenna and me. I decide on "I'm looking at every bit of you. A man would be a fool not to."

Jenna fashions a sultry smile, a sexy turn, a come-hither wave of her right arm, and says, "Well, come to the bed and maybe you'll get a closer look."

I accept the invitation, although I don't always, lately. I still love Jenna, despite everything. As we move in a familiar sexual choreography typical of long-married couples—every step of the dance is practiced, unsurprising, yet comforting—I try to force out the insidious thoughts: Jenna isn't making love but, rather, engaging in a victory fuck; she's been sleeping with wealthier, more powerful, more attractive men; why do we have sex only when she's been drinking?

Finally, an intrusive echo of David Sullinger's last answer on redirect:

Jenna: David, as you sit here today, how do you feel about your wife?

David: I still love Amanda, despite everything.

THE BAILIFF

BRADLEY KOBASHIGAWA

"Showtime, Kobash."

These mumbled words rouse me from sleep. What's majorly weird is that the cheesy announcement comes from my own lips. It happens a lot. Weird. Majorly weird.

Am I sleepwalking? Am I awake when I say these words? Maybe it happens in that sliver of existence between awake and sleeping. That's the one time when you can control your dreams. Whichever, the words are a great internal clock and calendar. They don't wake me on weekends, holidays, or vacations.

I haven't told anyone about my special talent. Not my son or ex-wife. Not the police-force shrinks they made me visit after the incident. No way them.

Once, when I patrolled the streets for the sheriff's department, I was one of the good guys. I loved being one of the good guys. Not because people looked up to me, which they did. But because I *was* doing good, and when you're doing good, life has a rhythm. I had a musical life back then. Each day was a kind of concert, and while I was never the lead singer, I was in the band. That's how I looked at it.

Show time, Kobash!

Then I was no longer one of the good guys.

I look at the clock. Yep, five-fifteen. My internal ring announcer came through again. Why does the early-morning weirdness continue to torture me?

I get out of the bed, take a shower, and tie my tie in a Windsor knot. When I turned twelve, my father insisted I learn how to tie a necktie three ways: Windsor, reverse Windsor, double Windsor. The mark of a cultured man, he said. The mark of a man who society takes serious. He was so disappointed when I became a cop. He didn't come out and say it; that wasn't his way. What he said was, "You'll only need to tie one kind of knot for that job."

I get in my car and drive to the coffeehouse for a latte and an orange-ginger scone. A perfect breakfast on a cold day. My ex-wife hated that I wasted money on such minor extravagances. She ended up hating most things about me. Of course, that was after my fall from grace.

I arrive at the courthouse a little before six-thirty. I take the elevator to the sixth floor, where the deputies assigned to court-house duty share a tiny office. The other bailiffs are either rookies paying their dues in anticipation of promotion to more exciting jobs, or has-beens like me. I nod a hello to the others, who give not-so-friendly nods back. They can't afford to be friendly where I'm concerned. I get my sidearm and my keys and go down to the courtroom. As usual, I'm the first one to arrive. I go into the jury deliberation room and turn on the light.

Oh, my God. The night crew hasn't cleaned the room. The jurors shouldn't be subjected to unsanitary conditions, especially on the first full day of deliberations. I gather up Styrofoam coffee cups, mostly in the place where the Foreperson sits. Then I go back to chambers. The judge is sitting in her office, signing orders.

"Good morning, Bradley," she says. "I have the cupcakes for the jurors. Jonathan and I baked them."

"You mean you and Mick, Judge?" Why did those words come out? Not because it's early. I'm a morning person.

"Isn't that what I said?"

"Maybe I—"

"That's what I said. Mick and I."

"I must've misheard you, Judge."

"Yes. You did," she snaps. "People seem to be mishearing me right and left these days. Listen more carefully." Judge Quinn-Gilbert can get like this. She's a nice person, but she's also a judge.

I stand at attention. "Yes, ma'am."

She lets go of her pen. It's not good when she lets go of her pen. "How many times have I told you not to call me 'ma'am'? It's 'Judge' or 'Judge Quinn-Gilbert.'"

"Yes, Judge. I'll take care of those cupcakes."

The truth is, she's never, ever told me not to call her ma'am.

THE COURTROOM CLERK

MICK REDMOND

The judge and Mick's ingredients for maple-bacon cupcakes:

12 bacon strips
1 stick of butter (8 oz.)
1 teaspoon pure leaf lard (Durham's preferred) or use the bacon fat, cooled and congealed
2 eggs
6 tablespoons pure maple syrup (Vermont preferred)
2 tablespoons brown sugar
1½ cups all-purpose flour (sifted)
1½ teaspoons baking soda
1 tablespoon vanilla extract

Jonathan would give the judge such a hard time about putting bacon in the jury's cupcakes.

"Insensitivity to the religious dietary laws of minorities," he'd say in that rich voice that drew you to him despite the substance of the words. The fact that we'd always bake other kinds of cupcakes sans bacon so that the jurors would have a choice didn't discourage him from making such remarks. Sometimes, he would even level the criticism while scarfing down a maple-bacon cupcake he had stolen while Natalie wasn't looking. Jonathan Gilbert was one of the few people whose smart-ass remarks could truly be endearing. Smirking, she'd tell him to mind his own business. Then she would order him out of the kitchen. Yet I always felt that for some reason, this light, affectionate banter stung her. Only after Jonathan died did I realize why. Three weeks after the funeral, at the end of a particularly grueling day in court, the judge called me into chambers and confided that Jonathan had put a clause in his will providing that he was to be buried in the county's only Jewish cemetery and that she can't be laid to rest next to him. Oh, she can be buried in the cemetery, she said—the operators are Reform Jews—but only in an area reserved for interfaith couples, and that isn't where Jonathan's mortal remains remain. Apparently, Jonathan's asshole of a father had objected to the marriage because the judge is a gentile. As a quid pro quo for his father's agreement to accept the marriage, Jonathan promised to be buried, when the time came, in the family plot in the county's only Jewish cemetery.

"At least, my father-in-law has never called me a shiksa," the judge said. "Well, that I know of."

So-the-fuck-what that he didn't call you a shiksa? I wanted to reply, but I didn't, because this was just another example of Judge Quinn-Gilbert's capacity to forgive, and I admire that.

My face must have registered anger, because she said, "I don't blame Jonathan. I truly believe he was going to fix it after his father passed. Who could have known he would die so young, especially since his parents lived so long?" She shrugged.

Jonathan Gilbert's father has outlived him. The loathsome old man is ninety-six, lucid, and heartbroken. Jonathan's mother passed away four years ago at ninety-one. I suppose Jonathan thought he had longevity on his side. The moral of the story: careful when you wager on genetics, because sometimes a thoroughbred breaks down in the blink of an eye.

As executor of Jonathan's will, the judge could have ignored the stipulation about the place of his burial. I checked with one of my fellow clerks. She works in the probate department, and she says testamentary provisions like that are nonbinding. *Hortatory*, the lawyers call it. But the judge followed the terms of the will because she didn't want to disrespect Jonathan's wishes. She's no religious zealot, my boss, but she's a romantic who, despite her education, high intellect, and rational judicial mind, can be superstitious. She doesn't let rocking chairs rock without someone seated in them, because an empty rocking chair that rocks means someone will die; she throws spilt salt over her left shoulder; she holds her breath and makes a wish while driving through a tunnel. She believes that if she and Jonathan aren't buried together, they won't find each other in the afterlife. Why would she sacrifice her eternal future for principle? Because she's a lawyer and a judge, damn it. Lawyers live to follow the rules, and judges exist to enforce them. So sad that she couldn't break a rule just this once.

JUROR NO. 43

THE CLERGYMAN

The judge and her clerk baked cupcakes for us jurors. Although I should not consume sugar because of my type 2 diabetes, or bacon because of my high cholesterol, I must note that the two pastries I ate were scrumptious. The cakes were fluffy and pure, and the bacon cooked to perfection, neither overly crisp nor fatty-rare.

The jurors appear in good spirits this morning. All except the Foreperson, that is. Presumably, we will vote for an acquittal based on Lacey Sullinger's testimony and then adjourn. I suspect the Foreperson will miss the excitement. I am ready for this to end. An end will ease the burden, although it will not lift it entirely.

The Foreperson pours herself a second cup of coffee, which smells orders of magnitude better than it did yesterday. It is still courthouse coffee, however. The Foreperson seems to have forgotten to bring in her own brew.

"I guess we should get started," the Foreperson says, her voice shaky, her tone funereal.

If I sounded so morose at funerals, I would never again be asked to officiate.

"There's ..." She inhales deeply and turns splotchy pink from the neck up, as if she's had a severe allergic reaction to a fruit berry. She reaches into her purse and takes out some sort of document, then looks directly at me.

"I found this picture on the internet last night," she says, the words shooting out with the cadence of bullets fired from an automatic weapon. "I think that's you. Isn't that a picture of you with Amanda Sullinger at some charity event for your church, or something? I'm raising it because I wanted to give you a chance to explain. That's my job as foreperson, right? Or should we just tell the judge, or the bailiff ... or ...?" She looks up and down the table for help.

"Holy shit, my mom was right!" the Express Messenger says.

The Foreperson stares at him in confusion.

"Surfing the net about the trial," he says. "It's a sucky thing to do."

"I was *not*!" the Foreperson says. "I was looking up stuff about us, since I know our names. The public doesn't know our names, so there's nothing in the stuff about the trial. I was just curious, since ... I would never break the judge's rules."

The Housewife whispers something to the Architect, who nods her head and smirks. The Grandmother and the Jury Consultant sit up stiffly in their chairs. The Student regards me morosely. So there it is. My secret discovered. Seven heads turn in my direction, Torquemadas all, and for the briefest of moments I know how David Sullinger feels.

I rise from my chair and stand to my considerable height, walk around the table toward the Foreperson, who cowers slightly, and pick up the photograph. I make a show of studying it, return it to the table, and use my hand to iron out any creases. In my best

Southern-TV-evangelist, *thou-hast-wronged-me-sinner* voice, I say, "If you are implying that I withheld information from the judge, I resent the defamation of character. I know nothing about that photograph except that it appears to have been taken at a fund-raiser, not for my church but for Amnesty International. I was one of the honorees for my good works. There were several hundred people at that event, including many from Sepulveda County. A candid photograph was obviously taken of Amanda Sullinger standing next to me. Along with three other individuals."

I return to my place, sit down, and cross my arms, my eyes locked on my accuser. I am a good liar.

As I suspected would happen, the Foreperson has turned beet red. "I … I still think maybe we should tell the judge," she says, barely audible from across the room.

"I don't think we need to go to the judge with this," the Jury Consultant says. "There's a rational explanation. The voir dire question was whether any of us *knew* Amanda. He doesn't."

"I agree," the Housewife says. Addressing the Foreperson, she says, "I don't think you should worry about what other jurors do. You looked at the internet, and we're not supposed to look at the internet."

Fascinating. I took the Housewife for a stringent moralist who would line up against me. Not so. She knows we are about to vote her way and acquit David Sullinger, and she does not want to do anything that could change that outcome. The prospect of imminent victory causes many to shunt morality to the side. That is exactly what should happen, morally—I should have to answer to the judge.

The Foreperson looks to be on the verge of tears. "I was only … I didn't do anything wrong."

I shut my eyes, attempting to mask the discomfort from the all-too-rapid heartbeat which threatens to send me into atrial fibrillation.

The Foreperson puffs herself up like some kind of albino land fish. "Anyway, when we left off yesterday, we were all in agreement and were going to vote. So I think we can vote now."

"I'm not ready to vote," the Jury Consultant says. "There's more to talk about."

"What more is there to talk about?" the Housewife says. "We all agree Lacey was a believable witness. You said so yourself."

"Excuse me, but I didn't say Lacey was a believable witness," the Jury Consultant says. "I said she was an *effective* witness. Not the same thing as credible. The judge instructed us to rely on life experiences in coming to our decision, and I can't help doing that. I make my living teaching people how to be effective witnesses in front of juries, and Lacey was *too* effective. Especially for a twenty-year-old."

"You want to penalize Lacey for being too good a witness?" the Housewife asks.

"I don't want to penalize anyone," the Jury Consultant says. "I just want us to reach a just verdict."

"Let's hear her out," the Foreperson says. "We haven't been going at this very long."

I am intrigued. I found Lacey to be a truth teller. I am a good judge of truth tellers. It takes a liar to know one.

"Here's what I observed," the Jury Consultant says. "Lacey was always leaning slightly forward while testifying, which is the very first thing we jury consultants train a witness to do. That posture helps a witness appear earnest and engaged—and truthful. Normally, a witness who's on the stand as long as she was will get tired and lean back or slouch, but she never did that, even after an entire day on the stand."

"Now, *that's* a stinging indictment," the Housewife says. "Prevarication by dint of posture—is that what you expert jury gurus would call it?"

"There's no need for sarcasm," the Grandmother says. "As Madame Foreperson pointed out, we really haven't been at this very long."

"Speak for yourself," the Architect snaps. She is grouchy this morning. Even more so than usual. I have noticed over the course of these weeks that the Architect is not what one would call a morning person.

The Grandmother glares at her.

"Lacey's posture is no biggie in and of itself," the Jury Consultant says. "But did you also notice that she'd always look at the questioner and never at us? We drum that technique into witnesses—look at the questioner. *Except* when you're giving a long answer or making an important point. Lacey followed that rule without fail. Another thing—when Lacey made eye contact with each of us, she'd start with Madame Foreperson and move down the line in strict numerical order. Truthful testimony isn't mathematical like that."

She is correct, our Jury Consultant. The edges of truth are jagged, not linear.

"I understand your point," the Grandmother says.

"I don't," the Architect says. "Another two minutes for Lacey in the penalty box for appearing truthful."

"I taught many students in my time," the Grandmother says. "Young people Lacey's age are rarely so poised when speaking to a group, even under the best of circumstances. Still, that doesn't mean I believe she was lying. On the contrary. I still find her credible."

"You taught high school kids," the Housewife says. "Lacey is in college."

The Grandmother turns to the Student. "You and Lacey are about the same age. What do you think?"

"I still feel like she was believable," the Student says. "But …"

We wait respectfully. The poor young woman is so nervous. Obviously equivocating. This is indeed an interesting and surprising development, this crack in Lacey Sullinger's seemingly impregnable armor of credibility. Interesting, surprising, and most distressing.

"Go ahead, honey," the Grandmother says, patting the Student's arm.

The Student inhales deeply. "It's just that, honestly, I mean, if my dad killed my mom, self-defense or not, and I had to testify in court …" She hugged herself. "Oh, my God, I wouldn't have been so calm and logical, and neither would any of my friends. I know people who've seen a lot of gang violence growing up; violence was part of their lives, and I doubt they'd testify as calmly as Lacey did. I mean, she was kind of mechanical, when you think about it."

"That's what you jury consultants teach witnesses to do?" the Express Messenger asks.

"Oh, my God, you're just speculating that Lacey was trained by a jury consultant," the Housewife says. "Anyway, it's not evidence."

"Actually, I'm not speculating," the Jury Consultant says. "She was trained by a competitor of mine, Jerome Marks from Chicago. He's good. I know it was Jerry, because he was in the courtroom. Only twice—when David was testifying and when Lacey was testifying. The dark-haired man in the blue blazer, khaki pants, no tie, sitting in the third row behind the defense table? Did anyone else notice him?"

No one else had.

"Is that evidence?" the Housewife says. "That's not evidence."

"Well, what if Dr. Phil had walked into the courtroom and sat in the third row?" the Jury Consultant asked. "Would you have noticed him?"

"Dr. Phil the talk show guy?" the Express Messenger asks. "My mother loves him."

"I do not," the Grandmother says.

On this, the Grandmother and I agree. I do know where the Jury Consultant intends to go, however. Dr. Phil and I both went to school in Texas.

"Phil McGraw was a jury consultant," the Jury Consultant says. "He met Oprah Winfrey on a trial involving the beef industry."

"My mother loves Oprah, too," the Express Messenger says.

"Much better," the Grandmother says.

"What's your point?" the Architect asks, sighing impatiently.

"My point is that if a celebrity walked into the courtroom, you'd notice. You couldn't put it out of your mind. I couldn't help recognizing Jerry Marks. I'm not saying he did train her—only that he was there and that Lacey Sullinger was undoubtedly trained.

"I still say, *so what*?" the Housewife says. "Trained or not, Lacey was a terrific, credible witness. No glitches."

"Not so," the Jury Consultant replies. "The girl slipped up at least once. Remember when the prosecutor was hammering her on cross-examination about how she'd never complained to her friends or teachers about her mother's supposed abuse? She glanced at Marks for help. The only glitch in a full day of testimony, but a telling one—a sure sign a witness thinks she's going to be caught in a lie." The Jury Consultant half smiles. "Poor Jerry wanted to crawl under his seat. I know how he felt. I've been there."

"I think this is inappropriate consideration of evidence that didn't come in," the Housewife says. This is felicitous—another accusation of juror impropriety, which further deflects attention from my infraction. "Anyway, none of this changes my mind about Lacey." She leans in closer to the Jury Consultant. "No offense, but by making these points, you're dissing your own profession. Anyway, I think all this stuff about verbal cues and demeanor is junk science. You either believe a person or you don't. I listened to Lacey's testimony, and she proved to me that her mother was a psychopath just waiting for an opportunity to murder David. So unless there's some hard evidence that Lacey wasn't credible—"

"There is," the Jury Consultant says. "The letter."

Ah, yes. The letter. Interesting. I had concluded that the letter worked to David Sullinger's advantage by bolstering Lacey's credibility as a sincere, devoted daughter who wanted to right a grave wrong done to her father. Perhaps I have missed something.

CHRISTINA KELLEHER, CSR

SUPERIOR COURT FOR THE COUNTY OF SEPULVEDA

	)
PEOPLE	) JURY TRIAL—DAY 22
v.	)
DAVID BENNETT SULLINGER	) Case No. 16-382
	)
	)

BEFORE: Hon. Natalie Quinn-Gilbert, Superior Court Judge

APPEARANCES: JOHN Y. CRANSTON, ESQ.
Assistant District Attorney,
Sepulveda County
On behalf of the People

JENNA MARIE BLAYLOCK, ESQ.
On behalf of the Defendant

TRANSCRIPT OF PROCEEDINGS

Reported by Christina Kelleher
Certified Shorthand Reporter

Cross-examination of David Sullinger by John Y. Cranston, attorney for the People (excerpt):

Q. You were incarcerated in the Sepulveda County Jail for some months?

A. [The witness nods.] It was horrible.

Q. And during that time, you received a letter from your daughter, Lacey?

A. Lacey wrote me a ton of letters. She's supported me from the beginning of this nightmare. I owe my life to her.

MR. CRANSTON: Your Honor, I'd like the clerk to mark as People's Exhibit N a one-page letter from Lacey Sullinger to David Sullinger.

MS. BLAYLOCK: Objection. Hearsay.

MR. CRANSTON: Offered to show motive, Your Honor, not for the truth of the matter.

THE COURT: Overruled. But keep your questions limited to that, counsel.

Q. Mr. Sullinger, let me read to you a letter that your daughter sent to you while you were in jail, and, at the same time, project it on the screen for the jury.

[Exhibit N projected on courtroom monitor]

Hi Daddy

I miss you. I'm doing everything I can to get you out of there. I promise, and you know your little girl never breaks her promises no matter what. The lawyer says we're making progress. No details, you never know who might be reading your mail. I'll just say she's confident. After that, I'll do whatever it takes to make sure you don't ever have to go back to that terrible place or anywhere like it. I'll make sure you get back what belongs to you. We'll finally be happy and free.

See you very soon!

Love,

Lacey

A. As I said, I owe everything to Lacey. For a kid her age, she was—

Q. Wait until I ask a question, sir.

A. I just—

Q. Wait, sir.

MS. BLAYLOCK: I object to counsel's attempt to—

MR. CRANSTON: I'm only trying to ask my—

THE COURT: Sit down, Ms. Blaylock. Mr.

Sullinger, don't talk until you're asked a question. Did your daughter send you Exhibit N, Mr. Sullinger? Yes or no.

A. Yes, she did, Your Honor.

By Mr. Cranston:

Q. And in this letter, Lacey wrote that the "lawyer says we're making progress," correct?

A. Yes. Just like it says on the page.

Q. By "the lawyer," she meant Jenna Blaylock, didn't she?

A. Yes.

Q. She's a pretty expensive attorney, isn't she?

MS. BLAYLOCK: Objection.

THE COURT: Sustained. Don't do that again, Mr. Cranston.

MR. CRANSTON: It goes to motive, Your Honor.

THE COURT: Not the way you phrased it.

Q. You didn't have the money to pay a lawyer, did you?

A. No. At first I was represented by the public defender.

Q. And you didn't have money to post bond.

A. Correct. I was rotting in jail for something I didn't do.

Q. And you couldn't use your wife's money, could you?

A. No, because of the false charges.

Q. It's called the slayer rule, isn't it, Mr. Sullinger? The slayer of a person can't inherit their money?

A. I don't know. I'm not a lawyer.

Q. Then your daughter, Lacey, turned eighteen and gained control of Amanda's assets?

A. Yes.

Q. And Lacey used that money to hire Ms. Blaylock and post bond.

A. Yes, thankfully.

Q. And if you're acquitted, you stand to gain control of Amanda's money.

A. I told you. I'm not a lawyer.

Q. Isn't that what Lacey meant when she wrote, "I'll make sure you get back what belongs to you?"

A. I wasn't in Lacey's head. But the way I read it was that I'll get my life back. My dignity back. I don't care about Amanda's money. I never did. Jesus, when we first … when I first met her, she was a teacher.

Q. A teacher who you stalked for years after?

A. Absolutely not. That's ridiculous.

Q. Amanda's mother is a liar?

A. My mother-in-law … Let's say, she's never had a grip

on reality when it comes to Amanda. She stood by and let Amanda abuse her grandchildren.

MR. CRANSTON: Move to strike that last sentence as nonresponsive, Your Honor.

THE COURT: Denied. You went there, counsel.

MR. CRANSTON: Your Honor, I … May I have a moment to confer with my colleagues?

THE COURT: Keep it brief.

THE COURT: Mr. Cranston?

MR. CRANSTON: Just another brief moment, Judge Quinn-Gilbert.

THE COURT: Speed it up, Mr. Cranston.

THE COURT: Do you need a recess, counsel? If not, I'll infer that you've finished your cross-examination.

MR. CRANSTON: No, sorry about the delay, Your Honor. Mr. Sullinger, let's go back to the letter. You wrote… I mean Lacey wrote… never mind. Withdrawn. Uh, uh … Let's move on to, uh, another subject. Did you …? On second thought, Your Honor, maybe we should take that recess now.

THE COURT: Members of the jury, we'll take a fifteen-minute recess. During this recess, I remind you not to discuss this case with anyone, including your fellow jurors.

JUROR NO. 33

THE GRANDMOTHER

I've always been an irascible woman—my mother claimed that I was an irascible child—but I'm particularly grumpy this morning. The reason is no mystery. Last night, my husband's waltz—a brief, tantalizing dream of normality—transformed back into the nightmare that has become our reality. He didn't want to stop dancing after thirty minutes, didn't understand or care that my hip was aching. He became agitated and then hostile when I insisted that I had to stop. When Ligaya intervened, he shoved her so hard she fell to the ground and sprained her wrist. She quit, the poor girl. Quit right on the spot. I don't blame her one bit. Only my tears and a call to the doctor for an increase in my husband's medication got her to agree to stay until the agency finds a replacement.

Thank God for the long-term-care insurance I forced him to get. Oh, how he resisted, and what a row we had over it. Things weren't going well between us at the time, and he accused me of wanting him to get sick. But he eventually did what I wanted when I invited that insurance broker over—a very nice, very pushy gay man who gave my husband just the right push by reminding him that men get sick and die earlier than women and that a husband has a duty to provide for his wife. Implied it's unmanly not to. This happened so long ago, I don't even recall the man's name—Alan or Edward or something? He was at least ten years older than my husband. He's probably gone by now.

In any case, I'm grumpy. I thought these deliberations would be over this morning, and that's not happening. We're talking about the short note that Lacey Sullinger wrote to her father when he was in jail, and that makes me grumpier, because I wanted to hear more about it at trial, and the prosecutor Cranston bollixed up the whole cross-examination. At least, the heater is off and I can hear what the others are saying.

"We heard tons about that letter during the prosecutor's closing argument," the Housewife says. "It doesn't change anything."

"Not much about it during cross-examination," I say. "Thanks to Mr. Cranston's blunders."

The Student nods in agreement, nods a little too long for my taste. I like the girl very much, but now I wonder if she's patronizing me because I'm an old woman. Or, how do I explain it? Maybe she's grabbing on to the hem of my skirt because she's afraid to stand on her own two feet. Kids today are so dependent.

"The David-killed-Amanda-for-her-money theory?" the Housewife says to the Jury Consultant. She lets out a verbal scoff, a kind of half sigh, half snort. "Ridiculous. David and Amanda were in a violent confrontation that had nothing to do with money. It was the forgotten anniversary and the name calling and the accusations of adultery with her best friend; it was … she accused him of sleeping with her best friend. The letter says nothing about David wanting money. He didn't want money. On top of that, as Lacey so perceptively noted, this is a community-property state. Half of it was his, frozen or not."

I lean in close to comprehend, and at the same time the Housewife leans back, breathing heavily, borderline hyperventilation. In my days as a teacher, I taught quite a few students for whom a discussion wasn't about communicating but about winning. The trait was particularly prominent in the bright, unpopular, awkward children who were desperate for a moment in the limelight. Little did they realize that their insistence on forcing themselves front and center alienated the very people they wanted to impress.

"It's not about the money," the Jury Consultant says in a soft voice. What a patient woman she is. She stands, walks over to the credenza, riffles through the evidence binder, and retrieves the document, then reads the letter to us and passes it around.

"I think it's important that we all look at the letter again," she says. "Study the words, the handwriting."

Hi Daddy,

I miss you. I'm doing everything I can to get you out of there. I promise, and you know your little girl never breaks her promises no matter what. The lawyer says we're making progress. No details, you never know who might be reading your mail. I'll just say she's confident. After that, I'll do whatever it takes to make *sure you don't ever have to go back to that terrible place or anywhere like it. I'll make sure you get back what belongs to you. We'll finally be happy and free.*

See you very soon!

Love,

Lacey

"The letter proves that Lacey is a devoted daughter who loves her father," the Housewife says. "You're implying that he was a duplicitous murderer, a monster. She wouldn't love a monster."

There are nods of agreement from some of the others, but not from me. The Student starts to follow suit, glances sidelong at me, and stops midnod. Annoying.

"People love monsters all the time," the Jury Consultant says to the Housewife. "David testified he still loves Amanda, and you seem to believe that *she* was a monster."

"Apples and oranges," the Housewife says. "David is the classic battered spouse—codependent on his abuser, according to the defense expert."

"Unless Lacey was abused by David and has an unnatural affection for *her* abuser," the Jury Consultant says. "That's the problem with the apples-and-oranges cliché: they're still both fruit."

"I'm not sure what that means," the Housewife says.

"Both sides had psychologists," the Student says. "Who are we supposed to believe?"

"The defense psychologist was better qualified," the Housewife says.

"Also expensive as hell," the Express Messenger says. "Kind of a whore, if you ask me."

"No one asked you," I snap. "And there you go again with that mouth."

"Yes, no profanity in the jury room," the Foreperson says.

"'Whore' is not profanity," the Express Messenger says like an argumentative teenager. "'Whore' is in the dictionary. But okay. The defense expert is kind of a prostitute." The kid was a smart aleck in high school, and he's a smart aleck now. Look where it's gotten him.

"Could we get back to the letter and talk about the psychologists later if we need to?" the Foreperson asks. Most of the time, the woman follows the deliberations like a kitten trying to capture a moving beam of light—just a bit behind and always ready to pounce.

"The important thing about this letter," the Jury Consultant says, "is that Lacey *promised* she'd get David back home, and *swore* she wouldn't break her promise. She made it her business to add the words 'no matter what.'"

"I see your point," I say. "Why didn't the prosecution bring that out?"

We sit in fraught silence, as if we're trying to figure this out, though we all know the answer. Leave it to the Express Messenger, who says, "It's because Cranston sucks hind tit as a lawyer."

Now we sit in embarrassed silence.

"Stop it," the Student says. "Just stop it."

"Yeah, just stop it," the Foreperson says.

The Express Messenger points his thumbs to his shoulders, lets his jaw go slack, and gapes at us with a *What? Who, me?* look.

"Does anyone else find it creepy that Lacey, a grown woman, calls her father 'Daddy,' and herself his 'little girl'?" the Foreperson asks.

"Not me," the Student says. "I call my father 'Daddy.' A lot of girls my age call their fathers that."

"Creepy," the Foreperson says, at which point the Student looks down at the table. "And look at that handwriting. It's like she's writing a love letter or something. Cranston didn't bring that out, either."

"Oh, he tried, but the judge shut him down," the Jury Consultant says. She's being cryptic and civil, but I know what she's getting at: the incest thing. I don't like to think such thoughts. It's hard to explain, but when my husband bought my daughter that new car for her sixteenth birthday, the way they were so close, made me wonder ... It was absurd, of course—the bizarre, perverse fantasies of a frustrated wife. He would never, and David and Lacey, well ... The thought of that topic makes me want to gag. I'm glad the judge didn't let that testimony in.

"Well, *I* read the letter the way the defense attorney does," the Housewife says. "A touching note from a supportive, loving daughter to a father who's been wrongly accused. It's disgusting to characterize this letter as evidence of some kind of twisted relationship between David and Lacey. Cranston tried to go there, and the judge shut him down. And it's inappropriate for anyone to bring it up here."

"The letter speaks for itself," the Jury Consultant says.

"Yes, it does," the Housewife says. "It's irrelevant. We're talking about guilt beyond a reasonable doubt here. David isn't guilty."

"Let's leave the sleaze behind and get back to the original point," the Express Messenger says, the sarcastic lilt so contrived that he undoubtedly received a D-plus for *sarcastic technique* in one of his acting classes. "You could read this letter as Lacey saying she'd lie for Daddy."

"I feel like I agree," the Student says. "You could read the letter that way. Or it could mean nothing."

The Express Messenger grins at her—his way of trying to be charming, I guess. Has he no shame? She's too young for him. And I know this is old fashioned of me, nothing I'd share publicly, but there are the racial differences. I'm not a biased person, taught many minority students, but even in this day and age, mixed relationships are difficult. That aside, she's a nice, bright girl, and he's a ne'er-do-well. Good thing she has a level head on her shoulders.

"Should we vote again, or something?" the Foreperson asks.

"It's far too soon for that," I say. "I find this discussion illuminating. I'm not ready to draw any firm conclusions yet."

The Housewife lets out an audible sigh of frustration. How rude of her! How irritating. She's making me grumpy.

"Let's take another five-minute break and talk about it after," the Foreperson says.

"Good idea," the Express Messenger says. "I have to take a lea … I have to use the little boys' room."

THE HONORABLE
NATALIE QUINN-GILBERT

Two knocks on my door, a pause, and two more. The pattern repeats. All the court personnel know it: the signature greeting of Edison Halleck, presiding judge of the Superior Court for Sepulveda County. It's an affectation he views as endearing and that everyone else but me views as narcissistic. It's not narcissism but, rather, a deep-seated nerdism that Ed has managed to hide from most of the world. Many dislike Ed Halleck, mostly because he's an effective administrator. I'm a fan of Ed Halleck. It's just that since Jonathan died—Jonathan was my husband—I can't stand to be in Ed Halleck's presence. There are two reasons for this.

"A moment, Natalie?"

I invite him in, though I don't really have a moment. There's the motion to suppress evidence I've had under submission for eighty-two days, and if I don't decide it by the ninetieth day, the State will withhold my paycheck until I do. I have several other motions that might also be running up against the ninety-day deadline. I don't know; I'll have to ask Mick Redmond.

You'd think I'd get a pass because of this Sullinger trial, but the august superior court bureaucracy, under the stewardship of one Edison Halleck, doesn't give passes. That's the first reason I don't want to be around him: it's his job to scold us ordinary judges about tardiness and clogged dockets. I never thought of this before, but he reminds me of the time when I was a seventeen-year-old girl, working a summer job at a long-defunct burger place called "Next Door," which required us to take an order and cook a hamburger by the time the customer was at the cash register. "Push 'em through!" the manager, a gropy, vindictive junior-college dropout named Jerry, would holler at us. "Push 'em through!" I still don't know whether he was talking about the customers or the burgers, or both. Anyway, that's Ed Halleck's role in this courthouse: get the other judges to push the cases through.

He flashes what he believes is an endearing smile, and the smile *is* endearing, but not for the reasons he thinks. Ed thinks he's debonair, and mostly he's right. He has a firm jaw, Roman nose, full head of silver-white hair, and imperial bearing, as if he came out of central casting. (Jonathan went bald at a young age.) Ed's smile, however, reveals upper front teeth reminiscent of Howdy Doody, or perhaps Alfred E. Neuman. The smile is a leavening feature that gives this dignified man an improbable boyish quality.

"So, your jury is finally deliberating," he says. "Word around the courtroom is that it'll be a defense verdict."

"Blaylock is as good as advertised. As good as she advertises herself."

He chuckles and then looks solemn. Here it comes: the lecture about managing my caseload more efficiently.

"Sit," I say.

Rather than sitting, he walks behind my guest chairs, half leans on the edge of the credenza, and crosses his legs.

"Now that the trial is over, I was wondering about a dinner," he says. "To celebrate this court's biggest trial in … well, in forever."

Which leads me to the second reason I don't enjoy seeing Ed Halleck. Ever since Jonathan passed, he's pursued me romantically. Well, not *ever since* Jonathan passed. Ed waited the socially acceptable minimum period. Minimum, maximum—there is no socially acceptable period where Jonathan is concerned—no timetable, no expiration date.

"Ed, we've been over this. I'm just not ready to date yet. I don't know if I'll ever be."

He looks at me sadly. I've hurt his feelings.

"Natalie, are you …? I meant, a group of us will have dinner. Judge Kroft, Judge Dudnik, Judge Strenger, Commissioner Ward, your courtroom clerk and bailiff …" He shrugs. "It was just a thought. No obligation if you're fatigued or have other plans, or … I certainly wasn't trying to …"

"Of course you weren't. I'm so embarrassed."

He straightens up and dismisses my concern with a wave of his hand.

"The dating thing is …" I say. What is the dating thing? I force myself back on track. "It's just that so many people are trying to fix me up all the time, trying to force me to join those computer-dating sites. So I assumed that … Knee-jerk reaction, you know. I'm so tired from the trial, I … Saturday night would be lovely. If there's room, let's ask Christina Kelleher, the court reporter, to join us. She did a terrific job under trying circumstances. Blaylock insisted on dailies when they were totally unnecessary. Poor Christina was transcribing late into the night—probably didn't get any sleep."

"I'll have my assistant arrange it," he says, smiling—no, forcing—a boyish smile. He's out the door without another word.

My head is spinning from the humiliation of assuming Ed was asking me out. He's asked me out before, but … Hasn't he? Of course not. What would his wife, Ellen, think?

THE HONORABLE
NATALIE QUINN-GILBERT

I find Mick in the courtroom, at his desk, processing papers. Without him, I couldn't have survived, wouldn't be surviving. And I'm not talking just about my job.

"Judge, why are you wearing your coat?" he asks. "The heating is back up, and it's very warm in here. If you're cold in chambers, I could—"

"I'm going for a quick walk."

"You can't do that, Judge!" His face registers pure horror. Bottle-cap eyes, Jonathan would call them. "The jury's out. What if they come back with a verdict?"

Poor man. I know he's worried about me. He doesn't have to be. I understand his shock. I've never before left the courthouse, possibly have never left my chambers, while a jury was deliberating. Well, to every thing there is a season. I reach into my pocketbook and pull out my cell phone.

"I'll tell you what, Mick," I say. "I'll carry this appliance with me, and if the jury comes back, you just call me, and I'll come running. I'm going to the park."

"You won't go far, Judge?"

"Just the park. I promise."

"Shouldn't Bradley go with you?" he asks, his brown eyes still wide with fear and devotion.

"I'm afraid it's Bradley who can't leave. The jury is his responsibility for now. If something happens, call me."

I leave the courtroom, make a right down the corridor, and almost collide with Assistant District Attorney Jack Cranston, who regards me with a look of horror on par with Mick's.

"Is there a … a … a something, Judge?" he asks, just as inarticulate now as he was during much of the trial. "Are you looking for us … me?"

"The *something* is that I'm taking a walk, Mr. Cranston. The jury is still deliberating. I'll be within walking distance with a cell phone if anything changes."

"Thank you, Your Honor," he says, forcing a smile. "Pretty day outside."

"I wouldn't know. That's why I'm taking a walk. To find out firsthand."

"If you'll excuse me, I have to be in Judge Halleck's courtroom now." He turns and scurries away. He doesn't like me much these days. I can't say I blame him. My rulings went against him on some major issues.

"We'll see each other in due course, Mr. Cranston," I say.

Jonathan liked Jack, thought Jack was a good lawyer. Jonathan also recognized that Jack isn't a politician. Of course, everyone recognizes that Jack Cranston isn't a politician—except Jack Cranston. He thought he'd prove otherwise through his prosecution of David Sullinger, but he was wrong. The DA should never have pressed murder charges. Manslaughter, maybe, but not murder. Not after interviewing Sullinger's daughter.

I proceed down the hall, avoiding any further awkward encounters, leave the courthouse through a back entrance available only to court personnel, and walk out onto the street. It's a chilly February morning, in the high thirties.

I told Mick I was going to the park, which is only a block away from the courthouse. It's a welcome oasis amid a desert of concrete and glass, the gardens well maintained by the city. There is a homeless problem. I wish our government would do something to help those poor souls. They say there's no money, but you can always find money to do the right thing.

I pass the park and go another seven blocks to the river. The walk is easy. I do love these catwalk flats I bought online from StylishShoes.com. Mick told me about the website. The shoes are functional yet formal enough for court. Not stylish, but fortunately, judges don't have to be fashion plates during court days. The black robe makes its own statement.

The tourists, panhandlers, boaters, and anglers congregate at the end of Gallatin Street, but I know a quiet spot down London Road. The street looks, to the uninformed, like a cul-de-sac, but a concealed gate provides access to the river. The path down is rocky, through a glade of willows and white alders. Then, if you walk along the shore for about a hundred feet, you find an old gazebo. The county hasn't maintained it, so it's a little rickety, but it has a lovely view over the river. Now, in the February cold snap, the splintery beams creak and moan in the gelid wind—a counterpoint to the rustle of the trees. Jonathan and I met on this gazebo, although we told people we'd met at a State Bar conference in San Diego. I was never sure why we did that—maybe to keep private one small part of our very public lives.

Like me, he found this a convenient place to escape from the constant disputation that is the American justice system. "Disputation"—what a Jonathan word.

A renaissance man, Jonathan could distinguish the migratory birds from the indigenous ones. The winter before he passed, we saw snow geese, dunlin, Clark's grebes, and American coots. "I thought you were the original American coot," I said, and he laughed. Now I wish I hadn't said it. I don't know why I wish that.

I pull my coat tight around me and try to identify the birds, but the only species I recognize is a crow, probably the same fellow who perches on the telephone pole outside my chambers window and laughs at me (*haw, haw, haw,* not *caw, caw, caw*) as I sit cooped up at my desk, parsing sentences in search of a truth that really doesn't exist in words.

There's a rustle of underbrush, a soft, uneven thump of footsteps, and I turn to find a disheveled man gaping at me. He's got the old-before-your-time complexion of so many homeless—leathery and pallid at the same time. And yet, he has a youthful aura that intensifies the tragedy. I'd guess he's no older than thirty. I take a step to leave, but he moves in front of me, blocking the path.

"Excuse me, sir, I need to pass by," I say firmly. I'm over the momentary shock. As a criminal-courts judge, I've encountered hundreds of dangerous people, perhaps more, many of whom I've sentenced, many of whom have been released from prison, and they haven't hurt me so far. In this, I was much braver than Jonathan, who was otherwise a courageous man. Jonathan feared that someone would retaliate one day. Perhaps that was another, unspoken reason he never became a judge himself.

The homeless man steps aside as if I'm the one who's startled him.

"You're Judge Gilbert, right?" he says in a surprisingly congenial voice.

"Judge Quinn-Gilbert." Why in the world would I correct him? Years of habit on a point that seemed important for so long but now is trivial.

He takes his grimy Cubs cap off and half bows—a gesture that's both obsequious and courtly.

"My late husband was a huge Cubs fan," I say.

"I like the Padres. I just wear this one because ..." He puts the cap back on his head. "It's Timothy Morales, ma'am. I'm doing really good."

I scrutinize the haggard face but still don't recognize him.

"Good for you, Timothy," I say. It seems the prudent response under the circumstances, though I wonder about this fellow's definition of "really good."

"Yeah, I'm still on the streets, but I'm staying away from the meth like you told me to."

"Are you staying away from the alcohol, too?"

He half shrugs and holds his shoulder to his cheek for a beat, embarrassed. The eccentric shrug triggers the memory. He was arrested for possession of methamphetamine and pled guilty. Thanks to a pretty good public defender—they get a horrible rap in the movies—he cleaned up well in court, looking almost like a fresh-faced college student. He was articulate and, I felt, truly remorseful in pleading for leniency. I decided to sentence him to time served and a diversion program.

"I just want to thank you, Judge Gilbert, for what you done for me."

"You can thank me by laying off the wine and going to your meetings. I'm still counting on you, Timothy."

"Yes, ma'am."

"Excellent," I say, and head back up the dirt path to the street.

No, Timothy Morales isn't doing *really good.* Perhaps I should have given him more jail time. Perhaps more time would have scared him straight. Not that I regret my decision. A judge shouldn't spend energy questioning her past decisions. Judges who do that eventually flame out. No, you do the best you can, hope you haven't punished the innocent or exonerated the guilty, and move on. That's another reason Jonathan never became a judge: he couldn't let his past mistakes be—always blamed himself when matters didn't go his way.

If I believe this, then why do I feel I'll blame myself no matter what the jury decides about David Sullinger?

I arrive back at the courthouse in twenty minutes and go inside to find my clerk. He's sitting at his desk and speaking on the telephone. When he sees me, he bolts up out of his chair, shouts into the phone, "Bradley, she's back!" and slams the receiver down.

"Judge, we've been trying to call you for the last forty minutes," he says. "My God, where have you been?"

"Strange. I didn't get a call." I dig into my purse for my cell phone and check for messages. It's powered off. "I guess I forgot to turn it on," I say without embarrassment or apology, because, after all, I am the judge.

"Well anyway … the jury—they have a note. They've been waiting."

JUROR NO. 52

THE EXPRESS MESSENGER / ACTOR

Half the jurors hate me, but fuck 'em, they'll get over it. I didn't start it. The Foreperson started it by asking me straight out, "Do you want Dillon's testimony read back?"

"Yeah, I think I do," I replied, making the Architect, the Housewife, the Foreperson, and even the Student groan. The fricking Foreperson, who asked me the question in the first place, groaned. The Grandmother huffed. *What's the rush?* I wondered. I want to hear some of the testimony because Dillon was such a bad witness that I'm not sure I really listened to what he was saying. The substance, you know? Isn't it partly about substance, not just appearance?

"Let's ask to have it read back," the Jury Consultant said, coming to my rescue. "That's what we're here for."

So now we're sitting here waiting because the bailiff says the judge had an unexpected matter come up.

The door opens. Finally. The bailiff says, "Line up numerically," and we comply and march into the courtroom. The judge is on the bench, the lawyers are at their tables, the court reporter is at her machine, and the girl with the tattoos, Kelsi Cunningham, is the only reporter present. David Sullinger isn't here. As always, when we walk into the room, everyone stands, including the judge, and they don't sit down until we do.

"The jury has sent the court a note," the judge says. "Is that right, Madame Foreperson?" The judge looks weird. Her cheeks and nose are all red, like she's sunburned or something. Or like she's been drinking.

The Foreperson hops out of her chair the way my mom does when one of her bowling teammates rolls a strike. "The jury would like to have Dillon Sullinger's testimony read back."

"Which part of it?" the judge asks.

The Foreperson glances around, her eyes glazing over with confusion. "All of it, Judge?"

Jack Cranston smiles. Why is he smiling? He's losing. Dillon was his key witness, and Dillon was terrible. I just want to hear the testimony one more time, that's all.

Judge Quinn-Gilbert shakes her head, and she, too, looks like she wants to smile. "Unfortunately, Madame Foreperson, we can't read back the entirety of Dillon Sullinger's testimony. He was on the stand for half a day. Is there any particular portion of the testimony you want to hear?"

The Foreperson's cheeks get splotchy, and she starts to say something, then looks at me, as do the other jurors. I slide over and whisper in her ear, "The stuff about the time he protected his mother, the tuna casserole stuff, and the nine-one-one call."

"The stuff about the time he protected his mother, the tuna casserole stuff, and the nine-one-one call," the Foreperson says.

"Can you find that, Christina?" the judge asks the court reporter.

"It'll take a moment, Your Honor." The court reporter inputs something into her computer and then types some more. She's a hot chick. She's wearing jeans now—I guess she didn't expect to come to court—but sometimes when she wore a skirt or a dress to court during the trial, it was hard not to steal looks at her legs, especially when the hem creeped up. She's got that court-reporting machine between her legs, and I couldn't help wondering about her … Then I'd think of my mom and what she'd say about me sleazing it up in court, and I'd look away from the court reporter's legs and pay attention again. Maybe I'll run into Christina someday, out shopping or at one of the two movie theaters. I've always liked the name Christina. I wonder if her friends and family call her Tina or Chrissie or Chris. I wonder if she has a boyfriend.

"Ready, Your Honor," Christina says.

"Proceed, Ms. Kelleher."

Christina straightens up in her chair and leans forward. "Reading from the transcript of the direct examination by Mr. Cranston:

Question: Dillon, did you ever see your mother strike your father?

Answer: Yeah, in self-defense when he was trying to beat the shit out of her.

Question: Can you give us an example?

Answer: Yeah, there was this one time when I was in middle school, and I got an F on a social studies test. I didn't know the state capitals. Who gives a crap about the state capitals?

Anyway, my mom started screaming at me, said I was a fuckup, said if I didn't shape up I was going to end up a loser like my father.

Question: Your mother said that to you?

Answer: Yep.

Question: That wasn't very nice.

Answer: Like I said before, my mother could be a bitch sometimes. No denying that. I have a fucked-up family. It didn't mean she hit my father. It was the other way around.

Question: What happened on this occasion … or on the occasion … uh, that occasion?

Answer: My father was sitting at the table drinking Scotch or gin or whatever he drinks. He screamed out, 'I'm sick of this bullshit.' He stood up so hard, he knocked his glass off the kitchen table and broke it. Then he walked over and hit my mother in the arm.

Question: With a closed fist?

Answer: I think … I think it was open, but he hit her with, what do you call it …? [Witness gestures]

Question: The heel of his hand?

Answer: Yeah. The heel of his hand. Hard. My mother yelped like a hurt dog.

Question: What did your mother do next?

Answer: She told my father to get the fuck out, that he needed psychiatric help.

Question: In a loud voice?

Answer: In a tough voice. My mother was tough. Also scared.

Question: What happened next?

Answer: My father grabbed my mother by her blouse and started lifting her off the ground. She was wearing one of her work blouses, buttoned up to her neck, and he was choking her. She was gasping for air, and her eyes were bugging out, you know, like in one of those horror movies, but it was real. Like, swinging, but not swinging …

Question: Flailing?"

Christina stops reading testimony—kind of a shock, because there's a rhythm to her reading, and it's been broken. She hesitates, then looks up at the judge and says, "Your Honor, then there was an objection that was overruled."

"Go ahead with the next answer, Ms. Kelleher," the judge says.

Christina nods and says, "The witness answered, 'So, I went over to my father and shoved him. The good thing was, he let go of my mother. The bad thing was, the dickwad hit me in the stomach really hard.

Question: Were you in pain?

Answer: Damn straight I was in pain. I was only fourteen. But when my father turned back to my mother, I picked up a knife and told him to get away from her. And he did it, just left the house and took off in his car. Fucking coward, hitting a woman then running away when I challenge him. After that, he never fucked with me again.

Question: What happened next?

Answer: My mother came over and hugged me. She started crying. It was freaky, because my mother wasn't a crier and wasn't a hugger, but this time she did.

Question: Was your sister, Lacey, present when this occurred?

Answer: Yeah.

Question: What was she doing?

Answer: What she always did when my dad was abusing my mom—smiling or laughing or just sitting there like nothing happened. Then freaking out and screaming at me when I protected my mother.

Question: Are you aware that Lacey testified that your father never struck your mother or you or her?

Answer: That's what Lacey tells everyone. She was the only one who didn't get hit.

Question: Do you believe Lacey is a liar?

Answer: Lacey is a fucking liar. She'll do anything to protect my father.

Question: Why?"

"Then another objection by Ms. Blaylock was overruled, and the witness answered, 'Because Lacey and my father have this perverted—'"

Christina takes a deep breath and looks at the judge. "Your Honor, at that point, the court stopped the witness from answering. And, I believe, that ends the first segment of testimony that was requested by the jury."

The courtroom stays quiet. Jenna Blaylock is thumbing through a loose-leaf binder like she couldn't care less about what the court reporter read. I think she cares about Dillon's testimony. I've never felt that before. Meanwhile, Assistant DA Cranston is sitting straight up, trying to look dignified, which the man cannot do.

Wow. When Dillon Sullinger testified in real time, I didn't believe him for a second. What a sleaze the kid was. Is. I think he was stoned on the stand. And then, on cross, Blaylock crucified him, just crucified him. Got him to admit that he'd washed out of his first private school after getting busted for possession of marijuana with intent to sell. Only Amanda's money and connections kept him out of juvie and got him into a drug diversion program. He'd gone back to rehab twice more after that. Blaylock also got Dillon to admit he was shitcanned (Dillon's word, not mine) from another private school for writing over and over on his American history exam, "I'm stoned on 'shrooms, I'm taking this test on 'shrooms." No, Dillon had no credibility with me, with any of the other jurors except the Jury Consultant. But now, when the words came out of the court reporter's mouth, they seemed credible, even though the court reporter sounds like a robot.

So Dillon seems like a better witness when you just listen to the robotic words. Does that matter? I don't know. We're supposed to consider not only the witness' words but also his demeanor and reputation. But his testimony is so detailed. Where does that leave us?

"Reading the next requested passage," Christina says. "For the record, Your Honor, this was during the prosecution's rebuttal on February seventh."

"Thank you, Ms. Kelleher," the judge says.

"Question: Are you aware that your sister, Lacey, testified about an incident involving a tuna casserole?

Answer: Yeah, I heard about that. I wasn't in court, because the judge said witnesses can't be, but … Anyhow, more Lacey bullshit.

The Court: Dillon, I've tolerated your profane language during previous appearances on the witness stand. That was my mistake, in hindsight. Watch your language this time, or there will be consequences."

Answer: Yeah, okay. Sorry, Judge.

The Court: Is there something funny about my admonition, Mr. Sullinger?"

At this point, Cranston stands up, interrupts Christina, who stops reading, and says, "Your Honor, the People object to the court reporter reading the colloquy between the court and the witness. It's not evidence."

"That objection is sustained," the judge says. "Ms. Kelleher, please just read the questions and answers and not colloquy between the court and counsel."

"Sorry, Your Honor," Christina says, blushing.

"It is I who was asleep at the wheel," the judge says. "Please proceed."

Christina raises her arms and stretches and then looks back down at her screen.

Question: Did your mother get upset at your father or you kids for calling the dish tuna casserole rather than tuna à la king?

Answer: Nope, never. I never even heard the à la king shit until the lawyer that works with you, Alicia, told me that my father testified about à la king. He must've gotten that word from the internet. He didn't get it from my mom.

Question: Did your mother ever throw a hot bowl of tuna at your father and burn him?

Answer: Nope.

Question: Did your father ever go to the emergency room with a burned face?

Answer: Yeah, because he was drunk, got down on the floor to look for something in the bottom drawer under the stove, and tipped the pot over on his face.

Question: Did your sister and your mother ever have a confrontation over a tuna casserole?

Answer: Only when my sister one time ordered it in a restaurant we went to and my mom got upset because Lacey was getting fat. I told you, my mom could be mean. But nothing like Lacey says."

Christina pauses and types something into her keyboard. "Your Honor, I believe that ends the second segment of testimony that was requested," she says. "The third was the nine-one-one call. Should I read the transcript of that recording, or—?"

"No, that's not necessary, Ms. Kelleher," Judge Quinn-Gilbert says. "We'll play the recording itself again for the jury. Mr. Redmond, are you ready?"

"Yes, Your Honor," the court clerk says. He punches a button on his computer, and the courtroom sound system powers on.

Dispatch: *Nine-one-one emergency.*

Dillon: *I need an ambulance … I … I need the cops to come to my house, and the paramedics, or … I need the fucking cops.*

Dispatch: *Calm down. What's your name?*

Dillon: *Dillon Sullinger.*

Dispatch: *Pardon?*

Dillon: *Dillon! I'm Dillon! I need an ambulance, damn it! I need the police. My dad killed … I think my father killed my mom. The asshole … I think she's dead. Her head is split … and all the blood. Please send an ambulance, damn it!*

Dispatch: *Is your father there now?*

Dillon: *Yeah. He has an ax and a knife.*

Dispatch: *Is he there now? Are you in danger?*

Dillon: *I don't … No. He's just sitting there in the kitchen, crying. Right where she is. Oh, my God, there's so much blood, and she's not moving, and her eyes are open. Does that mean she's dead? I think she's dead. Please. Please, send an ambulance."*

Dispatch: *The other dispatcher is dispatching the police and the paramedics to where you're at right now.*

Dillon: *We live at five—*

Dispatch: *We already have your address, okay?*

Dillon: *Okay.*

Dispatch: *Okay, stay on the line with me and don't go near your father. Help will be there soon.*

Dillon: *Okay. Okay. Okay.*

After that, all you could hear was Dillon whimpering until the authorities arrived at his house.

We heard the recording only once during the trial. It didn't affect me so much then, but it does now. On the stand, Dillon sucked as a witness, but on the recording, he was a scared, vulnerable kid.

I'm glad I asked for a replay of Dillon's testimony and that recording. I wanted to hear Dillon once more, to be fair to him before we tore him apart in the jury room. Still, I don't know what any of this proves. All I know is that the whole thing sucks.

THE PARALEGAL

SAUL MEADE

After sitting through as many trials as I have, you learn that trying to divine the significance of a jury's note has as much scientific validity as tasseography, but without the Jungian insights and meditative benefits that staring into a cup of tea brings. Nevertheless, you try to read the jury's mind. Now, after the judge sent the jury back into the deliberation room, we sit at our usual booth in the Sepulveda River Grill, our hangout away from home, and deconstruct and reconstruct the jury's note with an intense scrutiny worthy of a Marxist/Freudian critique of the later works of James Joyce.

Jenna's nonpartner-partner and associate maintain that the note is good for us because the jury simply wants to consider for a final time the prosecution's best evidence, which isn't very good.

"They'll be back with a defense verdict within the hour," the nonpartner-partner says.

"Ditto," the associate says. "Maybe in a half hour. An hour at the most."

They truly believe this. Their true belief comes from the fact that this is the truth Jenna Blaylock wants to hear.

"What do you think, Saul?" Jenna asks.

I answer the way I've answered such pointless questions recently: with gratuitous cruelty. "I have no opinion. I'm just the paralegal." Then I add a new gloss on this spiteful response. "*Que será, será.*"

"Jesus, don't fucking quote Doris Day to me," Jenna says, taking a long swig of her second glass of Chardonnay. Yes, she's drinking at lunch. No, she didn't drink at lunch until recently. "Of course you have an opinion. And I know what it is. You think we're losing. That they're crediting that lying kid. Saul Meade, Mr. Glass-Three-Fourths-Empty. Mr. Passive-Aggressive."

Passive-aggression is defined as indirect resistance to the demands of others. I consider my behavior to reflect aggressive-passivity—indirectly assaulting Jenna emotionally when she's made no demands on me. Is it my way of getting back at her because she's outshone me? Because I'm no longer her unsung hero, the wind beneath her wings? Because she's growing ever more self-centered with each passing month? Marital annoyance works both ways.

Or maybe I'm being mean to Jenna because I thought that she gratuitously inflicted pain on Dillon Sullinger during her cross-examination of the kid, asking questions calculated to elicit foul language, cataloguing the boy's academic and socialization problems, hammering home ad nauseam at his drug use. She even convinced the judge to admit into evidence a record of one of Dillon's drug convictions that had been under seal and shouldn't have come in. I doubt it's a reversible error, but what do I know? I'm only a paralegal.

"I've concluded no such thing," I say. "And Doris Day was an unsung prophet of the 1950s and '60s."

The nonpartner-partner and the associate both smile at this, which draws a piercing glance of rebuke from Jenna. I'm encouraged—they finally seem to have acquired an appreciation of Doris Day, an underrated talent.

"We can debate the note from now until next autumn," I say. "But the jury will return a verdict soon, and whatever we conclude about the note will be insignificant. So this is a pointless discussion."

"Here's what's not pointless," Jenna says. "I expected the jury to be back this morning. Apparently, that's not going to happen. I need to call the people in Boston and tell them I can't make the fund-raiser." She finishes her wine and leans toward me. "Since you're the paralegal, please get on the phone and tell them I can't make it. Extend my apologies."

"I'll do it right after lunch," I say.

"No. You'll do it right this second."

"Yes, Ms. Blaylock." I rise from my chair, pull out my cell phone, and walk out of the restaurant and onto the sidewalk to make the call. The air is dry and crisp, the traffic sparse. Quiet for a town center at noon. Nice place, Sepulveda County. Green hills and a clear river. I wonder whether I could move here and escape.

THE PROSECUTOR

JACK CRANSTON

"The jury asking that Dillon's testimony be reread—a great sign, right?" I say.

I look at Bauer, who shrugs.

I look at Alicia, who shrugs.

I look at Cole, who shrugs.

"Shit," I say.

JUROR NO. 11

THE STUDENT

The bailiff takes us back into the jury room. While we were out, they brought in lunch: deli sandwiches, some gloppy coleslaw, gloppier potato salad, and soft drinks. I'm not a fan of cold cuts or carbonated drinks. I don't eat beef, pork, or poultry—nothing that walks or flies. I hope I can get a tuna-fish sandwich. I know they have them—the room smells like tuna fish already.

"Well, that was useful," the Housewife says as soon as we sit down. She's being sarcastic. She looks at the Jury Consultant. "Even if you don't believe Lacey, how could you believe Dillon? You can't believe them both, and he's an obvious liar. Even with the court reporter reading the cold, hard transcript, he's an obvious liar."

"I agree completely," the Architect says. She and the Housewife are still a team, I guess.

"I feel like that's true," I say. "Dillon has no respect for anything or anyone. I find his bad language really annoying. This trial is like a game to him."

"Sure, Dillon has his troubles," the Jury Consultant says. "But he was actually more credible than his sister."

"I can't wait to hear this argument," the Housewife says, and then she snickers out loud. She's been passionate up until now, but this time she was downright rude.

"It's not an argument; it's a discussion," the Grandmother says. "Let's be respectful. We owe it to the defendant and the victim."

"Dillon had no witness training, and he's not nearly as articulate as Lacey," the Jury Consultant says.

"That's for sure," the Architect says.

"Let's focus on the words," the Jury Consultant continues. "Substance, not perception. Lacey testified that her mother was the devil and her father was a saint. Black and white. Dillon testified in shades of gray. He agreed that his mother was overbearing and critical and often cold, that she made no secret about the fact that she was bitterly disappointed in David, and that she was afraid that Dillon would grow up to be just like his father. He admitted that his mother had a temper. While Dillon testified that his father was unpredictable and full of rage and physically abusive, he also said he understood his father's frustrations. Dillon gave the evenhanded, forthright testimony. People who are telling the truth concede weaknesses in their position. Dillon did that; Lacey didn't. He was telling the truth when he said that David was the abusive one. If it weren't true, if Amanda abused Dillon, why would he support her and testify against his father? It makes no sense."

"It does if he's mentally ill," the Housewife says.

"Nothing anyone says can make me believe Dillon," the Foreperson says. "I've got a druggie brother, and he couldn't recognize the truth if it slapped him in the face."

"What if we don't know who's telling the truth?" I ask. "Isn't that reasonable doubt?"

"Bingo," the Housewife says.

"It's not that simple," the Jury Consultant says, looking at me. I hate to be singled out, but her eyes are kind. "We have an obligation as jurors to decide which witness is telling the truth. That's why we had the long instruction on witness credibility. If jurors shirked their responsibility to make credibility determinations, every criminal defendant would be acquitted, innocent or guilty."

I feel my cheeks flush, and the Jury Consultant detects my unease, because she reaches over and touches my arm. "I didn't mean to imply that you or anyone else in this room is shirking their responsibility," she says. "Far from it. We're all trying to do the best job we can. It's hard to decide, especially in a case like this, when a person's very future is at stake. And it *should* be hard. Be that as it may, we have a responsibility to decide."

"I couldn't agree with you more," the Housewife says. "It's also our responsibility to use common sense. Common sense dictates that a poised, articulate, consistent witness like Lacey is far more likely to be telling the truth than a demonstrable delinquent like Dillon."

I glance at the Clergyman. He's looking down, picking at his fingernails. He's been unreadable as a slab of slate so far, but now he looks upset about something. He won't talk. Why won't he talk?

"Dillon sure didn't sound like a liar on the nine-one-one recording," the Express Messenger says.

"What was there to lie about?" the Architect asks. "He came home, found his mother dead, and called."

"That recording humanized him," the Express Messenger says. "I don't know why I didn't feel that when it was played during the trial, but it humanized him. The kid found his mother dead, which sucks. Jesus Christ." He visibly shudders.

"No one's saying he's not a human being," the Housewife says. "Don't get me wrong. He's as much of a victim as anyone. He's like an abused dog who craves its owner's attention and approval. That's why he's still protecting his mother even after everything that's happened. He still seeks her approval, even after her death."

"I don't see it that way," the Jury Consultant says. "I know that I'm dissing my profession in a sense, but sometimes, the untrained witness shows credibility through his or her flaws."

"I don't believe that druggie for a moment," the Foreperson says. "Now, I think we should take a break so we can eat our lunch. I got dibs on a tuna sandwich."

JUROR NO. 1

THE FOREPERSON

Just as I'm about to call the jurors to order, I see the Housewife checking her cell phone. Again. I should report her to the bailiff. I really should. But I'm not that kind of Foreperson.

"Let's get going, people," I say. "Times a-wastin'."

Everyone sits down but the Housewife and the Architect, who ignore me like I'm air. The bitches are standing in the corner drinking their expensive bottled water. I wish I could afford water like that, but I'm stuck with drinking contaminated county tap water.

"Let's get going, people!" I repeat.

The Housewife checks her cell phone, looks up at the Architect, and rolls her eyes.

"Another snarky text from Jared?" asks the Architect, talking loud enough for all of us except the Grandmother to hear. It's like none of us exist except the two mean girls.

The Housewife nods.

"We're in the home stretch," says the Architect. Is it my imagination, or does she sound impatient with her buddy?

"God, I hope so," says the Housewife. "But at this rate …"

"We're making progress," says the Jury Consultant. "But even if we're here for another week, you don't rush justice." Good for her—she refuses to be ignored, just like I do.

"You have a daughter as I recall, living in Oregon?" the Housewife asks. "A sixteen-year-old?"

"Good memory," says the Jury Consultant.

"I'm sure you haven't forgotten how needy small children are. I have three little ones. The baby is seven months old. My husband has a full-time job managing twelve people on four different projects, and since this trial started, he's been working from home because we can't afford a nanny. He's overtaxed with his job and with taking care of the children. I need to be with my husband and children." She sighs. "I still can't believe the judge wouldn't excuse me. My husband thought I should make up a lie to get off the jury, but I just couldn't do it. So don't you worry, I'm definitely here because I care about justice."

Interesting. As I remember it, the Housewife did lie to try to get off the jury. Or was that the Architect? Anyway, why does the Housewife think she's so special? We all have our issues. I've missed work for a month, and I told my bosses I'd be out two weeks. The law says they can't fire me for going on jury duty, but they're pissed that I'm not there. They'll probably find some other excuse to let me go if they want to, but if that happens, I'll sue them, maybe even hire Jenna Blaylock on a contingency. Anyway, you don't hear me complaining about the time this trial has taken.

"I've been thinking," I say. "Let's take a vote to see where we are. Any objection?" I wait. "Hearing none, let's vote."

"Absolutely not guilty," says the Housewife, although I didn't call on her.

"Not guilty," says the Architect.

"Not guilty," grunts the Clergyman.

"Not guilty," says the Student. "I'm not sure which sibling to believe anymore, but I guess I have reasonable doubt."

"Not guilty," says the Express Messenger.

"Guilty," says the Jury Consultant.

"Guilty," says the Grandmother.

"Not guilty," I say. "Which makes it six to two, and we have a ton to talk about." I pause. "That's right, six to two?"

"You get a gold star for arithmetic," says the Architect. Says the bitch.

"Here's why I've changed my vote," says the Grandmother. "As you all know, I was going to vote 'not guilty' when I walked in here, but changed my mind because Lacey's testimony wasn't nearly as strong as I thought it was at first. That letter and that immature promise she made to David—immature promises foster lies. When Dillon's testimony was reread, if you just consider his words, he sounds credible. Unrehearsed. The pathetic, tortured child we heard on the nine-one-one tape—he was not the smirking kid we saw in court. That was the real person, someone traumatized yet able to take necessary action.

"I just can't agree," says the Housewife. "If you compare Lacey and Dillon, we—"

"We've been through all that," says the Express Messenger.

"Please don't interrupt me," says the Housewife. "If you compare Lacey and—"

"It's a waste of time to talk about the siblings," says the Express Messenger. "Let's talk about another witness. Let's talk about the cop."

"Yeah, the cop," I say.

The Housewife shuts up. Finally.

THE HONORABLE
NATALIE QUINN-GILBERT

My husband, Jonathan, once called a jury trial the legal equivalent of an M. C. Escher drawing: the impossible intersection of a judge sworn to remain fair and unbiased; a prosecutor whose job it is to ensure punishment for lawbreakers; a defense attorney who must protect both the innocent and the guilty; and a group of jurors with no expertise in law, forensics, abnormal psychology, or much of anything else important in a trial. Wouldn't you know? The uninformed jury gets to decide. It's enough to drive a lawyer or a judge batty.

I can't bring myself to come down too hard on Jonathan's father. My father-in-law might not have approved of our "mixed" marriage, but he's always been civil, even warm in recent years. He wasn't the executor of Jonathan's estate; I was. What else could I do but carry out Jonathan's wishes regarding burial? Refusing to do so would have violated my moral duty, would have dishonored Jonathan's memory. My decision won't matter in the end; I know it won't. If, by some divine miracle, Jonathan and I are reunited in the afterlife—if there is an afterlife—he'll respect me for doing what he asked, for not being selfish.

My father described Jonathan as a "conniving Jew lawyer," and my mother didn't reproach him for it. Mother's reticence was *not* a case of the traditional, subservient housewife reluctant to defy her husband. My mother stood up to my father on many occasions. But not on this one, and that's what I found galling. She never said it aloud, but she believed no good Catholic girl marries a Jew, much less a Jew who doesn't want children. What my family didn't know is that *I* was the one who didn't want kids.

Because of the tension with my parents, I became estranged from my siblings. Well, not estranged, but formal and distant. Jonathan's friends became my friends. As the years passed, my parents offered an olive branch. Hell, they offered an entire tree. But I'm a bullheaded Taurus. Olive tree rebuffed, and now my parents are dead.

When he had that damned aneurysm, we were alone, watching a baseball game. I had to call 911 (I'm glad they never played *that* recording in court); I had to watch him die; I had to keep a stiff upper lip; I had to bury him in a place where I'm considered a trespasser. It's hard to reach out to others for support, because I'm an introvert at heart who took on a public role only because I fervently believe that a world without justice is a world without God.

JUROR NO. 6

THE ARCHITECT

"I'm not a fan of Deputy Beckermann," the Student says, sounding more confident than she has at any time during these deliberations.

Beckermann is the detective from the sheriff's department who first arrived at the scene of the killing, led the investigation, and eventually arrested David Sullinger.

"It's one reason I'm voting not guilty," the Student continues. "I feel like he arrested David to get publicity. I feel like Becker-mann railroaded David."

"I don't know if 'railroaded' is the right word," the Express Messenger says. "But I agree. I didn't like the guy. He's an arrogant prick."

Like you're not, Mr. Express Messenger / "Actor"? Still, despite the source of the comment, I, too, found Beckermann to be an arrogant prick. He's one of those people who try to act like a good guy but don't know how. Smiling at us as if we're his buddies; pleading nervousness when he clearly wasn't; calling Jenna Blaylock "ma'am." Bragging about shooting a homeless man to death, which was awkward, because this is a small county, and we all—well, those of us who read or watch the local news—realized that he and the bailiff had been partners on that day, holy shit. I don't like Beckermann, and I like the bailiff. Of course I like the bailiff—I wouldn't want to fuck a man I didn't like.

"Beckermann botched the investigation," the Housewife says. "The patrol officers were very careful not to handle evidence, not to contaminate the crime scene, and then Beckermann shows up and moves the pickax with his shoe. He moved the murder weapon with his *shoe*! He says it was an accident, but who knows? Only God knows what else he moved or stepped in. Just like Blaylock argued in closing, moving that pickax contaminated the crime scene. Worse, he has the bad sense to move the pickax back to where he *thought* it had been. Without wearing gloves. Then he gets distracted with whatever and lets Dillon stay in the house unsupervised while David sits in the patrol car. Who knows what Dillon tried to do with the evidence? Not even the crime-scene investigator could cover up for Beckermann. She was embarrassed to be on that witness stand."

"Poor Cranston," the Jury Consultant says. "Did you see the look on his face when all that came out? Beckermann blind-sided him."

"The guy's a moron," the Express Messenger says.

"Which one?" the Housewife asks.

"I was talking about the cop, but both," the Express Messenger says.

"I'm not okay with that word," the Student says.

"What word, 'cop'?" the Express Messenger says.

"No, I meant . . ." The Student exhales. "You know very well what word I meant. It's offensive. You're not clever or funny." The Student is finally showing some balls.

The Express Messenger's smirk and dark-circled eyes make him look like a half-man, half-raccoon video game character.

"You are a smart-ass," I say to him. "Not only are you not funny, but your behavior is unattractive. You've made some good points, but you fuck yourself with the attitude."

"Hear, hear," the Grandmother says.

He holds up his hands in submission. The smirk remains on the lips, but the sting of our insults has caused his eyes to glaze over. So the wisecracker is sensitive. Aren't they always.

"Let's all calm down," the Foreperson says.

"Who's not calm?" the Express Messenger says.

"Some of us," the Foreperson says. "Including you."

If one more person criticizes him, I bet he'll cry. I'm ambivalent about whether I want that to happen.

"How could Cranston not have known about Beckermann's mistake?" the Housewife asks. "Just another example of the prosecution's ineptitude."

"Ditto that," I say. I'm impatient today. I want to get out of here and see if I can resuscitate my drowning architectural-design practice. We're almost done. Why am I so impatient?

"No disagreement from this end of the table," the Foreperson says. "I don't like Beckermann, because of what he did to our bailiff."

"What did he do?" the Express Messenger asks, and surprisingly, the Housewife also looks puzzled. The Clergyman comes out of hibernation for a moment and nods.

"We're not supposed to discuss that," the Jury Consultant says. "It's not evidence."

The Foreperson puts a hand to her mouth. "I'm sorry, you're right. I instruct the jury to disregard that. Well, I can't instruct, but … You know what I mean. I shouldn't have mentioned it. It's just that if you live in this county, you—"

"Or if you surf the internet looking for info on the cast of characters," I say, making the Foreperson recoil. Why do I do things like that? My ex, putting it kindly, would say I don't suffer fools gladly. It turns out that his words weren't so kind, because the full verse from the Bible is "For ye suffer fools gladly, seeing ye yourselves are wise." Which means, according to my ex, that I see myself as *un*wise. Maybe, maybe not. Maybe it's simpler. Maybe I'm just a bitch.

I don't know which book of the Bible that quotation comes from. I'm not one for the scriptures. I'd much rather look at paintings by Raphael or Velázquez for my spiritual sustenance. El Greco's *The Tears of Saint Peter* brings *me* to tears. The mystical, communicative silence that is visual art—that's what I aspire to create in my own painting. My paintings are just noise, the grating shriek of the untalented.

"So, what do you think of Deputy Beckermann's testimony?" the Housewife asks the Grandmother. "You've changed your vote to guilty, so I assume either you don't think he was so bad or you don't care."

"I see the problems with his investigation, and I certainly care," the Grandmother says. "Which doesn't change the fact that David brutally killed Amanda." She writhes as if in pain and then points an index finger at the Express Messenger. "I want to add this. I respect the police and what they do for us, how they protect us, and it's disgraceful for anyone to call an officer of the law a moron."

Interesting. The Grandmother is a law-and-order freak. I didn't see that, especially with her early "not guilty" vote. But it stands to reason. She was a high school vice principal—a cop in her own way. This is a bad development. I thought the old woman would be easy to flip back to "not guilty" once we all talked this through and the Jury Consultant got off her high horse. Now I'm thinking we'll be here until April.

"I'm tired of all your insults," the Express Messenger says, springing up out of his chair. He points at the Grandmother. "Especially from you. This isn't high school, and you're not the vice principal anymore. Do you know what us students called you? 'The Warden.' Well, I'm not your prisoner anymore. I'm entitled to my opinion just as much as you are. At least, I haven't flip-flopped. Beckermann *is* a moron, whether you like the word or not."

"And you're still a rude child," the Grandmother says.

"People, I just want to say, can't we all get along?" the Foreperson asks, and it's all I can do to stop myself from asking, who does she thinks she is, Rodney King? The Foreperson probably doesn't even know who Rodney King is. I'm not sure why I want to embarrass her, but I do. But I'll try to get along.

There's a grunt-snuffle at the end of the table—a kind of wide-awake snore that comes from a partially successful attempt at stifling a guffaw. The Clergyman remembers the Rodney King riots, too. Riots? Uprising? Is that the politically correct term these days? Who the fuck cares?

"I'm not a fan of the Sepulveda County Sheriff's Department, to be honest," the Student says. "There have been successful lawsuits against them for harassment, especially of minorities. I'm especially not a fan of Deputy Beckermann."

The Student knows the story behind Beckermann and Deputy Kobashigawa, too.

"Oh, I didn't think you were one of those," the Grandmother says with an acerbic trill that's almost a cackle. Along with the stunned silence in the room—along with the Student's expression of the newly wounded—comes the Grandmother's recognition, evident from her open mouth and closed eyes, that she's revealed something unpleasant about herself she's made every effort to hide. No matter how much we practice, we can't consistently hide our prejudice, which, like a virulent strain of herpes, lies dormant until the next unexpected outbreak comes.

"You didn't think I was one of *what*?" the Student says.

The Grandmother flaps her jaw. After several false starts, she says, "I didn't mean … Of course I didn't. I just have respect for the police, and I …"

"Yeah, right," the Student says.

"That sucks," the Express Messenger says.

"That was a patently racist thing to say," the Clergyman says, slapping a meaty hand on the table, the sound of flesh on wood like the slamming of a car trunk. Many of us jump. I do, as much from surprise that the Clergyman spoke as from the loud noise.

"Please, please," the Grandmother says, shaking her head rapidly with a range of motion so slight, you'd think she was suffering from some kind of palsy. "Please. I meant no offense. I meant no offense." She looks at the Student as if she expects her to say, "None taken." Well, that's not happening.

I glance at the Housewife, who nods slightly. We suspected it, the way the Grandmother kept telling the Student she was a nice *girl.* It wasn't just about the age difference.

The Grandmother makes a pathetic attempt to reach out and touch the Student's shoulder, but the younger woman recoils, swivels in her chair, and turns her back.

Silence. All I'm thinking is, this is bad, because the Student and the Grandmother won't agree on a verdict, out of spite for each other, and we'll be here until June.

"Let's take the Foreperson's advice," the Jury Consultant says. "Let's get along, put aside our differences. Jury deliberations are stressful. Let's forgive and forget. Soon, we'll all be out of here and go our separate ways."

"At this rate, we'll never get out of here," I say. Why am I so antsy to leave? Is it simply habit? In here, I'm doing something most of society considers useful. I'm not sure how useful these deliberations really are, but I do know there's nothing more important going on outside the room, at least for me.

"Even if we're here another two weeks, it's nothing in the grand scheme of things," the Jury Consultant says. "Here's my thinking. Jenna Blaylock did a masterful job of making Deputy Beckermann look bad. No, Beckermann did a masterful job of making himself look bad, and Blaylock ran with it. The fact remains that this case is about what was in David Sullinger's mind. What Beckermann did or didn't do in the investigation can't change that. I believe Dillon and not Lacey, which means that David was the abuser and murdered Amanda with malice aforethought. That's why I'm voting guilty despite Beckermann's incompetence."

"I'm not changing my vote," the Housewife says.

The Jury Consultant politely ignores her.

"Okay," the Foreperson says. "Still six to two for not guilty. We should ..." She appeals to the Jury Consultant. "What now?"

"Do you think a break is in order, Madame Foreperson?" the Jury Consultant asks.

"I think a break is in order," the Foreperson says, as if she had the idea herself.

THE BAILIFF

BRADLEY KOBASHIGAWA

Mick frightened me when he told me Judge Quinn-Gilbert wandered away. Made me think of my grandfather, who once wandered away. He was found on the banks of the river, trying to fish without a pole. The judge says she didn't wander away. The judge says she took a walk. Did she?

In my time with her, she's never left a jury hanging like that. Not once. Mick says she's never done it in his time with her. He's been working for her for years. Worse, she forgot to turn on her cell phone. She promised to turn it on, Mick says.

The problem with this job is that there's too much time to think. When I was on the street, you had to think, but you also had to act. Lately, I've been thinking about what I've tried not to think about.

What's self-defense, anyway? Suppose you get a call. You're dispatched to confront a homeless guy who's threatening pedestrians near the docks. It's summer, so tourists are there. We get there, and it's Shoeless John, a regular. Harmless most of the time, but now he's off his meds and not so harmless. Because he's black, he's more intimidating to some people. There aren't many African Americans in Sepulveda County, and people get scared, prejudiced. I know Shoeless John, but my then partner, Beckermann, is new to the county. He was most recently with the Fresno PD. He moved here to join our force. Shoeless John is swearing at pedestrians, mixing up God with the president, the internet with aliens. Can you believe a couple of punks stood around and gawked and laughed? Taunting a paranoid schizophrenic? We park the car and get out. I tell Beckermann that I know the guy, I'll talk him down, that I have before. Not that Shoeless John couldn't be a danger to himself or others. He was in the Gulf War.

Too much time to think.

Suppose you and your new partner get out of the patrol car. Approach the subject as slowly and as nonthreateningly as possible. Just like we're trained to do.

"I'll do the talking," I say. "You don't talk." That's to keep Shoeless John's sensory overload to a minimum, just like we're trained to do. Besides, I've talked Shoeless John down before.

"Hey, John," I say.

John looks at me and says, "You're with them."

"Who?" I say.

"The dark web paramilitary. They've infiltrated my frontal lobe."

"John, it's me. Deputy Kobashigawa. I don't understand the situation, but I can see it's upsetting you. How can I help?"

He looks at Beckermann. "Who the fuck are you? Are you with them?"

Beckermann snaps to attention, aggressively, and says, "C'mon, now, nobody's after you; it's just your imagination.

You're going to have to come with us. We can do it the easy way or the hard way."

Wrong thing to say. Adrenaline on overload, Shoeless John hurls a string of obscenities at Beckermann and feints like a boxer but doesn't come any closer. I start to talk to John, quietly, but Beckermann reaches for his radio, and not calmly. He calls for backup. We don't need backup yet. Wrong move. Who the hell trained him?

Suppose Shoeless John pulls a knife, doesn't approach, just brandishes it, and Beckermann and I both pull our service revolvers, and Beckermann commands John to drop the weapon, and when he doesn't comply, Beckermann shoots him dead.

The board of inquiry exonerated Beckermann, found that he acted in self-defense. Beckermann was twenty or so feet away from John. A gun doesn't do all that much good within twenty-one feet of a suspect with a knife once the suspect advances, an expert testified. The expert testified to a myth. We were in no danger.

We were in no danger, and Beckermann wasn't in fear for his life. He was trigger-happy. That's what I told Internal Affairs. The civilian witnesses who testified didn't see it my way. The board of inquiry didn't see it my way. My fellow officers don't see it my way. Bradley Kobashigawa, turncoat. Bradley Kobashigawa, pariah. Can't fire me, of course. I just gave my opinion, called it as I saw it. They put me in Judge Quinn-Gilbert's courtroom, off the streets and away from the cops who hate me. They promoted hero Beckermann to detective, where he arrested David Sullinger for lying about acting in self-defense. As my son puts it, "How ironic."

This is what I think: Beckermann didn't reasonably fear that Shoeless John, admittedly a knife-wielding psycho, was going to kill him, which means that Beckermann murdered John. David Sullinger reasonably believed that his small, weaker wife was going to kill him with a pickax, which means that David should go free. Doesn't make sense? Stories don't have to make sense. Once, I was a patrol cop with a loving wife. Now I'm a divorcé and a turncoat working as a bailiff and worrying that a fine judge has gone mental. We're not always the heroes of our own stories. Sometimes, we're the chumps.

There's too much time to think on this job.

JUROR NO. 33

THE GRANDMOTHER

I meant no offense. I meant no offense. I don't think I heard what was said, because my hearing aids … What I meant was … No offense intended. Was I so wrong? Is there not reverse racism, reverse bias, a disrespect of law enforcement among some minorities that were long oppressed but now are as free as the rest of us—more privileged in many ways, no offense intended? The Student isn't a product of the ghetto, for heaven's sake. Her father owns the biggest fabric store in the county, and her mother is a teacher. She grew up more privileged than I, whose father worked in a picture-frame factory and whose mother was a housewife until she had to go to work in the school cafeteria when my father lost his job because the factory closed and the work was outsourced to Japan. Wasn't the Student wrong to suggest that Deputy Beckermann is a racist, that the sheriff's department is racist? That's not evidence.

The homeless man was threatening Beckermann with a knife. The homeless man just happened to be black, and the officer of the law protected himself. That's what the investigation found. Hardly Selma, Alabama, in the sixties. Racism has nothing to do with this trial. The Student is a very nice girl—I mean, woman. She dislikes me now. They all dislike me now. Even the Clergyman dislikes me. Perhaps not the Jury Consultant. What hurts most is that even after all this happened, the Student helped me out of my chair when we went on break. She helped me back to the table when the break ended. She didn't say a word, turned her back on me when I was settled, but she helped me. How cruel of her.

JUROR NO. 1
THE FOREPERSON

I can't believe the Student helped the Grandmother to her seat. The girl's face looked like she was cleaning up dog poop when she grasped the older woman's elbow, but she still helped. A second later, the Jury Consultant took the Grandmother's other elbow and smiled in gratitude at the Student. Was this infighting my fault? I'm the foreperson. Could I have stopped it? Where's my cell phone? I check my pockets, my purse, look on the floor and under the table. Others help me look, but no luck. Why were the Architect and the Clergyman smiling after I told everyone we should get along? Isn't that my job? They smiled like my blouse was unbuttoned and my right boob was hanging out. During the break, I looked in the bathroom mirror, and my boobs were in their proper place.

"I want to ask a question," says the Housewife to the Jury Consultant.

"Wait a minute," I say. I hop up and hurry to the bathroom. There it is—my phone is right there, sitting on the sink. I'm always losing things.

"Sorry," I say when I get back. "My phone was ..." I look at the Housewife. "You had a question?"

"Other than Dillon's testimony, what evidence is there that David was a violent man? There's plenty of evidence proving Amanda was violent, but nothing about David. Zip."

"Splitting your wife's head in two with a pickax is pretty good evidence of a propensity for violence," says the Jury Consultant.

"That begs the question," says the Grandmother, her voice breathy. "It assumes that David didn't act in self-defense."

I expect the Jury Consultant to say to the Grandmother, "Whose side are you on?" or something like that, because the Grandmother voted guilty the last two times and her response implies not guilty. But the Jury Consultant doesn't say that. It takes me a sec, but I get why. The Grandmother had to say something, anything, to try to become one of us again. It won't work.

"There's the testimony of the head of the cooking school," says the Jury Consultant. Before we can all laugh, the Jury Consultant raises her hand and says, "I understand why you're smiling, but please hear me out on this," and we don't laugh, because this case isn't a laughing matter. Oh, my God, it was so hard not to laugh in court at the cooking-school guy's testimony. It was about one of David's many attempts to get a job. Even though I think David is innocent, I don't get why he never held a real job longer than a few months. I'd like to be a chef or a singer or have my own jewelry design shop, but I have to work in the real world. Doesn't matter that I hate the file room—I have no Amanda to support me.

I check my juror notes. I'm a great note taker, probably took more notes than any of the other jurors, even though the judge instructed us not to take too many notes, because we might not pay enough attention to the witnesses' demeanor and stuff like that. But I'm such a great note taker and multitasker that I did both things at once.

> ADA Cranston calls Anton La Pierre (ALP) to stand. Owner of French cooking school in Tapia Beach. Academie de la Jambe du Cochon San Franciso (witnes spells). French accent. Cute. David enroled in his cocking school July 2014. Prof track. Pastrie chef. David lasted 3 wks, couldn't take criticism, temper. ALP critisized David's profitarolls, said they tasted burnt. Profitarols=creme pufs. David shoved ALP. ALP shoved David. David went for palett knife. ALP ran, David expelled.
>
> X-exam Def atty Blaylock. Academie de la Jambe du Cochon means pig leg school in English. Lol! ALP is expert in pork dishes. No school in SF, ALP just thought it gave school presteege. Denies lying about SF part. Lie. ALP real name Aaron Rees. Never lived in France. Doesn't speak french. Says accent real cuz he watched so many french cooking shows. Lol! Cullinery certificat from unacredited online school!!! Never lived out of state. Blaylock calls him liar, says David droped out because bad teaching. ALP gets upset, loses most of French accent. LOL!! Temper Blaylock establishs ALP never called cops re David's aleged knife assalt. No further Qs. No re-direct by Cranston. Bad witness for DA.

"Blaylock skewered the guy on cross-examination," the Jury Consultant says. "No doubt about it. LaPierre—"

"You mean, Reese?" the Architect says, arching her eyebrows in sarcasm.

"LaPierre, Reese, whichever you prefer," says the Jury Consultant in a professional tone. "Blaylock is cagey, brilliant. She tore the guy apart without ever challenging anything substantive about his testimony. Which stands uncontradicted—David got mad, picked up a knife, and brandished it."

"Your theory doesn't hold water," says the Housewife. "Blaylock got that clown to admit that he never went to the police after David supposedly went for the knife—which was a dull palette knife, by the way, as anyone who's ever baked knows. If David really threatened to stab him, Reese would've called the police."

"I don't agree," says the Jury Consultant. "Most of us have been confronted at one time or another over the course of our lives with potential threats of violence yet didn't call the police. Is there anyone here who hasn't been the victim of road rage, the target of some crazy person swearing or giving you the finger? Yet despite that, you didn't call the police?"

"Road rage is totally different from threatening someone with a knife," says the Housewife. "Someone flips me the finger on the street, it happens. Someone picks up a knife and threatens to stab me, and I'm calling the police and reporting them. Reese didn't do that."

"I don't think there's that big a difference," says the Express Messenger. "You all know that when I don't have an acting job, I drive a truck. There are some real nutcases out there. In a way, I'm more afraid of a two-ton vehicle than some joker wielding a flimsy baker's knife."

"Reese lied about everything else, so he obviously lied about David pulling a knife," replies the Housewife.

"Maybe it *did* happen. Maybe the reason Reese didn't call the police was because he was scared of David and didn't want to make him madder," says the Student. "I have a friend, and this guy at her prior college was stalking her, and she didn't call the cops, because she thought he'd get violent, so she quit school and moved back home to get away from the guy. Sometimes, it's better not to escalate a situation."

"I don't see how anyone could believe Reese," says the Housewife. "He lied about—"

"When David was on the stand, he never refuted Reese's testimony," says the Jury Consultant. "The subject never came up in the hours and hours of direct."

"Reese was such a poor witness that David didn't need to refute his testimony," says the Housewife. "David isn't on trial for assaulting Reese with a palette knife."

"Or …" says the Grandmother, then slumps her shoulders.

"Go on," I say.

"Well, I recall that Cranston tried to ask Dillon about what David told the family regarding the culinary school incident. But the judge sustained Blaylock's relevancy objection. So we never got to hear the answer. David obviously said something to the family about the fight with Reese. What if David admitted to his family that he picked up a knife? If he later testified about the incident under oath, claimed it didn't happen, wouldn't Dillon's testimony then become relevant because Blaylock opened the subject up? Is that why Blaylock didn't go into it with David, because she knew David was lying and Dillon would say so on rebuttal?" She looks at the Jury Consultant for guidance.

"I'm not a lawyer," says the Jury Consultant. "We shouldn't be speculating about evidence that wasn't admitted. All we know is that David never denied the incident on the stand. Something for us all to think about."

I'm so confused. Why didn't the judge let Dillon testify about the incident? As the foreperson, I can't let the other jurors know that I'm confused. I'm sure most of them are just as confused as I am. More.

"Yes," I say. "Food for thought."

THE HONORABLE
NATALIE QUINN-GILBERT

Two knocks on my door, a pause, and two more. The pattern repeats. Ed Halleck.

"Another moment, Natalie?"

Another? Was he here before? When ...?

"Of course," I say.

As the presiding judge, he has the job of scolding us ordinary judges about tardiness and clogged dockets. I never thought of this before, but he reminds me of the time when I was a seventeen-year-old girl, working a summer job at a long since defunct burger place called "Woody's Smorgasburger." We had to dress up in blue-and-yellow Swedish folk dresses, take an order, and cook a hamburger by the time the customer paid at the cash register. "Push 'em through!" the manager, a horrible, gropey, vindictive junior-college dropout named Jerry, would say to us. I still don't know whether he was talking about the customers or the burgers. That's Ed Halleck's role: move the cases through quickly. *Push 'em through!* I've never thought about that before.

"I hope this isn't about my walk," I say.

"Excuse me?"

"I took a walk this morning, and the jury sent a note while I was gone."

"Not the end of the world. We're not chained to our desks."

"It's unusual for me. My clerk and bailiff panicked, got the idea I had wandered off in some fog."

He strokes his chin and says, "Oh," drawing out the word with a heterodyne lilt. Ed's signature "oh" is at once an acknowledgment of what you've just said, an expression of surprise, an empathetic moan, and a noncommittal reservation of judgment. There's brilliance in Ed Halleck's "oh's."

"I'm fine, Ed. It was a walk. So you don't need to—"

"That isn't why I've come to see you, Natalie. I've come because of this."

He hands me several sheets of paper. I put on my glasses and start reading. Printouts from the website of reporter Kelsi Cunningham, who almost flimflammed me until Mick Redmond showed up at my house and came to my rescue.

When I finish, I look up at Ed and say, "Good Lord. What do I do now?"

"I'm sure you know exactly what to do," he says. "I'm sorry I had to bring this to your attention."

JUROR NO. 43

THE CLERGYMAN

These deliberations are not proceeding as I had thought they would, as I had hoped they would, and that eventuality has caused me to face a moral and ethical choice unlike any that I have ever faced. Since the writing of the Old Testament, the concept of good and evil has been binary, but for me, in the Sullinger case, it is ternary. In one corner is the law. In the other two corners, we have right and wrong, which do not necessarily coincide with the law. My trilemma is, which option do I choose? I had surmised that the law and the right would coincide, but that will not necessarily happen. It would seem my choice is obvious—the right, the good—but that is not so. It is never so. II Corinthians 11:14: "No wonder, for even Satan disguises himself as an angel of light."

I rue the day I met Amanda Sullinger.

JUROR NO. 11

THE STUDENT

The Express Messenger raises his hand like we're in a classroom, and I wonder if he's doing it to annoy the Grandmother, who I guess was his teacher or vice principal or something back in the day. Whatever happened between her and me, she's old and sick, and we shouldn't be mean to her. Having her prejudice exposed is causing her pain. Maybe I'm not a nice person deep down, but I feel like that *should* cause her pain. That's her punishment. We don't need to punish her more.

"Yes, sir," the Foreperson says, delighted to be in charge again.

"I'm changing my vote to guilty," the Express Messenger says. "David should've said something about the cooking school incident. He should've answered Reese's allegations. He should've explained what happened in the kitchen."

The Housewife rolls her eyes, and the Clergyman takes a huffing breath.

"Anyone else changing their vote?" the Foreperson asks. Everyone shakes their head but me.

"I'm not changing, either," the Foreperson says.

So, excluding me, it's four to three. The Housewife, the Architect, the Foreperson, and the Clergyman are still voting not guilty. The Jury Consultant, the Grandmother, and the Express Messenger want to convict David Sullinger. All eyes are on me—even the Clergyman's—which frightens me.

What to do? (Oh, my God, I sound like my mom. She says that all the time.) The Jury Consultant and even the Grandmother have made good points about Lacey not being all that credible and about David not refuting the cooking school chef's testimony. So that favors a guilty verdict. But I'm not a fan of either Dillon or Beckermann, the racist cop, and that makes me lean toward voting not guilty. I'm just not sure. I feel like it's not right to convict a person on *not sure.*

"Not guilty," I say. "Reasonable doubt still. It's all so fuzzy, and I can't convict on fuzzy."

The Clergyman smiles at this, but it's a pained smile, with downcast eyes and tight lips.

"Amen," the Housewife says. "Reasonable doubt. Other than doing some name-calling, we haven't really talked about the expert psychologists. The defense expert, who's far more qualified, testified that David exhibited all the symptoms of a battered spouse. Amanda constantly criticized him. Even Dillon confirmed that, so no factual dispute there. And she was constantly accusing David of cheating on her."

"He did cheat on her," the Express Messenger says.

"We'll get to that," the Housewife says. "Amanda punished the kids when she was angry at him. We know about the horrible violence—kicking, hitting, biting, not to mention scalding him with a hot pot and pushing his hand down on the grill. Classic behavior of a female abuser."

"If you believe that really happened," the Jury Consultant says.

"Of course it really happened," the Housewife says. "The expert testified—"

"You can hire an expert to testify to anything," the Grandmother says. "Especially if you're Jenna Blaylock. I'm beginning to agree with my colleague on the other side of the table that the defense expert *is* a whore." She tilts her head toward the Express Messenger, obviously desperate to make friends from any quarter. I can't help giggling at that, and it's not the time to giggle. The Grandmother forces a smile, but from the way she straightened her back, I can tell she didn't like my laughter.

"According to the psychologist, David believed Amanda was omnipresent and omniscient—that she still is even though she's dead," the Housewife says. "David often referred to Amanda in the present tense while he was testifying. He even said Amanda would be alive today if he'd been a better husband and father. A classic abused spouse."

"How do we know he wasn't faking it?" the Grandmother says. "I think he was faking it."

"The defense psychologist checked for that," the Housewife says. "His examination of David turned up no indication of fakery."

"Except, the prosecution's expert testified that David is a psychopath," the Grandmother says. "How did she explain it? Two of the symptoms of a psychopath are the ability to charm and the ability to lie effectively. Also irresponsibility, inflated self-worth, unrealistic goals. David couldn't hold a job, because no job was good enough for him. I'd say that was irresponsible, that he has a huge ego."

"The prosecution's expert comes from outer space," the Housewife says. "She doesn't believe a man can ever be a battered spouse at the hands of a woman. Her radical feminist theories aren't mainstream. *She's* the sexist."

"I don't see it that way," the Grandmother says.

"Me, neither," the Express Messenger says.

Strange bedfellows, as my dad would say.

There's a knock on the door that makes me jump and makes everyone else go quiet. The bailiff sticks his head in and says, "You're all going to go on break for a while."

"It's still early in the afternoon, Deputy Brad," the Foreperson says. She calls him Deputy Brad because she can't pronounce Kobashigawa. "We're going hot and heavy here, so maybe ...?"

"The judge ordered you to take a break," he says in a stern tone I've never heard him use before. He points toward someone at the head of the table. "The judge would like to speak to you in chambers."

JUROR NO. 52

THE EXPRESS MESSENGER / ACTOR

I haven't bitten my fingernails in six years. I was this close to getting a recurring role in a TV series once, but at my final audition, the casting director noticed I was a nail biter and dinged me for it. So I stopped. Now I'm doing it again. I've already chewed two nails to the nubs, and my fingers sting like hell, yet I'm still biting my fucking nails.

I changed my vote to guilty. I really did it. When I walked into the jury room, I was so sure David was innocent. That stuff about the cooking school and pulling the knife on the chef affected me. All the deliberations have affected me. But what sucks is that I can't get my mother's words about Jody Arias out of my mind. Jody claimed self-defense but, during the sentencing phase, admitted she killed her boyfriend. It turned out the whole self-defense thing was bullshit. I worry that David Sullinger is a bullshitter like Jody, and I can't let a bullshitter get away with murder.

I told my mom over and over not to talk to me about the case, damn it. I love her to death, but why can't she ever listen to me?

Shit, my pinky finger is bleeding. I suck on it, the taste of blood both nauseating and comforting.

Why did the judge order this break? We've been waiting half an hour. We're like prisoners, because even though it's supposed to be a break, the bailiff made us stay in the jury room. It's freaking me out. I'm not the only one. Us jurors aren't talking to each other. Just sitting, milling around, fiddling with our phones, drinking coffee or water, staring off into space. Or biting our nails.

There's a knock on the door, and the bailiff walks in. Finally.

"Line up in numerical order," he says. "We're going into the courtroom."

The Foreperson says, "But the …" and stops herself.

We file in. The judge is on the bench, the attorneys are at their tables, and the clerk is at his desk. The court reporter is here, wearing a short dress, which is awesome in this cold weather. No David Sullinger. The Clergyman hasn't rejoined us.

The judge gazes at us with a solemn face. The color is out of her cheeks. She stares at us so long without blinking that I actually begin to wonder if she's eyes-open asleep or worse. Finally, she says, "Members of the jury, I've called you in here to inform you that juror number forty-three has been excused. You'll continue deliberations without him. You will not speculate about the reasons I excused him, and you will not discuss it. You may reach a verdict with seven jurors. As I previously instructed you, your verdict must be unanimous."

Shit. The Clergyman is gone. Not that he added much, but still. What did he do wrong? That photo the Foreperson brought in. Was it that photo? Did another juror bust him? Maybe he owned up to it. But he said he knew nothing about Amanda, that it was a coincidence they were in a picture together. Should we have said something to the judge as a group?

Maybe it's not the photo. Maybe he's sick. He was always taking some kind of pill. Whatever.

Whoa. That makes the vote four to three for acquittal. Jesus, my fingers sting. Like my mom always warns, I'll probably come down with some bacterial infection from putting my fingers in my mouth. This courthouse is filthy.

CHRISTINA KELLEHER, CSR

SUPERIOR COURT FOR THE COUNTY OF SEPULVEDA

	)
PEOPLE	) JURY TRIAL—DAY 21
v.	)
DAVID BENNETT SULLINGER	) Case No. 16-382
	)
	)

BEFORE: Hon. Natalie Quinn-Gilbert, Superior Court Judge

APPEARANCES: JOHN Y. CRANSTON, ESQ.
Assistant District Attorney,
Sepulveda County
On behalf of the People

JENNA MARIE BLAYLOCK, ESQ.
On behalf of the Defendant

TRANSCRIPT OF PROCEEDINGS

Reported by Christina Kelleher
Certified Shorthand Reporter

Direct examination of Annalise Rauch by Jenna Blaylock, counsel for the Defendant (excerpt):

Q. You and Amanda Sullinger were friends?

A. Amanda didn't have friends, but I was the closest thing. She was like my boss. Well, not literally, we're both real estate brokers, but she trained me. She handled much more expensive properties. I was someone who Amanda vented to.

Q. Vented about what?

A. About the sorry state of the world. About the unfair cut of our commissions that the owners of our agency took. About the obnoxious clients. About David.

Q. David being David Sullinger, her husband?

A. Yes.

Q. What did she say about David?

A. That he was a loser. A bad father. Messy. Stupid. Not good in bed. Overweight. Among other things.

Q. Did she use the word "overweight" when describing David?

A. You want her exact words?

Q. Please.

A. She called him a fat pig, a fat slob. Her favorite was "fat sow," because she could attack his appearance and his manhood at the same time.

MR. CRANSTON: Move to strike everything starting with the word "because." Speculation.

THE COURT: Motion granted. The jury is instructed to ignore everything after the words "fat sow."

MR. CRANSTON: Your Honor, the Court's last comment … Oh, never mind. Withdrawn.

By Ms. Blaylock:

Q. But Amanda did call David a fat sow in your presence?

A. All the time.

Q. You told us that Amanda would call David stupid. Tell us more.

A. She hated that he didn't get a college degree, said he was lucky to have graduated high school, wouldn't have passed her history class if she … if she hadn't … sorry for this, if she hadn't been fucking him. She'd refer to him as "the imbecile" in normal conversation. Even in front of other people at the office, even sometimes in front of clients. I think she lost some sales because she said things like that, and I think she knew it and blamed David for it. She said he couldn't hold a job. She said he was a bad influence on the kids, was holding them back—particularly their son, Dillon. Things like that.

Q. What did she tell you about her sex life with David?

A. She said he was a bad lover, but she used an obscene word instead of bad. She said he couldn't get it up without Viagra, if then. She said she wasn't attracted to him, because his fat belly disgusted her. That he had a small dick—sorry, a small penis.

Q. Did Amanda Sullinger ever tell you that she cheated on David?

MR. CRANSTON: Objection. That calls for hearsay.

MS. BLAYLOCK: Offered not for the truth, but for the fact that Amanda would demean David to third parties.

THE COURT: On that basis, the objection is overruled. Members of the jury, I instruct you to consider the evidence only to show the statement was made and not to show the truth of Amanda having affairs.

THE WITNESS: Should I answer?

MS. BLAYLOCK: Please.

A. Amanda bragged about sleeping with other men. She said she'd tell David about it to make him jealous in the hopes that he'd clean up his act.

Q. When she said this, what was her demeanor?

A. Sometimes, like it was nothing. Sometimes, she'd laugh at David for letting her get away with sleeping with other men.

Q. Ms. Rauch, putting aside what Amanda Sullinger might have told you, do you have any firsthand knowledge that she cheated on David?

A. Yes.

Q. Please tell us what that knowledge is.

A. It's … I'm sorry, just a second, it's embarrassing.

Q. Take your time.

A. Okay. Okay. About a year before all this happened—I mean Amanda dying—she and I went on a business trip to Denver. A potential client was looking into developing town houses riverside here in Sepulveda County, and Amanda and I hoped we could get hired as the brokers. We had drinks, the client was very handsome, and he invited Amanda and me up to his hotel room. One thing led to another, and we both had sex with him.

Q. Did Amanda have sexual intercourse with this man?

A. Yeah, we both did.

Q. Did you observe anything unusual about Amanda's behavior during this encounter?

MR. CRANSTON: Objection. Irrelevant.

MS. BLAYLOCK: Goes to pattern and practice of Amanda's abusive behavior.

THE COURT: The objection is overruled. You may answer, Ms. Rauch.

A. I—

THE COURT: Just a moment, ma'am. Mr. Cranston, is there anything you want to say to the Court?

MR. CRANSTON: No, Your Honor.

THE COURT: Because if you have an issue with my rulings, you can take it up on appeal. But you will not scoff or make sotto voce complaints to your colleagues.

MR. CRANSTON: Judge Quinn-Gilbert, I wasn't—

THE COURT: Oh, yes, you did. Proceed, Ms. Blaylock.

Q. Did you notice anything unusual or strange about Amanda's behavior when she was having sex with the prospective client?

A. Amanda got dominant with the guy. Giving orders.

Then she got rough with him. At one point, she bit his nipple hard, and he yelled, told her she was hurting him. She drew blood.

Q. Ms. Rauch, did you at any time enter into a sexual relationship with David Sullinger?

A. Yes.

Q. How did that start?

A. Amanda asked me to sleep with David.

THE COURT: Everyone, calm down, or I'll clear the room of everyone but the parties and the news media.

THE COURT: Good. Anyone who reacts to the testimony will be removed from the courtroom by the bailiff. Proceed, Ms. Blaylock.

By Ms. Blaylock:

Q. How did this request come about?

A. We were coming back from a showing of a home late one night. Sometimes, we show luxury properties late, after the prospective buyer gets off work, so … On this night, Amanda asked if I wanted to grab some dinner. I said yes. You couldn't turn her down without her getting … Anyway, we had quite a bit of wine, and she started talking about David's sexual problems with her, and then told me that she thought he was cheating on her.

Q. Was this the first time she'd suggested David was having an affair?

A. No. It had come up before. It was crazy—she'd brag about her affairs, tell me how unattractive David was, and then get really jealous when she thought David was doing the same thing.

Q. How do you know she was jealous.

A. She'd say things like if she caught him she'd kill him, cut off his balls … violent things like that.

Q. And yet, she asked you to have sex with her husband?

A. Crazy, but yeah.

Q. Did she tell you why?

A. She said she wanted to find out once and for all if David was cheating on her.

Q. What was your response?

A. I thought she was joking at first, drunk. Then it became clear she wasn't joking and she knew exactly what she was saying. She got really adamant about the whole thing. So eventually, I said yeah, I'll try to seduce David. It was wrong, but I …

Q. Why ever would you agree to something so wrong?

A. You have to understand. Amanda … She was real powerful at my office, and she especially had power over me. If I displeased her, she could've ruined my career. And then, we shared this kind of weird bond … I don't know if it was because of what she and I did in Denver, but … It was exciting, you know? And there was something about trying to seduce David that was exciting. The truth is, David and Amanda would hang out a lot with my boyfriends and I, and I got to know David, and he seemed like a real nice guy. Seemed to love Amanda a lot, strangely enough. I actually thought I'd be doing them both a favor, because I didn't think he'd cheat on her, so I'd prove to Amanda that he was faithful and get him off the hook at the same time. Stupid, I know now. Warped. Amanda could make your thinking warped.

Q. How did—?

THE COURT: Either stand up all the way and object or sit down, Mr. Cranston.

MR. CRANSTON: Apologies, Your Honor. On second thought, no objection.

By Ms. Blaylock:

Q. Did you eventually enter into an intimate relationship with David Sullinger?

A. Yes.

Q. How did that come about?

A. David is a good carpenter, good at fixing things. Amanda suggested I ask him over to my house to do some repairs, you know, to install some undercounter lights, a spice rack, replace a loose toilet seat. Stuff like that. Amanda said she'd approve it, because he'd ask her approval before doing it. So he came over to my house, and I acted sexy, was just dressed in my little silk robe. And I guess I tried to seduce him.

Q. You say you *guess.* You did try to seduce David, didn't you?

A. Unfortunately, yes. I'm so ashamed of it.

Q. How did he react?

A. He resisted. He said he was married, it wasn't right. He said it wasn't me, that I was beautiful. He said that if we did anything and Amanda found out, things would go very bad for him. He started doing the chores he came over for, but he didn't leave, and I knew … I was persistent, kind of aggressive. Amanda told me to be aggressive, that David was into that. So I was, and David finally gave in. And I don't think … He hadn't had sex in a long time, so the frustration made him let his guard down.

Q. Did you tell Amanda about your encounter?

A. Sort of.

Q. What do you mean, sort of?

A. I lied and told her David wouldn't sleep with me, that he was totally devoted to her. It's totally what she wanted to hear. She got tears in her eyes.

Q. Were you and David intimate only the one time?

A. Unfortunately, no. We started an affair that lasted three months until David ended it. He said Amanda was getting suspicious, and if she found out, she'd kill us both.

MR. CRANSTON: Objection. Hearsay.

THE COURT: Overruled.

Q. Did you think David was exaggerating, like people sometimes do when they use the word "kill"?

A. At first. But he said he totally believed Amanda would kill us or use her money to hire someone to do it.

MS. BLAYLOCK: No further questions.

THE COURT: Cross-examination, Mr. Cranston?

Cross-examination of Annalise Rauch by John Cranston, attorney for the People (excerpt):

Q. Ms. Rauch, I take it that during your romantic relationship with David Sullinger, you saw him naked?

A. Uh … yes, of course.

Q. Did he have any scars?

A. Did he …? Not that I noticed. I mean, nothing ugly or anything like that.

Q. And you found yourself attracted to David Sullinger?

A. Yes, of course. Otherwise, I wouldn't have—

Q. Your relationship with David was romantic, not just sexual, true?

A. Yeah. That's true.

Q. He gave you presents?

A. He did. He brought me flowers. He made me some jewelry. He's very artistic.

Q. Were you in love with David?

A. I was infatuated.

Q. You weren't in love with him?

A. I wasn't *not* in love with him, if that makes any sense. It was difficult. You have to understand, there was a lot of guilt on both our parts.

Q. Well, poor you, Ms. Rauch.

MS. BLAYLOCK: Objection.

THE COURT: The jury will disregard Mr. Cranston's sarcasm.

Q. You say David feared that if Amanda found out about your affair, she'd kill you both. Were you afraid of Amanda?

A. I was … I mean, from a work standpoint and what she could do to my career, yes, but from a physical standpoint, no.

Q. Did you believe David when he said Amanda would kill you both?

A. I knew *he* believed it.

Q. Did you believe it?

A. It gave me pause, yeah.

Q. Did you believe it, Ms. Rauch?

A. I'm not sure. I knew Amanda was cheating herself, so …

Q. At any time, did David tell you that Amanda was physically abusing him?

A. He implied it.

Q. Did he say Amanda was physically abusing him?

A. He said she was a mean bitch, and I knew already that she verbally abused him to me. She'd call him fat, stupid, sexless, all kinds of things, so that's abuse to me.

Q. Are you done with your answer?

A. Yes, sir.

Q. Will you listen carefully to my next question?

A. I will.

Q. At any time, did David say Amanda was physically abusing him?

A. No.

JUROR NO. 1

THE FOREPERSON

We return to the jury room gloomy, as if we're soldiers and someone in our platoon went missing. I think it's my job to say something nice about the Clergyman. He was one of us, right?

"So I'd like to say that our departed juror—"

"He's not dead," says the Architect. "He's lucky it's over for him and he doesn't have to make this decision. Let's follow the judge's advice and not speculate about why he's gone. Right now we've got a deadlocked jury, four to three, and I haven't heard anything that's going to get me to change my vote."

I'm about to demolish that rude woman with words. I can be very biting when I have to. Before I do that, the Jury Consultant says in a quiet voice, "I think it would be a good idea to move on. There's still more to talk about. I have an open mind."

"Me, too," I say. "That's what we should do. Keep an open mind. Keep open minds. We've done most of the important witnesses. Except Annalise Rauch."

"No credibility," says the Housewife.

"An immoral, weak-willed woman whom you couldn't believe

if she told you the sun will rise tomorrow," says the Grandmother.

"Ditto," says the Architect.

"No argument from me," says the Jury Consultant.

"What a sleaze," says the Express Messenger.

The Student nods in agreement.

Wow. I didn't think Rauch was *that* bad. Yeah, she's a slut, but does that make her a liar? Well, she is a liar, but that doesn't mean she committed perjury on the witness stand. The fact that she's weak-minded makes her less likely to lie, I think, because weakness can sometimes work like a lie detector machine. Who's more likely to cave and tell the truth: the person with a backbone, or the weakling?

"Yeah, she's a liar; can't trust a word she says," I say, because there's been too much disagreement between us already. I glance at the Architect and can't help myself. "You know, Rauch kind of reminded me of you a little bit."

"What the fuck is that supposed to mean?" says the Architect, pointing an index finger at me, real aggressive. "What the fuck is that supposed to mean?"

"I just ..."

Oh, my God, she's standing up. She's tall, and she works out, and I sit in an office all day, and she's younger than me. The Housewife puts a hand on the Architect's arm to restrain her, and the Architect pulls away from the Housewife aggressively but, luckily, sits down. The Architect gives the Housewife a dirty look. Wow, maybe they're not such good friends anymore.

The Architect overreacted. I only meant that she and Rauch look alike, which is a compliment, because Rauch is attractive. Considering the violent reaction, maybe I should've compared the Architect to Amanda Sullinger.

"The neighbor," says the Housewife, saving me some more.

"We haven't talked about the neighbor. On the night of the killing, the neighbor only heard Amanda shouting threats to David and not vice versa. Which means she was the aggressor."

"The neighbor is of my generation, even older than I," says the Grandmother. "He and I have something else in common. We both wear hearing aids."

"I remember that," says the Express Messenger. "Good point."

"I wouldn't be surprised if he suffers from low-frequency hearing loss, which would mean he couldn't have heard David's deeper voice on the afternoon of the murder," says the Grandmother. "David could have been shouting and the man wouldn't have heard it."

"Even if David was quiet, it doesn't help his case," says the Jury Consultant. "If he truly feared for his life, he would have been shouting to high heaven. Who would be quiet during an event like that except a cold-blooded killer?"

"That's exactly what I was thinking," I say.

"There's something else I haven't mentioned," the Grandmother says. "Another reason why I'm voting to convict. David is a man—stronger than Amanda was."

"Not a large man," says the Housewife.

"He was strong enough to take the pickax away from her," replies the Grandmother. "Why didn't he take the knife away from her, too?"

"He couldn't, because he was holding the pickax, and she picked up the knife and was slashing at him," says the Housewife. "The ax is bulkier; the handle is long—much easier to grab. The knife is almost all blade."

"I have an idea," says the Jury Consultant. "Madame Foreperson, may we ask the bailiff to bring in the pickax and the knife?"

"We may," I say, and then I go to the door and press the green button.

JUROR NO. 52

THE EXPRESS MESSENGER / ACTOR

The knife that Amanda Sullinger allegedly attacked her husband with has a nine-inch, layer-hammered Damascus stainless steel blade and a magnolia handle. Of Japanese origin, it cost two hundred and seventy-nine dollars on sale and was a gift from Amanda to David when he decided to enroll in culinary school. The tool that caused Amanda Sullinger's death was a pickax with a thirty-four-and-a-quarter-inch fiberglass handle and a stout steel head that combined a pick and a cutter. David Sullinger killed Amanda with the cutting end. A sucky way to die.

When the bailiff walks in and sets the pickax and the knife—which is sheathed in its original wooden-block holder—onto the conference table, the Architect visibly shudders, and the Student hugs herself. The Foreperson twists her mouth in a grotesque grimace, making her look like she's wearing an albino Halloween mask and kinky-blond wig. It's the first time I've seen the weapons up close—we didn't get to hold them during trial—and they look bigger and sharper than I remember. When I catch myself biting my nails, I drop my hand onto the table with a thud that makes the Student jump. The Housewife, the Jury Consultant, and the Grandmother don't react to the weapons or my thud—tough women, like my mother.

When the bailiff leaves the room, the Jury Consultant places the holder containing the knife on the credenza. Next, she picks up the pickax. "I'll play the role of David," she says. "Who'll play Amanda?"

"This is absurd," the Housewife says. "And dangerous. The Sullingers were under intense pressure when the killing occurred. Everyone agrees one or the other of them was bent on committing murder. We can't recreate that scene."

"We won't need to," the Jury Consultant says.

"I wish the prosecution had done something like this during trial," the Student says.

"The demonstration might not have been admissible," the Jury Consultant says. "Or things could have gone wrong, like the bloody glove in the O. J. Simpson trial. Or, even if the demonstration worked, it could have looked fake. Blaylock would have torn Cranston apart for grandstanding. We're objective." She looks at the Student. "Would you mind playing Amanda? You're about her size and height."

The Student hesitates until the Grandmother says, "I'd like to see where this takes us, so I'll volunteer to do it."

The Student shakes her head and lets out an exasperated sigh. "I'll do it."

I'd like to help out, but I'm a man, much bigger than Amanda. I could play David, but that wouldn't work, because I don't know what the Jury Consultant has in mind. Even in this room, I can't get an acting gig. Why doesn't the Architect or the Housewife or the Foreperson step in and save the Student? Because the demonstration might prove that David is guilty, and they're the not-guilty faction? Is winning more important to them than justice?

The Jury Consultant situates the Student to the right and slightly ahead of the knife holder. The Housewife and the Architect grudgingly agree that the Student is standing in the right place. The granite countertop in the Sullingers' home was about six inches higher than the credenza, so the Jury Consultant uses two evidence binders to raise the level of the knife holder.

Still carrying the pickax, the Jury Consultant moves so close to the Student that the Student cowers. The Jury Consultant pats her on the shoulder. "Sorry," she says. "I promise it will be okay."

The Student smiles, but it's forced.

"I'm having us stand only about six inches apart because David testified that he wrestled the pickax away from Amanda and that Amanda immediately drew the knife from the holder and started slashing," the Jury Consultant explains. She hands the ax to the Student. "When you say ready, I'll take the pickax from you. And, for heaven's sake, please, please, please don't resist. Then, as quickly as you can, go for the knife. It should end up in your left hand. Amanda was left-handed, and David testified that she brandished the knife in her left hand. You'll notice that because the holder is on the right, Amanda had to either twist her body to draw the knife with her left hand, or transfer the knife from her right hand to her left. Either maneuver would have taken a bit more time than if she'd gripped the knife with her right hand. Plus, the medical examiner testified that Amanda's left cheek was bruised because of a blow to the face. David testified that he hit her so he could take the pickax from her. The punch would have slowed Amanda down even more."

"Or made her more murderous," the Housewife says.

"On your signal," the Jury Consultant says to the Student.

The Student bends her knees in a warlike pose and raises the pickax. The Jury Consultant steps forward, but then the Student cries, "Wait!" and lowers the weapon.

The Jury Consultant reaches out and pats the Student's arm. "Look, if you're not up for this, maybe Madame Foreperson—"

"It's not that," the Student says. "I'm an anthropology major, and biological anthropology is related to archaeology. I've gone on some digs." She holds up the pickax. "Everyone's been calling this thing a pickax. It's really a mattock. That's because the head has an adze and a cutter. A pickax has a pick instead of an adze, and a hatchet has a hammer instead of a pick." She goes over to the credenza and leafs through an evidence binder.

"What are you looking for?" the Architect asks impatiently.

"That receipt," the Student says. "It was ..." It takes her another couple of minutes to find Amanda's purchase receipt from a home supply megastore not far from the Sullingers' house.

"This is the receipt for the mattock," the Student says. "Amanda also bought a trowel, a plastic bucket, a half-dozen exterior flood-lights, two rolls of masking tape, a pack of AAA batteries, and some household cleaning supplies. A mattock, trowel, and bucket are tools used for archaeological digs."

"Neither of the lawyers mentioned this," the Housewife says. "Can we even talk about it?"

"It's in evidence," the Jury Consultant says. "We can consider whatever is in evidence."

"I'd like to hear more about this," the Grandmother says, smiling shyly at the Student.

The Student turns slightly away from the Grandmother. That's too bad. My mom taught me how important it is to forgive—not just for the other person's soul but also for your own.

"Please continue," the Jury Consultant says to the Student.

"Okay. I feel like maybe Amanda bought the mattock because one of the kids was going on a dig. Even my public high school had an archaeology club. I bet the private school those Sullinger kids went to had one, too, or maybe even offered an archaeology class."

"What's your point?" the Housewife asks.

"Isn't it obvious?" the Jury Consultant says. "Her point is that this receipt, and the fact that the pickax is actually a mattock, proves that Amanda had a benign reason for having the tool in her home. She wasn't planning on using it to murder her husband. It was the other way around."

The Housewife shakes her head, starts to say something, but can't seem to get the words out.

"Why didn't the cops figure this out?" the Student asks.

"I'm sure they did and determined there was no such dig," the Housewife says. "If there was some kind of dig at school, the police would've discovered it. Lacey or Dillon would've testified to it."

"Now you're the one who's speculating," the Grandmother says. "If there's one thing that's become clear in this trial, it's that we can't begin to fathom the motivations of the Sullinger children. Maybe they didn't mention the archaeology dig, because they were never asked. Maybe Lacey was the one going on the dig, and she knew that if she mentioned it, she would convict her father. Who knows?"

"The prosecution wouldn't miss something like this," the Housewife insists.

"Cranston wouldn't?" I say. "Sure he would. Not to mention screwup Detective Beckermann."

"Cranston missed a lot of things, and Beckermann made it worse," the Jury Consultant says. "The lawyers in the district attorney's office have a lot of trial experience, but they're no match for a high-priced private defense attorney like Jenna Blaylock. Look at all the celebrities who've gotten away with murder over the years. Famous private practitioners against assistant DAs."

The Student picks up the mattock and takes her place near the knife holder. "Let's do this."

The Jury Consultant gets in her face. The Student waits a beat and then shouts, "Ready!"

The Jury Consultant jerks the pickax or mattock or whatever the hell it is out of the Student's hands, spins around, and runs out the door to the courtroom. When the door slams, the Student hasn't yet drawn the knife from the holder.

THE COURTROOM CLERK

MICK REDMOND

I'm on the phone with my husband, Eric, talking about *Star Wars*. No, not talking—arguing. For the umpteenth time in the past three weeks, he and I are debating whether the *Star Wars* canon should still include the previously released material about the Expanded Universe. Eric says it was okay for Disney to redefine the canon, because they acquired the copyright from George Lucas. I say you shouldn't change the canon, that you can't go back once the cat's out of the bag—and the Expanded Universe is out of the bag. He gets pissed when I call him Mickey Mouse's myrmidon. That's a word I learned from the judge's late husband, who was a walking dictionary and loved using exotic words. Eric doesn't know what "myrmidon" means, but he's pissed about it anyway, and he's raising his voice.

This isn't some trivial argument, not on your life. We both love *Star Wars*, one of the many things we have in common, but if this disagreement continues, we'll have to seek counseling. I just bought my nephew some *Star Wars* Legos—they're for six and up, and he's four, but I doubt he'll choke on a block, and you can't start a kid too early on *Star Wars*—and I can't have Eric poisoning the child's young mind about the canon.

My husband is making some unconvincing point about the Sith when a juror runs into the courtroom. She looks crazed and is carrying a pickax. Not only a pickax, but *the* pickax, as in the murder weapon, holy hell. Why would the judge let them take the thing inside the jury room in the first place? I told Bradley to talk her out of it, but … Damn it, Bradley!

I hang up the phone while Eric is in midsentence—an action that will be hard to explain later. I doubt he'll believe I had to go because a juror ran into the courtroom with a pickax. Deputy Kobashigawa, who's helping me process some papers, springs out of his desk chair and places his hand on his holster. This is the closest I've ever seen him go to his service revolver.

I don't know the jurors as well as he does, but from what I do know about them, I would have expected antics like this from the Express Messenger or the Architect, or maybe the Foreperson if someone egged her on. This is the dignified Jury Consultant, and not only is she brandishing a murder weapon, she's laughing.

"What's going on, ma'am?" Kobashigawa asks, his tone commanding and sharp, like the sound of a club hammer striking dense metal. This must have been the voice he used while patrolling the streets.

Between giggles, she says, "I'm so, so sorry. Just part of a discussion of the physical evidence." She glances at the pickax as if she only now realized she's holding it. "I think we're done with this." She offers the weapon to Bradley, and once he takes it, she smooths out her black skirt, takes a couple of deep breaths, and, without the trace of a smile, walks back into the jury room.

"What do you think that was about?" Kobashigawa asks.

"Probably releasing the tremendous tension they've been under."

"Do you think I should go in there?"

"I didn't hear any bloodcurdling screams."

He shrugs, walks over and pokes his head into the deliberation room, lingers a moment, and then shrugs again before going back to his desk.

I pick up the phone and call Eric back. Before I can apologize and explain why I had to go, he hangs up on me. "Jesus," I say.

"Another *Star Wars* argument?" Kobashigawa asks.

"He's so damned stubborn."

Kobashigawa shrugs. "One man's apocrypha are another man's canon."

Coming from him, the statement startles me almost as much as the Jury Consultant's entrance did. Bradley Kobashigawa is a complex man.

"Don't look so surprised," he says, clearly reading my expression. "We talk about canon at church. Adult Sunday school."

"Where do you stand on the issue?"

"I follow the rules as set down by the church. It's simpler that way."

"Simple is no fun. Simple is fascistic."

"By that, you mean …?"

"No freedom. If you capitulate, you're on the side of the Empire. I prefer being part of the Rebel Alliance."

"You lost me there, Mick."

"Not a *Star Wars* fan?"

"I like *Star Trek* better. Because my son does, not that I know much about it. So, have you ever seen anything like that?"

"Like what?"

"A juror running out of the deliberation room carrying a murder weapon and looking like she's about to go on a killing spree."

"I've seen crazier things. I'm sure you know about Judge Halleck jumping over the bench in his robe to help his bailiff tackle a defendant who was trying to escape during sentencing. I was his substitute clerk that day. Then there was the guy who came to court dressed in one of those old-fashioned black-and-white-striped prison uniforms to try to get out of jury duty. Judge Quinn-Gilbert was great. She toyed with him, used all her techniques to keep him around as long as she could. She was masterful. Ultimately, the prosecutor challenged him. Oh, there was never a judge who could control a courtroom the way Judge Quinn-Gilbert did."

He nods sadly, and I want to cry—truly, I do—because I realize I inadvertently used the past tense. We can't have this discussion in the courtroom, not with the judge so close by, but what will we do? Is it our obligation to report the judge's confusion to Presiding Judge Halleck? Do we wait it out? With these thoughts, I feel like the betrayer Lando Calrissian. No, wrong gospel—I feel like Judas. Judge Quinn-Gilbert's life was her husband and the bench, and now that Jonathan is gone, to deprive her of the bench would be …

Melodramatic? Maybe. But melodrama can still be true.

JUROR NO. 52

THE EXPRESS MESSENGER / ACTOR

It's 4:12 in the afternoon when the Jury Consultant comes back inside the jury room. She's empty-handed.

"I gave the mattock back to the bailiff," she says. "I hope no one minds."

The Student has been holding the knife all this time. Not much time, in one sense—two minutes at most—but long in another sense. Long enough for the demonstration to sink in. She puts the knife back in its holder and returns to her seat. The Jury Consultant also sits down.

"I change my vote to guilty," the Student says. "I feel like Amanda bought the mattock for one of her children. And David could've run. Should've run, if Amanda pulled a knife at all."

"Guilty," the Foreperson says.

"The so-called demonstration was meaningless," the Housewife insists. "A farce. Besides, David didn't have to run. He had the legal right to stand his ground. That's what we were instructed."

I have to say this for her: she doesn't back down. Sort of like my mom, but not.

"David's ability to run means he didn't reasonably believe that deadly force was necessary to prevent imminent death to himself," the Jury Consultant says.

"You're not making sense," the Housewife says. "If he had an obligation to run, there wouldn't be such a thing as the stand-your-ground defense."

That's not a bad point. Not good enough to change my mind about the guilty verdict, though.

"Anyway, the legal rule is irrelevant," the Jury Consultant says. "Based on what we just learned about the archaeological tools, it's clear that David had planned to murder Amanda for some time and was just waiting for his opportunity, and the self-defense and the battered-spouse story is just that: a story he concocted to cover up his crime. His opportunity came when Amanda bought the mattock, and he realized he could use her innocent purchase to set her up and claim he killed her because she attacked him."

"Let's regroup," the Foreperson says. "It's five to two in favor of conviction, right?"

"Six to one," the Architect says, her voice barely audible.

The Housewife winces as if she's been stabbed with the knife. She leans close to the Architect and whispers something. The Architect turns her head away and lifts her eyes to the ceiling, like someone who wants to make another person disappear but can't.

"Did you just say, 'We agreed?'" the Grandmother asks the Housewife.

"I didn't say anything," the Housewife says indignantly.

"With my poor hearing, I've learned to read lips," the Grandmother says. "You definitely—"

"What did you agree to?" the Foreperson asks. "Because if you two discussed this case before the end of trial or made a side deal, you broke the judge's rules. As the foreperson, I'm going to make sure the judge hears about it."

"I didn't say anything," the Housewife says.

The Architect folds her arms across her chest. "Nobody made any agreement. It's only that you all have convinced me that David didn't act in self-defense."

Did they really make a deal before the verdict? My mom said that's what people do on juries, but I didn't believe her. How gullible am I? This makes me kind of sad. Very sad. I respected the Housewife. Now I can't.

The Housewife gets out of her chair and takes a seat at the end of the table, as far away from the others as she can get without leaving the room—the seat the Clergyman occupied before he was kicked off the jury. What would he have said about all this? I know: *nothing*.

JUROR NO. 1
THE FOREPERSON

I thought about doing a demonstration like the Jury Consultant did, but I didn't want to take over. I'm the foreperson, and it's my job to bring out the best in everyone, right? I am doing a good job as a foreperson, I think. No, I'm sure I am.

If the Housewife would only get off her high horse, we could get out of here and put that murderer behind bars forever. Or for the rest of his life, anyway. If we reach a verdict, they'll talk about this at the insurance agency tomorrow—if I decide to go back to work tomorrow. Maybe I'll take the week off. I deserve time off, even though I need the money. On second thought, if I'm interviewed by the reporters today, I'll go in to work first thing. No one likes to talk about old news.

How about those mean girls, huh? So judgmental, and it turns out they're the ones who broke the rules. I'd tell the judge if I had proof, but they're liars, and they'll deny they made an agreement between them. They made an agreement between them, no doubt.

I stare hard at the Housewife. "You're all alone. David Sullinger is guilty."

"This is a hung jury," says the Housewife. "Let's tell the judge we're hopelessly deadlocked, and then we'll all go home. Because I'm not changing my vote to convict an innocent man."

"I can't believe your arrogance," says the Architect. "The evidence isn't the way we first saw it. I'm big enough to admit that and do the right thing. That's what this process is about: doing the right thing, not winning."

The Housewife crosses her arms over her chest so hard that her plump boobs pillow up. "I'm the one who's doing the right thing. I find people who cave in to peer pressure disgusting."

Whoa. Trouble in paradise between these two. I hate to admit it, but great!

"You know, your husband, Jared, seems kind of abusive himself, from what you've told me," says the Architect. "Like David Sullinger's mini-me? Maybe you're projecting and voting not guilty to justify your own husband's behavior."

The Housewife freezes in surprise like a guy who's just been kicked in the balls but hasn't felt all the pain yet. The Architect just crossed the line. I'm not loving this conflict quite so much now, because it's too mean. I'm not a mean person like them. It goes to show, friends can become the bitterest of enemies in the blink of an eye. Maybe it's a good thing I don't have many friends.

"What a horrible thing to say," says the Housewife, the color gone from every part of her face except for a red splotch under her left eye. "It's not true. Jared has never, ever ..." She glances over at the knife on the credenza, as if she's tempted to ... She wouldn't. *Would she?*

"That's definitely a rotten thing to say," says the Jury Consultant to the Architect. "Especially to a friend."

"Are any of us friends?" the Architect asks. "Do our youngest and oldest jurors have a friendship anymore?"

The Grandmother sniffles and crosses her arms, and the Student pushes her glasses up her nose twice.

"I doubt any of us will be meeting for cocktails after this is all over, or chumming it up on weekends," says the Architect. "No one calls me disgusting and gets away with it."

"That was wrong of her, but you attacked her family," says the Grandmother. "I'll overlook your attack on me. You don't speak ill of a person's family, whether that person is stranger, friend, or foe. Period."

"I'll second that," I say.

"It's true we're not friends in here," says the Express Messenger.

"We should move on," I say. "This is toxic."

The Express Messenger lifts his arm—a kind of peace offering—and I realize his eyes are glistening.

"I won't talk long. I know I have no friends in this room. I know you think I'm just a mama's boy, a scuzzy truck driver who has delusions about being an actor. Fine. Maybe you're right, maybe you're wrong. We don't have to like each other. A jury is supposed to be a cross section of the community, and that's what we are. Maybe it's better if we don't like each other, because maybe that means we're diverse like we're supposed to be. I say let's do the best we can to cooperate, so we can reach a just verdict."

Everyone is quiet. The Jury Consultant looks serious, but her eyes are smiling proudly at the Express Messenger.

"Hear, hear," I say.

The Jury Consultant leans in to the Housewife. "I appreciate your strong convictions. We all do. We're having an honest disagreement. Part of the process."

"Don't patronize me," says the Housewife. "You're trying to

use your expertise to poison this jury, and you're getting away with it."

"No one's being poisoned," says the Grandmother. "Most of us followed the judge's admonition, which she gave on the very first day of trial and repeated every time we took a recess, not to discuss the case among ourselves or draw conclusions before all the evidence was in. There's a reason for that: so you don't prejudge the case without hearing from your fellow jurors. It seems to me that you prejudged the case. You're the one trying to control us, Missy."

The Housewife's lower lip quivers. She looks like a teacher's pet who's just received her first-ever scolding. "Let's take another vote," she says. "I'll go first. Not guilty. Anyone want to change their vote?"

The Express Messenger groans. The Student shakes her head continuously.

"No one is changing their vote," says the Grandmother. "This should be over. The correct result is obvious."

What do they call a tie in chess? A stalemate? This stalemate has a rotten odor.

"You obviously love your children," says the Jury Consultant in a soft voice. "I just want to ask you this. Who made the nine-one-one call?"

For a moment, the Housewife looks like she's going to retreat further into her invisible tortoise shell, but she straightens up in her chair and says, "Okay, I'll humor you. Dillon made the nine-one-one call when he got home from school."

"He made the call ten to fifteen minutes after his mother was killed, right?"

"Undisputed," says the Housewife. "Get to the point."

The Jury Consultant takes a deep breath. "Dillon was scheduled to come home from school at that time. It wasn't like he showed up unexpectedly."

"Yeah, so?"

"Why didn't David make the nine-one-one call?"

"He testified that he was in shock, that he—"

"You're a parent. Put yourself in David's place. If you'd just defended your life by killing your spouse, felt as if you were defending the lives of your children—that's what David claimed: that it wasn't only *his* life that was in danger—would you ever allow your child to find your husband dead, brutally killed with a pickax? No matter how traumatized you were, no matter how dazed and anguished, no parent with an iota of feeling for his child would have let Dillon find his mother like that, much less put him through the hell of making the nine-one-one call. Think like a parent, not a juror. David Sullinger wanted Dillon to find Amanda's body."

The Housewife blinks several times, then shakes her head repeatedly. "The prosecutor never argued—"

"Probably some behind-the-scenes ruling the judge made," says the Jury Consultant. "A lot goes on behind the scenes that we don't know about. Or just another example of Jack Cranston's incompetence."

The Housewife withdraws further inside herself—the tortoise poked with a sharp stick. It's quiet in here, cold because the heater is out again. There's not even the sound of a machine to mask the silence of the Housewife's agony.

At last, she whispers, "Okay. Okay."

I walk over to the wall and push the red button.

THE PROSECUTOR
JACK CRANSTON

Things never turn out quite right for some of us. I beat the crap out of Jenna the Great, who claimed she'd never lost a case. Well, now she can't say that anymore.

But what did I win? According to the media, a discombobulated jury rendered an unjust verdict in spite of the assistant district attorney's pathetic courtroom performance. Kelsi Cunningham actually called my trial performance "pathetic." Her headline? justice undone.

I put a murderous psychopath behind bars, damn it. I took a dangerous killer off the streets. Yet I'm being treated as the criminal.

"I'm just so surprised," my wife said repeatedly on the night of the verdict. "I thought it was going to go the other way. I'm so happy for you, Jack." But there was no happiness in her eyes, only a kind of reproachful embarrassment that her husband was the instrument of injustice.

My son doesn't know what to think. Thirteen-year-old boys love winning, and he knows his father won, so he's proud of my victory. But he's a sensitive kid, and he also knows how his mother feels, how his teachers feel. He reads the internet. I overheard him say to my wife just two days ago, "I never want to be a lawyer when I grow up." Good. I don't want him to be a lawyer, either. Life isn't fun when it's all about winning and losing—at least, not for those of us who aren't Jenna Blaylock. But did he have to reject my profession so soon? Haven't I done *anything* he finds admirable? I put a murderous psychopath behind bars, for Chrissake. I took a dangerous killer off the streets.

When I was a kid, my grandfather would read me the Uncle Remus stories by Joel Chandler Harris, unaware that late twentieth-century critics would call the tales racist. My politically correct, pro–David Sullinger, anti–Joel Chandler Harris wife refuses to let me read the stories to our son, never mind that certain new-millennial critics have repurposed the stories, praising them as subversive and antiracist. Well, racist or not, one Harris story resonates with me now: the one about Brer Rabbit and the Tar Baby. The rabbit tried to engage the Tar Baby in conversation, but the Tar Baby wouldn't reply. Brer Rabbit got so mad at the Tar Baby for ignoring him that he punched and kicked it, becoming entrapped in the sticky tar. The rabbit was a fool because his rage was unfocused. I get angry at life for ignoring me, sure, but my rage is focused on doing justice. I took a killer off the streets. Why have I become ever more mired in a viscid bitumen of failure?

JUROR NO. 43
THE CLERGYMAN

"Do not be afraid; you will not be put to shame. Do not fear disgrace; you will not be humiliated." Thus reads Isaiah 54:4. I am not a brave man. I do fear disgrace. If I were a brave man, I would not persist in speaking as though I were reared in Laredo, Texas, when in fact I grew up in Cotati, California. I attended school at Southern Methodist University, however, where I quickly learned it is not only the education that makes the minister, but also the accent. It has served me well, except with my siblings, who mock me about it at every family gathering. My place of upbringing is not the only thing I lie about. If I were a brave man, I would go to the media and explain the truth. I sit silent, however, for otherwise, I would be put to shame, would be humiliated.

My chortle wakes up my boxer mix, who was sleeping under my desk. He looks up at me and whines, his censure of me justified. Biblical quotes, grandiose sentiments, bombast—all evidence that I do not believe a word of what I preach. The truth is, I am a flawed man and a coward, and I tried to do one brave thing—or at least, one right thing—and could not manage it.

As I informed the other jurors when the Foreperson confronted me, Amanda Sullinger and I met at a fund-raiser ten years ago, at which we were photographed together. What I failed to confess was that I *did* know Amanda quite well. Indeed, after meeting her at the charity function, I pursued her, charmed her, and pried a substantial charitable contribution out of her. She was a well-connected woman, a philanthropist, a progressive, even a bleeding heart—and, as the Housewife recognized, a monster.

I was riding high then, the pastor of the beautiful building on Whitesburg Street—my church before I quit in protest over the hierarchy's apathy toward human rights. (By the way, my resignation was not an act of bravery; it was an act of ego and, as such, constitutes no amelioration of my essential cowardice.) I am a masterful fund-raiser; my facility for prying money out of people is a gift from God. Amanda so wanted to help our causes that she connected me with people she knew in LA who might lend financial support for my church's attempt to foster tolerance of lesbians, gays, bisexuals, and transgendered individuals and to aid oppressed undocumented aliens. Ours is a small county. For that reason, Amanda demanded I keep her involvement in these good works a secret. I understood. Sepulveda County is politically conservative, and the outing of Amanda Sullinger as a liberal would have harmed her real estate business.

Approximately six months after she and I met, she appeared at my church unexpectedly. My office fronted the parking lot, and on this night, I was working late. There was the crunch of tires on gravel, and a gunfire-like bang of a car door slamming shut. Then a loud, frantic knock, and Amanda Sullinger walked in. As agitated as she was, her hair was still in place and her makeup was flawless. She was dressed in one of her designer business suits.

"I need to talk to someone," she said. "I didn't know where else to . . ." The timbre of her voice reminded me of an overwound guitar string—slightly off-key and about to snap.

I motioned for her to sit, but she stood behind one of my guest chairs and applied a two-handed death grip on the back. "I want to make sure our conversation will be confidential," she said.

"Of course it will. I have a moral obligation—"

"No, not just morally confidential. I mean *legally* confidential, like the Catholic confessional." Although she was seeking my help, her tone held an anomalous edge of hostility.

"Confidentiality is not only a tenet of my faith, but also mandated under the laws of the State of California," I replied pompously.

"To be clear, does that mean what I tell you will be protected by the privilege even if, hypothetically, I admit to actions some might find criminal?" The diction was unnatural, practiced, legalistic, though I didn't realize it back then. I was shocked and also intrigued. How perverse that the problems and flaws of others should bring excitement to our own drab lives.

"As long as you don't reveal you're planning to commit a crime in the future, whatever you tell me is privileged," I said.

"Now, that's rich. I can tell you about past acts, which you can't do anything about, but I can't tell you about future acts that you might be able to talk me out of. No wonder everyone hates lawyers." Then a question that turned out to be prescient: "Does the privilege survive the death of the penitent?"

"I am not an attorney, but I am quite certain that it does," I say. "Are you concerned about dying?"

She let out a loud laugh, the change in her demeanor so abrupt that I recoiled.

"Of course not," she said. "You pass the test." She had indeed been testing me, looking for any imperfections in my moral compass. She saw none, evidently. As things transpired, she was not an astute judge of character, about either her husband's survival instinct or my ethics.

Then she recounted to me what we jurors referred to as the tuna casserole incident, how thirty minutes earlier, she had burned David's eye and face, how she was not sorry, because he deserved it, how she loved him so. She recited a litany of similar past incidents. I became at first queasy and then nauseated. I advised her to seek professional help, even gave her the name of a therapist. I encouraged her to pray. She left my office calm and collected, the result not of my ineffectual advice but of her cathartic act of confession. Thereafter, she ceased all attempts to assist me with charitable efforts and political action, would not even take my phone calls. (Yes, I am so shamelessly mercenary that I kept pursuing her for money.) Eventually, she faded into my memory's recesses. David apparently had no clue Amanda had worked with me. Or perhaps, by the time of trial, he had forgotten.

And then I was called for jury duty, and instead of following the law and divulging my preexisting relationship with Amanda, I did what I thought was right, namely, allowed myself to be chosen so I could safeguard David Sullinger's freedom. It was the least I could do—an act of atonement, really, for I had failed to communicate anything useful to Amanda which would stop her from abusing David. I would remain silent for as long as I could, hopeful the other jurors would reach the correct result independently. At first, remaining taciturn was a simple task—the jury appeared certain to vote "not guilty," and all would come out as it should. Then the tide turned. I understand why: David was an exceedingly poor witness. As the guilty votes increased, I vowed to hang the jury. Let a future jury decide the case. At least, David would get two bites at the apple. I was wrong under the law. I was right in the eyes of God.

When the judge called me in after learning of the photograph, I used her chambers as my own confessional. As I spoke, she said nothing, simply nodded at me continually. I should have known something was not right when there was no court reporter present, when neither attorney was present. Not even her court clerk—just Judge Quinn-Gilbert and me. In hindsight, I do not think she comprehended a word I said. Or maybe I'm underestimating her. Under the law, she could not credit my extrajudicial testimony about Amanda. I assumed she would declare a mistrial, punish me, take steps to ensure that David would not be convicted of a crime he did not commit. She did none of those things. Did she believe David to be guilty? Did she spare me out of kindness because I confessed?

I should have been David's witness, not a juror, but I was afraid to breach the clergy-penitent privilege and lose the trust of my flock. I rationalized that as a juror, I could protect David better than I could as a witness.

I have consulted with an attorney and imparted these facts to her. She advises that even if I share what I know with the court and the media, it will not avail David. Judge Quinn-Gilbert excused me before the verdict was rendered, disinfecting any taint which I might have caused. Besides, there was no taint. My vote was to be "not guilty," and the jury voted "guilty." Which means that I had no influence whatever on the other jurors. I committed perjury by virtue of my failure to be forthcoming, tried to tamper with a jury. Both are crimes punishable by fines and imprisonment.

"Don't run your mouth and shoot yourself in the foot for no valid reason," my lawyer advised, her metaphors mixed but her point pellucid.

As I did in the deliberation room, I remain silent. I need an Aaron, though I am no Moses: *He will be as a mouth for you.* Perhaps I shall find him—or her.

THE HONORABLE
NATALIE QUINN-GILBERT

My siblings have been wonderful, Jonathan. My brother is driving me to specialists' appointments, and my sister has been staying with me. She says she'll stay on until we figure this thing out, but I tell her no and say that you, dear Jonathan, made sure I would have plenty of care if this happened, that she's not my caretaker. I've missed my siblings.

Ed Halleck, the presiding judge, has been wonderful, handing my most pressing cases off to other judges. As he says, I'm going to figure this thing out and return to the bench. Of course I will. Mick Redmond and Bradley Kobashigawa have been wonderful. Such good friends and employees, covering for me because I don't want anyone outside the courtroom to know why I'm taking a sabbatical. It's temporary, and attorneys lose respect for an infirm judge just as wolves turn on the wounded member of the pack. So you always say, Jonathan. I finally know what you mean.

It was an honest mistake, momentary confusion. I'm sure many others have made it. I mean, come on, what reputable builder would put the fourth-floor *women's* restroom precisely over the third-floor *men's* restroom and make the doors look exactly the same? Yet that's what happened in this architectural monstrosity. Something to do with the configuration of the building, the haphazard topography, the plumbing necessary for effective urinals—I don't know … The courthouse is a mess, as you more than once noted, Jonathan. Of course you did, so why am I telling *you* this? I became distracted with a legal issue and walked into the men's restroom on floor three, mistaking it for the women's restroom on floor four. As soon as I noticed the urinals, I backed out the door. It's not true that I tried to pee in a urinal, slanderous rumors to the contrary notwithstanding. I would have escaped unseen except that Mick Redmond happened to be walking over to Judge Halleck's courtroom carrying the transfer order I signed in another case, filed by a vexatious litigant Ed knows well and I don't. In any event, Jonathan, Mick caught me inside the third-floor men's restroom. It should have been okay—it was Mick, after all—but …

This is a mortifying confession to make, Jonathan.

"What were you doing on the third floor, Natalie?" Ed Halleck asked during the inquisition.

"I must have … the transfer order?"

"Your clerk was taking care of that."

"I thought I was in the fourth-floor ladies' room. This crazily constructed building."

"Why were you using a public restroom instead of the bathroom in your chambers?"

"The plumbing in this building …?"

"Was there a clogged toilet in your private bathroom?"

"I think perhaps there …"

"Maintenance found no plumbing issues."

"Well, that's … Goody for them."

"Why ever were you wearing your robe, Natalie?"

"I was not! Where did you get the idea—"

"Your clerk, Redmond."

"It was my black woolen coat, a gift from Jonathan when we traveled to Scandinavia. The courthouse heating system ..."

"You need to take a leave of absence while we sort this out."

"You can't make me."

"But you'll take a leave of absence, anyway."

We both cried, but he started to cry first, Jonathan. I'm sure of that. Mick Redmond is devastated. He believes he betrayed me by reporting me to the presiding judge.

He did betray me. I'll never forgive him.

Sometimes I take myself to task over my performance in *Sullinger*, but Ed Halleck says I did a wonderful job. What an unfortunate case.

I'm enveloped in fog, Jonathan. Not enveloped, but imprisoned in a thick, desiccated haze that surrounds me yet excludes me from its embrace, so that I feel utterly alone. Why won't the haze love me? It's the rest of the world, not me, who's in the haze, and in my isolation, I see things with perfect clarity. I see that I prefer a brain tumor over Alzheimer's, that I prefer insanity to a brain tumor, that I prefer death to insanity, that I prefer a life of forgetfulness to death, that my reasoning is at once circular, muddled, and rational and that I don't get a choice. How I wish that damn fog would embrace me. Or ... Have they diagnosed me yet, Jonathan? So many tests, so many neurologists and neurosurgeons and psychiatrists. It's all a misunderstanding. So confusing. What's wrong with me, Jonathan?

"The jury's still deliberating, Nat, so just relax and wait for the verdict. What else can you do?"

I'll accept the verdict. I believe in the jury system. Still, sometimes juries get it wrong.

My father-in-law, as old and frail as he is, came to see me. That wasn't easy for him, and he was wonderful. He says if I convert to Judaism, I can be buried next to you, that there's still room in the family plot. I'll have to get well first, of course, and then I'll decide. Plenty of time to decide. Something is nagging at me—some things, like persistent flies swarming and buzzing inside my head and beating against the back interior of my skull. I'm going to lick this thing once they figure it out, and then I'll remember, and the flies will stop buzzing, and that will be wonderful.

JUROR NO. 29

THE JURY CONSULTANT

Speak authoritatively and you alter perceptions, and once you accomplish that, you've altered the truth, and when you've altered the truth, you're a god.

I attended law school for one semester, until I realized lawyers are taught persuasion, not manipulation. Useless—life is about manipulation. I dropped out, enrolled in grad school, earned my PhD, and began my career as a jury consultant. Lucrative if you're good (I am), but each assignment is a short con—coaching witnesses, putting together mock juries, drafting jury questionnaires, helping with jury selection. Once the trial begins, you're irrelevant. So many times, the goddamn lawyers fuck it up.

I know how to get out of jury duty. I've avoided jury service many times. Then *People v. Sullinger* came along, and I knew how to get on the jury. It helped that the jury comprised mostly females. Bottom line, women dislike weak men no matter how sympathetic and genuine. That's why I knew that the Architect, despite her affinity for the Housewife, would get there on her own—eventually.

Poor David Sullinger. His wife forgot their anniversary, he got upset about it, and she ended up dead. Who cares if she forgot their anniversary? To condemn her for that was almost sexist—*was* sexist. Why shouldn't she forget? She worked; he didn't. She worked day and night. It could have been worse. My ex-husband was perpetually looking to succeed in a startup company in the days when people actually succeeded in startup companies. Except that he managed to fail every time and ended up never working much at all. How offended he got when I refused to renew our vows on our tenth anniversary!

"We agreed," he sniveled.

"Yeah, before the kid came along, before I got to know who you really are."

He cried real tears, grief-stricken over some silly romantic pact that became irrevocably broken six weeks after his daughter was born. "Force majeure," the lawyers call it—an act of nature that nullifies a contract. In the case of my "marriage," the force majeure was my pregnancy and all that followed. Amanda and David had their own force majeure.

Other than the Foreperson, the jury was intelligent—unusually so. Smart people often hold the naive belief that the justice system depends on dialogue and understanding. The Foreperson could have presented a problem. She has a chip on her shoulder, wanted to feel important, and intransigence can make a person feel important. Which is why I nominated her to be the foreperson. Upon being appointed the leader, she became the quintessential follower, precisely because she has no leadership ability. She aimed to please, and leaders can't aim to please.

Expertise impresses people, engenders trust. The expert announces that a witness has been coached, and *flip-flop.* When the expert makes up a story about a rival jury consultant being in the courtroom, the others don't question it—*flip-flop.* (If anyone checks, I'll just say the reporter from TrueCriminal.com looks a lot like Jerome Marks.) Sure, Lacey exhibited all the mannerisms and techniques jury consultants teach. We teach those techniques because they convey truth. Lacey is the prototype, not the product. Until I, speaking from on high, pronounced otherwise. And yet, credible or not, Lacey could lie. Truth tellers can lie, do lie, which means that truth tellers are figments. My own daughter, a daddy's girl like Lacey—oh, so much like Lacey—prevaricated about me. Apt word, "prevaricated." It comes from the Old French *prevari-cacion*, meaning disobedience. No matter what, a daughter must not disobey her mother; a husband must not disobey his wife. Lacey was disobedient and, so, a prevaricator. What is the truth, anyway, except what the decision makers say it is?

The principles of manipulation: Don't overstate your case. Give in sometimes. Use honey, not vinegar. (Poison the honey if you have to.) If the lead police investigator is inept, which Detective Beckermann was, acknowledge that fact and move on. The other jurors will admire your objectivity.

Perception is a delicate tapestry. Once a single thread snaps, the entire fabric unravels. After I ripped Lacey apart, the other jurors could believe that that drugged-out, publicity-seeking, bipolar, lying Dillon Sullinger was a truthful witness; that the right to stand your ground means you must run; that a traumatized man who's just killed his mate of thirty-four years would have any conception of time at all, much less remember that his son is soon due home from school.

Ah, the Clergyman. A block of inscrutable stone who was voting not guilty. Then a stroke of luck when the Foreperson found that photograph of him with Amanda Sullinger. (I'm not arrogant enough to believe that luck doesn't count in an endeavor like mine.) I couldn't go to the judge with the photo. Nor could I encourage the others to take the picture to the judge, because by empowering them I would have lost control of the proceedings. So I bided my time. Then more luck: discovering the Foreperson's misplaced cell phone on the ladies'-room sink, checking the screen, and realizing the phone was powered on and wasn't locked. I launched the browser app, found the photo of Amanda and the Clergyman, and used the Foreperson's email address to send the link to Kelsi Cunningham. Not only did I make it seem as if the Foreperson were the person who had busted the Clergyman, I also knew that Cunningham would protect her source at all costs. All of which meant that no one would finger me as the person who gave the photo to the media. Cunningham published the photo, of course, and as a result, the Clergyman's apparent relationship with Amanda came to the judge's attention. A judge like Quinn-Gilbert wouldn't let him stay on the jury even if that photograph was a coincidence, which I highly doubt. Wave goodbye to the Clergyman. I am surprised the media didn't find the photo earlier. But the internet still has little nooks and crannies that hide information in plain sight.

Smart woman, the Housewife. Foolish, needy, corrupt woman, the Housewife. She had talked too much before the trial ended, and counted on the support of the Architect, a shallow, enigmatic fashion plate with a mean streak. Poor judge of character, the Housewife—she hugged me before we left the deliberation room.

Too bad about Natalie Quinn-Gilbert. I like her; I sincerely do.

THE BLOGGER

KELSI CUNNINGHAM

I assured my loyal readers a not-guilty verdict was a slam dunk, a foregone conclusion, shooting fish in a barrel, a sure thing, open-and-shut, a dead certainty. As it transpired, the only certainty is that Amanda Sullinger is dead. I swear to God, I'll get to the bottom of this. The guilty verdict has embarrassed me with my editors and my readers and has emboldened my critics. The guilty verdict has made me look like a schmuck, and Kelsi Cunningham does not enjoy looking like a schmuck.

None of the jurors will talk to me. I guess it's not a surprise, because I've been hard on them. I coined the term "Simple-minded Sullinger Seven" in one of my articles, and some of the other media outlets picked it up. Worse, after the verdict came down, Judge Quinn-Gilbert advised them not to talk to anyone about the deliberative process, to keep their jury-room discussions confidential. The veteran reporters were stunned because, in the past, Quinn-Gilbert has been a big supporter of freedom of the press, and all that. The judge's "advice" was bad enough, but then, three days ago, I ambushed the Foreperson at her home, and before she ordered me off her lawn, she let slip that Judge Quinn-Gilbert's bailiff told the jurors they especially shouldn't speak with *me.* The bailiff called me unethical and untrustworthy, according to the Foreperson. I'm not unethical; I'm intrepid. Anyway, when I pointed out to the Foreperson how she'd trusted me before—trusted me so much that she sent me that photo of the Clergyman standing with Amanda Sullinger—the woman shouted that I was crazy and threatened to call the cops.

It's not the judge or the bailiff I blame for the jury's stonewalling. It's that court clerk, the son of a bitch.

I still remember Judge Quinn-Gilbert's look of betrayal, and the clerk's unbridled revulsion at my little subterfuge. I've gotten a lot of those looks in my short career. The memories of such expressions of disdain are insidious. No matter how hard you fight against them, they come back full force, like some kind of superresistant bacterial infection.

I tried to arrange an appointment with Judge Quinn-Gilbert and apologize for what I did. Of course, I had an ulterior motive: to convince her to advise the jurors to speak with the media. Her nasty court clerk informed me the judge has taken a leave of absence. He wouldn't divulge why. None of my sources who work in the courthouse will divulge why. I'm sure it concerns her mental state. I smell the stench of cover-up, which is fine with me, because I'm in the business of yanking covers off and exposing the underlying garbage.

Somewhere down the line, a juror will talk to me, reveal the truth, I'm sure of it. And then I won't look like such a schmuck. I need to flip only one of the Simpleminded Sullinger Seven. The problem is, *People v. Sullinger* isn't the O. J. Simpson murders or the Lindberg kidnapping, or even Jody Arias or the Menendez brothers. Those cases had legs. The public is already letting go of *Sullinger*, already moving on to the next salacious comitragedy. I report NEWS. My competitors fled Sepulveda County as quickly as they could. I'm scheduled to fly back home tomorrow.

The Simpleminded Sullinger Seven. What would I have called the jury if they'd remained at eight?

After the Clergyman got kicked off because of my article, he became something of a fifth Beatle. Only I and a couple of other reporters tried to talk to him, and like the other jurors, he declined to comment. Yesterday, on instinct or a whim, I called him again, and this time he invited me to visit his church and pray with him.

"A very private, very exclusive prayer service," he said in a big yet soft and enigmatic voice. "Perhaps both of us shall gain a bit of redemption and enlightenment."

Of course, I don't know what the hell he meant. I doubt he'll talk to me about the substance of deliberations, but I think I'll head over there now. What better way to kill time in this boring county?

Yeah, I'll head over and pray with the Clergyman—to kill time, dig up dirt, and, just maybe, get a booster shot of that redemption and enlightenment he talked about.

THE END

ACKNOWLEDGMENTS

Thank you: Andrew Auffenorde, Ariana Berlin, Hudson Hauser, Samantha Hauser, William Hauser, Ethel Rotstein, Jimmy Rotstein; Isabella Auffenorde for her insights on generational attitudes and dialogue; Daco Auffenorde and Matthew Sharpe for their comments and suggestions on early drafts; Jill Marr, Andrea Cavallaro, Derek McFadden, and Sandra Dijkstra of The Sandra Dijkstra Agency; Michael Carr, Lysa Williams, Greg Boguslawski, Lauren Maturo, Josie McKenzie, Sean Thomas, and Jeffrey Yamaguchi of Blackstone Publishing.